INTO THE
LIGHT

CAROLINE T. PATTI

Month9Books

INTO THE LIGHT by Caroline T. Patti
All rights reserved. Published in the United States of America by Month9Books, LLC.
No part of this book may be used or reproduced in any manner whatsoever without written permission of the publisher, except in the case of brief quotations embodied in critical articles and reviews.

ISBN: 978-1-942664-44-4

Published by Month9Books, Raleigh, NC 27609
Cover design by Monika McFarlane

Month9Books

To Jill Rice—
because you said, "Pick me. Pick me."

"Dare to reach out your hand
into the darkness,
to pull another hand
Into the Light."
-Norman B. Rice

Chapter One

Nathaniel

*N*athaniel stood on the bridge watching the sun rise over the hills. The tangerine orb drenched the sky, casting a yellowish-orange glow over the horizon. As if the beams were aiming directly for him, Nathaniel closed his eyes and let the warmth soak his skin.

"Gorgeous, isn't it?" Isadora mused as she gripped the railing.

"It's the same," Nathaniel lamented. "It's always the same."

"You're restless today." She nudged his shoulder. "What's going on in that head of yours?"

Nathaniel cast a downward glance. "I'm tired."

"We don't get tired."

"You know what I mean." Nathaniel turned his back to the sun. "I'm tired of the same thing day after day. Nothing ever changes."

Isadora stepped in front of him and held his face in her hands. "What is it that you want to change? Do you desire to scurry like a *human, rushing off from one chore to the next, never fully knowing the futility behind your actions?"*

Nathaniel blanched and backed away from Isadora's grasp. "If you came here to mock me, you can go."

"I came here to be with you." Isadora inched closer to Nathaniel. She ran her index finger along his arm.

"Isadora. Stop."

Her green-eyed gaze intensified. "No, Nathaniel." She gripped his chin fiercely. "You stop. Stop this foolishness before you get yourself into trouble."

He uncurled her fingers from his chin. "It's not foolishness."

"It is! It's ridiculous, this feeling of what? Jealously? Of humans?"

"You don't understand."

"I don't want to understand," she said sharply. "I want you to snap out of this. We could have everything together, be everything to each other. Why isn't that enough for you?"

The sun continued to rise as Nathaniel considered Isadora's proposal. She was offering him a position at her side, something he'd been mulling over for quite some time. Isadora was beautiful and passionate. She would make the ultimate queen, and she wanted him as her king. Isadora, as one of The Assembled, outranked him, and because of her position, she could have anyone, and she had chosen him. Nathaniel had played in her world for a while, but he could not overcome the nagging feeling in the pit of his stomach that somewhere out there, there might be more.

Being a Guide had been mostly satisfying. Nathaniel took his position seriously, helping souls cross from one realm to the next. He was good at his job too, which is what drew Isadora's attention in the first place. She'd told him how she admired him from afar, how she'd watched him care so meticulously for each soul. Nathaniel had been honored by her compliments, stoked by her affections, but not completely satiated.

Because he couldn't stop thinking about her.

Eleanor Jane Levinson, known as Ellie to those closest to her. Petite with blond hair, brown eyes, and a warm smile, she lived in a small village in the English countryside. She did not deserve to be dying. But she was. Inch by inch, minute by minute, her time ticked away slowly, painfully, dismally. The doctor had exhausted all efforts, but there was nothing to be done. Her condition was too far advanced. Yet through it all, Ellie smiled. She comforted her mother and father, sang sweet songs to her little brother, Will. Though she was the one suffering, she made it a point to be the pillar of strength her family needed. She was a captivating presence. And she'd caught the eye of Nathaniel Black.

He'd been watching from a distance, waiting for her body to give out so that he could properly introduce himself, and he would've stayed away if not for the night he heard her pray.

"Lord, I'm scared. I know that I should be looking forward to the kingdom of heaven, but I'm scared to die. I don't want to be alone. Please. Please, Lord, tell me that I won't be alone."

"You won't be alone," Nathaniel whispered through the darkness.

Ellie's head whipped around to the direction of his voice. "Who's there?" Fear crept over her face as she tried to see into the dark.

"Don't be frightened."

"Who are you?"

Nathaniel pondered his next move. He was treading on shaky

ground, hovering in the gray area of right and wrong. He was strictly forbidden from interacting with humans until their spirits left their bodies. So as long as he stayed in the dark where she couldn't see him, he wasn't technically breaking any rules.

When Nathaniel didn't answer her question, Ellie continued, "Are you an angel?"

"No," Nathaniel answered honestly. "I am a Guide."

"Are you here to take me?" Ellie could not conceal the worry in her voice.

"Not yet."

"Then why are you here?"

Nathaniel couldn't answer that, so he said, "You will not be alone. When it is time, I will come for you. I will walk you home."

Ellie's breath shuddered, and a faint whimper escaped her. "What's your name?"

"Nathaniel."

"It's nice to meet you, Nathaniel."

His name from her lips was the sweetest melody Nathaniel had ever heard. He was overcome with the urge to reveal himself fully, but instead he vanished. He should've kept to the rules and not returned until it was Ellie's time to go, but he couldn't stay away, and the next night he returned to her bedroom.

She appeared to be sleeping. But then she opened her eyes. "Nathaniel? Is that you?"

"I'm here."

"Is it time?"

"No."

Ellie relaxed against the pillows. "I was afraid to go to sleep."

He hadn't meant to worry her. "You can sleep tonight. You have more time."

"I don't want to sleep while you're here."

"I'll go."

"No." She reached out her hand. "Stay with me. Please."

Silently, Nathaniel agreed. Ellie took a few rattling breaths. Her time really was running out.

"What's it like?" she asked him.

"It's like home," he answered.

"It won't be home without my family."

"I know this is difficult, but I promise you there's nothing to fear."

"Will you be there?" she asked tentatively.

"No."

"That's too bad. It would've been nice to have a friend."

"Ellie?"

"Yes?"

"I would go with you if I could." He meant every word.

Moments later he heard the even sound of her breathing as she drifted off to sleep. He watched and waited, not wanting to leave her just yet. When he finally did go, he was met with an unwelcomed surprise waiting for him just outside.

"Isadora, what are you doing here?"

She stood with her arms folded across her chest, her eyes full of fury. "The question is, Nathaniel, what are you doing here?"

"You don't belong here," he reminded her. "It isn't right."

"Who are you to speak of what is right and what is wrong?"

"I can explain," Nathaniel tried.

Chapter Two

Gage

Stepping out of the shower, I towel off, rubbing the scar on my forearm where my Hunter's mark used to be and, for just a moment, mourn my former life. I miss the other Hunters: Jinx, Zee, and especially Rae. They were my friends, though when they were alive I never would've categorized them as such. We were more like brothers-in-arms. We fought alongside one another, risked our lives for each other, and in the end, they died for me. I often wonder if they are on the other side, if they are safe. I wonder if there was a Guide who welcomed them home. I hope so because the alternative—Purgatory, trapped between worlds—no, that couldn't happen. Not to them.

I survey the contents of my closet. It's strange to have so many choices, to know that humans take great pains in considering what clothes they wear. It seems insignificant to me, but Mercy and her friend Lyla say otherwise. So much to learn, they're always telling me.

In the months since Mercy made her deal with Isadora, I have been assimilating into my new life. Nathaniel and I found a small house to rent. It isn't much, and since domesticity is a trait neither Nathaniel nor I possess, I have little hope that our living conditions will improve. Mercy insisted we at least furnish the house and get a basic cable package.

On the day we moved in, Mercy unpacked boxes, organized our cupboards, and arranged our furniture. "You might as well enjoy being human," she said as she hooked the cable box into the television.

"This really isn't necessary," I insisted.

She gave me *that* look, the one that told me not to argue with her. "Gage, the whole reason I made this deal is so you can have a normal life. I'm not saying you need to become a couch potato, but there is something to be said for *Monday Night Football.*"

Mercy also stocked the kitchen even though I assured her Nathaniel and I could certainly survive on takeout.

"Speak for yourself, little brother." Nathaniel smiled wickedly at me. "Nothing will give me greater pleasure than seeing you in an apron."

"As if I would ever cook for you," I snapped.

Mercy stepped between us. "You're going to be able to do this, right? Live with together without plotting beheadings in your sleep?"

Nathaniel laughed. I did not share his humor. Having him for a roommate gave me more than a moment's pause.

"We'll be fine, won't we, Gage?" Nathaniel clapped me on the back. "Pretty soon it'll be keggers every Friday night!"

So far, we've managed without incident. It wasn't exactly a smooth transition, but we're trying. Part of what makes us successful is we never talk about Mercy. I mean, her name comes up in conversation, sure, but we never mention that we both love her. It's safer to keep that topic buried beneath the floorboards and several feet of denial. We don't have time to worry about our feelings for Mercy anyway. We have to stay focused for the day Isadora returns to collect on her bargain.

Isadora returned Mercy to her body, gave her back her former life, and agreed to leave us, Nathaniel and I, as well as Mercy's family and friends, unharmed so long as Mercy agreed to do Isadora's bidding. What that entails, we don't yet know.

What we do know is that Mercy is a Breacher, just like her mother. She can leave her body and occupy another. Yet, unlike other Breachers, Mercy doesn't need to kill her host in order to jump from one body to the next.

Since the day Mercy returned, we haven't discussed her plan to take down The Assembled. Every time I try to broach the subject, she shuts me down. She keeps telling me not to worry, that she can handle things. But as the weeks go by, and there's still no sign of Isadora, my anxiety level escalates.

My bedroom door bursts open and slams against the wall breaking my thoughts.

"Gage! You're not still asleep are you?" Mercy stops dead in her tracks at the sight of me in a towel. She quickly spins around, turning her back to me. "Oh my God. I'm so sorry," she says as she laughs.

"Just give me a sec," I tell her.

Slowly, she pivots back around. She's radiant. Her auburn hair is redder than it was just a few days ago. Her skin, sun-kissed and glowing, looks healthier than ever before. She wears little makeup, but she doesn't need it. Mercy is, by far, the most beautiful person I've ever known.

"Hey, kinda naked here," I say, holding the towel tightly around my waist.

She bites her lip and closes the door behind her.

"What are you doing?"

She starts toward me. "I need to tell you something."

"You can tell me after I put some clothes on," I say, backing away.

She continues her approach. "Actually, I think your current state of vulnerability works to my advantage."

"What?"

"Gage, for a while now, I've been thinking about everything. About me. About you."

My throat constricts, and I can't swallow. Mercy stands directly in front of me, within inches of my rapidly beating heart.

"You risked everything for me. You put my life before yours."

"Mercy, stop."

"Is that what you really want?"

"It's for the best. I think."

"You're absolutely sure about that?"

She tilts her chin. Her breath mingles with mine.

"Mercy."

"Gage." She winds her hand around the back of my neck and

crushes her lips to mine in one swift movement.

Need, desire—these are emotions that humans respond to. Humans are impulsive and spontaneous, the exact opposite of the controlled, thoughtful Hunters. But I am no longer a Hunter. I'm human, and my human body reacts before my brain can stop it.

The kiss is forceful and heated. All I want is the taste of her mouth. It isn't like me to lose control like this, and I expect Mercy to shove me away, but she doesn't. Her hands are on my waist, then up my spine. My body shivers, igniting parts of me I didn't even know I had.

Before I know it, we're stumbling toward the bed.

Her lips are everywhere: my jaw, my neck, my collarbone. I audibly groan when she kisses the hollow spot along my clavicle. I claim her mouth again, and I feel there's a strong possibility I will go on kissing her forever.

Abruptly, she stops and pulls away. She quickly scoots off the bed. "We can't. I'm sorry."

The entire room goes cold. "You're sorry?"

"I have to go."

The door slams. She's gone.

I flop against the bed and listen to the blood pumping in my ears. *What the hell just happened?* Self-doubt and worry take over as I wonder what I did wrong. Was I too aggressive? Too eager?

Footsteps come down the hall, and I sit up, hoping she's returned. "Mercy?"

Nathaniel opens the door. He assesses the situation, me in only a towel, my flushed cheeks and the embarrassed look on my face, the tangled bed sheets. My hair has to be a mess from when Mercy—I stop myself from finishing the thought.

His eyes narrow, and his mouth pulls inward. He leaves the room without saying anything.

Hurriedly, I make myself presentable, throwing on a pair of dark jeans and a black T-shirt. I find Nathaniel in the front room not watching television. He stares ahead.

Cautiously, I approach. "You're back early."

"Yep."

Gulping, I swipe my hand across the back of my neck. "Should we talk about this?"

Nathaniel rises from the couch. His coal eyes match mine in color and in shape, though his are more deeply set and, at present, burning holes into my face.

Retreating, I throw my hands up and say, "Or maybe we don't need to talk about this right now." He stalks toward me until I'm pressed against the wall. "I don't want to fight you, Nathaniel."

Briefly, a look of pain contorts his face, but he quickly recovers. Skulking back to the couch, he flops into the cushions. "Fine."

"Fine?"

"I don't want to fight with you either. It's been too quiet, and Isadora is just waiting for us to drop our guard." After a deep breath, he seems to mellow even further, but he's too calm, eerily calm. "But when this is over, mark my words, brother, there will be words about *this*."

"Knock, knock," Mercy says as she pushes the front door

open. She looks to Nathaniel, then to me, then back to him. "What's going on?"

Blush rises to my cheeks. I can't register the exact emotions I'm feeling at the moment. There are too many to count. "You came back," I say to her.

She looks confused, her auburn ponytail swishing against her shoulders as she continues to look at both of us like she's watching a tennis match.

"You can cut the innocent act," Nathaniel snipes at her. "I know."

Mercy's left eyebrow disappears beneath the hair that has shaken loose and fallen across her forehead. "You know what?"

Leaning toward her I grasp her elbow and whisper, "I told him the truth."

"The truth about what?"

"Seriously, you don't have to do this." I gesture toward Nathaniel. "I told him."

"Okay, somebody clue me in because I am completely lost."

I don't know which one of us figures it out first. Nathaniel and I exchange a look, the spark of truth transmitting between us. "Oh shit," we say in unison.

Releasing my grip on Mercy, I back away until I'm leaning against the wall. I need something to hold me up before I die of embarrassment.

"Still waiting for an explanation here," Mercy says. "Guys, what the hell is going on?"

Nathaniel, barely concealing a grin, says, "It seems as though Gage had a visitor this morning."

"Do you have to be an asshole about this?" I ask him. He smirks. Yes, apparently, he does.

"Your sister was here," he tells Mercy.

"Sister?" She shakes her head. "I don't have a ..." She gasps, her hand clamping down over her mouth. Lowering her hand she says, "She was here? With you?" Mercy's eyes are wide and frantic. "What happened?"

"I'll let Gage fill you in on the juicy details." Nathaniel's delight in my agony is annoying.

"I can't ..." Mercy inhales and exhales in rapid bursts. "I can't breathe." Her knees buckle, and before I can unglue my feet from the floor, Nathaniel is there, guiding her to the couch.

The scene quickly changes, and it's no longer about a brotherly squabble—it's about keeping Mercy from jumping.

"Relax," Nathaniel tells her. "I've got you."

"I'll get the kit," I say, springing into action. The hall closet is just a few feet away, and it doesn't take me long to locate the black box containing the binding agent we need.

I am only gone for thirty seconds, tops, but in that time, Mercy has gotten much worse. Nathaniel cradles her head and eases her into the cushions as her whole body begins to convulse. "Please don't do this," he says to her, his voice pained.

Pulling off the cap of the syringe, I flick the tube to make sure the liquid is ready. Nathaniel holds Mercy by the wrists while I dip the needle into her arm. Within seconds her body quiets, the tremors slow. She's no longer shaking. Her breathing steadies. Nathaniel props a pillow beneath her head.

"Did it work?" I ask him.

"I don't know," he answers tersely. "Mercy, can you hear me?" Her head lolls to the side.

I pace, wearing steady tracks into the carpet.

"Sit down," Nathaniel instructs. I obey.

Panic. That's the emotion I feel at precisely this moment. My skin crawls while my left leg jiggles. The relentlessly slow tick of the clock on the far wall drums in the silence. Five minutes. Ten minutes. Still no sign of her.

"What do we do, Nathaniel? How long do we wait?"

Calmly, Nathaniel strokes Mercy's cheek with his thumb. Then he says to me, "You're coming unglued."

He's right. "I'm never going to survive being human. How do you do this?"

Nathaniel stands and walks to the wet bar. When he returns, he's carrying a bottle of whiskey and two tumblers. "You adapt," he says. He pours himself a drink, and then he pours me one.

"You're suggesting I become a drunk?"

"I'm suggesting you calm down. This helps." He clinks his glass to mine, and with one quick tip to his lips, the brownish liquid is gone.

Grumbling, "Fine," I mimic his movements. Chugging the liquid sets the back of my throat on fire. I cough as the whiskey warms my insides. After a minute or two, my muscles unclench. But then I look over at Mercy, still unconscious, still unmoving, and my heart leaps back into my throat.

Mercy inhales suddenly, coughs, and tries to sit up.

"Easy," Nathaniel tells her.

She shakes her head and clears her throat. "I'm okay," she

says. "It worked then?"

"The binding agent?" I shift toward her. "Yes. It kept you from jumping."

"I still can't believe that type of thing exists," Mercy says.

"Rae's project," I tell her. "We have a limited supply. For now. I'm working on making more."

"My brother. The chemist." Nathaniel's mockery is both irritating and demeaning.

Mercy inhales and exhales deeply. "I'm sorry."

"Not your fault, love." Nathaniel runs his hand up and down her arm.

"Are you saying it's my fault?" I'm on my feet and ready to battle.

Nathaniel stands. "Your words. Not mine."

"She surprised me. I didn't know," I say, defending myself.

Mercy jumps up from the couch. Slightly unsteady, she wobbles before she is firmly rooted. "Guys! It doesn't matter. I'm fine. Everything is fine." Woozy, she teeters and then sits back down.

"What are we going to do about *her*?" I ask.

Nathaniel backs down from his attack stance. "Well, we can't have her running all over town impersonating Mercy."

"Yeah. That would be bad," Mercy echoes. "What if she shows up at my house? Or worse, school?"

"We'll take care of her," Nathaniel says reassuringly. "Don't worry."

The room is quiet for a few ticks of the clock.

Mercy sinks into the couch and tugs at the bottom of her

shirt. "Do you think this was Isadora's first move?"

Nathaniel and I both nod.

Suddenly, Mercy wraps her arms around her stomach. "Something's wrong." She expels a cry of pain. Her face contorts as she squeezes her eyes shut. Her jaw is clenched and strained.

"What is it?" I ask.

She moans. Dread sweeps her face distorting her beautiful features. "It hurts." Her eyes plead with me. "Gage, it hurts."

I kneel before her. "What can I do?"

"What's happening to her?" Nathaniel yells at me.

"I don't know!"

Mercy keels over and moans. "Make it stop!"

Adrenaline pumps through me as my heart hammers against my chest. "What do we do?"

Nathaniel knocks me over as he lunges toward Mercy. He's holding her by the back of her neck as her body shakes.

"Son of a bitch!" I curse.

Chapter Three

Mercy

The back of a hand connects with my cheek, and I reel backwards, my eyes popping open, my face smarting. I should've fallen, but my hands are clamped by handcuffs, which are bolted to a table. My legs are bound at the ankles. The thick chains chafe my skin. Gage and Nathaniel are gone. I am no longer in their house. *Where am I?* I don't know. What's worse, I don't know who I am either.

"I'm only going to ask you this one more time." A woman with close-cropped hair, no make-up, and a square jaw wags a finger in my face. "Where is the money?"

I steal a glance at my surroundings. I'm in a small, dark room with a large mirror. The woman glaring at me wears an ill-fitting pants suit and sensible, clunky shoes. On the waist of her pants hangs a shield. She's an officer or a detective or something. The pieces click together, and I realize where I am.

Holy shit. I'm in jail!

"Quit messing around!" Afraid she'll hit me again, I flinch. She exhales, and her short blast of tobacco breath hits me in the face. "Where did Louis hide the money?"

"I want my lawyer!" I blurt out, praying that all those hours of watching *Law & Order* reruns on the USA Network are about to pay off.

The detective reclines in her chair, nonchalant, like it doesn't matter what I've said.

"I want my lawyer," I repeat. "I'm not saying another word." I suck in my lips for added effect, which I realize too late, probably makes me look like toddler throwing a tantrum.

She wraps her knuckles on the two-way mirror behind her.

The door opens. Two hulking guards, thumbs tucked into their utility belts, approach me. One kneels and unshackles my ankles from the table while the other unhooks my wrists. I feel only momentary relief. They yank me from my seat and shove me out of the room.

Though they propel me forward, I can't make much progress with my ankles still cinched together. Doing all I can to not fall flat on my face, I press on down a long corridor lined with cells. This is so much worse than being in the interrogation room.

Jail on TV is nothing like jail in real life. The smell of bodies all jammed together, of toilets that haven't been scrubbed—I have to force myself not to vomit when the odors assault my nose. The other prisoners, all female, in bleak, gray, hospital-style scrubs eyeball me. A girl with a tattoo of a spider web on her left cheekbone winks at me, and a cold shiver ripples through my spine.

One of the guards digs his nails into my shoulder as he stops me in front of a cell. He slams me into the bars and holds me there while the other guard removes the ankle restraints. When he finishes, he barks at someone, whom I assume is my cellmate, to step back. The guard holding me jams my face and chest against the cold steel door and unclasps my handcuffs. Something sharp pierces my neck.

"What the hell was that?" I yell.

The guard holding me hustles me inside and locks the door. Without so much as a word, I'm left alone in jail with a girl that looks like a cracked-out version of Natalie Portman after she shaved her head for that movie. She eyes me as I slide over to the bunk beds. Since she's perched on the bottom, I guess the top is mine.

Climbing up, I crawl onto the barely-there mattress and fall against the pillow. *I will not cry. I will not cry. I will not cry,* I chant to myself until my resolve thickens. Below, Natalie Portman's lesser self chews her nails and spits them on the floor.

I have to get out of here.

Concentrating, I try to separate myself from this body. I imagine myself floating above, releasing into the air like steam, but when I open my eyes, I am still solidly attached to this body. *What the hell?*

Gage and Nathaniel have to be searching for me. But without the warehouse, without all that fancy technology, and without his Hunter's mark, Gage is without the skills and resources he needs. My hope falls to Nathaniel. He found me before, maybe he'll find me again.

I roll over onto my left side and find myself eye to eye with Faux Natalie. "Jesus Christ!" I sit up, scrambling to flatten myself against the wall.

Slowly, eerily, she tilts her head to the left. "There's something different about you." She rests her chin on the edge of my mattress. "You have a secret." She drums her fingers against the metal bed frame. "Someone's got a secret," she sings in a childish voice that reminds me of a scary movie.

Trying to sound brave, I threaten, "Back off. I mean it."

She responds by batting her eyelashes. "Or what?" The *ting-ting* of her nails against metal frame makes me shudder. "You're no fun," she whines. "I'm only playing."

My legs are shaking. They won't hold me in this defensive, squat position for much longer. "Just leave me alone."

"Come on. Play with me."

Every hair on the back of my neck stands on end.

Her eyes flash wildly. She spins around, dancing to a melody only she can hear. Swaying and laughing, she snatches the pillow from her bunk, and in a seductive and beyond creepy way, she reaches into the pillowcase and removes a long strand of plastic material. She twirls the strand like a lasso over her head and sings a song I don't recognize.

"No need to get excited,
The thief, he kindly spoke,
'There are many here among us,
Who feel that life is but a joke.
But you and I, we've been through that,

And this is not our fate.
So let us not talk falsely now, the hour is getting late.'"

She wraps the strand around her wrists until it's taut like a cord.

"Oh shit," I say as I realize what she's about to do. "Put that down!"

Smiling wickedly, she loops the noose around her neck and squeezes. I jump off the bed, lunging for her, but she's quick, and I miss. I crash to the ground and my wrist hits the concrete with a sickening *crack*.

"Stop!" I scream as she pulls the noose tighter and tighter. Her eyes bulge out of her head, and her face turns purple. "Stop!" Scrambling to the door, holding my injured wrist against my stomach, I yell down the hall, "Help! Someone help!"

She's on her knees now; the job is almost finished. I resume my cries for help. Finally, I hear someone coming toward us. The guards throw open the door. One of them pulls my obviously broken wrist, and I yelp as he secures my hands behind me. The other guard attends to my cellmate. She's limp and clearly not breathing. The guard holding me makes a plea using his walkie-talkie, and it isn't long before more people come running. A blur of uniforms pass me. Eventually, I am ushered from the scene.

My feet drag as I beg, "Please, my wrist is broken."

"Shut up!" the guard barks as he urges me forward. He opens a solid door at the end of the hall, unclamps my wrists, and tosses me into a very small, very dark, and very damp room. The slamming door cuts off my cries for help.

There's no bed, not even a cot, in this room. No windows, no light, nothing. Cradling my wrist against my body, I sink to the floor and pull my knees to my chest. My breath comes in short, rapid bursts, and I know what's about to happen. I am going to jump. *Thank God!* I close my eyes and give myself over to the urge. But nothing happens. When I open my eyes, I am still in the cell, still in this damaged body.

Shit!

I try again, thinking back to when I'd ended up in a dead body, and Nathaniel found me. He told me to concentrate on him, to reach for his hand. He isn't here in the cell with me, but I try to reach for him anyway. I imagine him coaxing me out of the body. But again: nothing.

Frustration builds, and I stomp, which makes my whole body jerk. I am in agony. My wrist needs to be treated. They can't just leave me in here. Can they?

It's unbearable, the sensation of needing to flee and being unable to. My skin crawls. Perspiration trickles and pools in my armpits and down my back. I shiver even though my palms are clammy, and my face is drenched in sweat. I lean back, close my eyes, and surrender to exhaustion.

When I wake, I'm curled in a ball on the dirty floor. My wrist is grossly swollen and purple, and though the pain is duller, it's still horribly uncomfortable. My mouth feels as though I've been sucking cotton.

I need to vomit. Scooting over to the toilet that, given the smell, hasn't been washed in decades, I dry heave until bile burns its way to the surface and spews forth. With my good hand, I wipe my mouth, and then I quickly retreat from the stank odor.

Completely disoriented, I have no idea how much time has passed. For all I know I could've been asleep for hours, or worse, it might have only been minutes.

The door opens, and someone barks, "On your feet!" It's slightly difficult to get off the floor using only one hand, but I manage. "Turn around. Hands behind your back," the guard instructs as he charges into the room. I try, but my broken wrist won't cooperate. "I said, hands behind your back!"

"I can't." I whimper and hold up my wrist. "It's broken."

He shoves me against the wall and yanks my arms behind me. White-hot pain flashes through me.

Down the long hall I walk with the guard hot on my heels. Tears splash my cheeks. Snot dribbles from my nose. I don't care. The guard leads me back to the interrogation room. He secures me to the table, but mercifully, he leaves my broken side unrestrained.

The guard moves to the corner of the room and stands watch. A door on the opposite end of the room opens. Isadora casually enters.

She addresses the guard. "I'll need a moment alone with my client." He exits, and we're alone. Gingerly she cups my wrist. "That looks like it hurts," she says, feigning sympathy.

"What are you doing here?"

She balks. "Would you rather I leave?"

Sadly, no.

Isadora sets a black briefcase down on the table, and then she sits across from me.

"How did you know where I was?" I ask. "Did you do this to me?"

Isadora smiles. Her green eyes light up like lightning bugs against a night sky. "It's my duty, my obligation, to know where you are at all times, Mercy. You are very precious to me."

In truth, I probably am precious to her, but not in a good way. Although Isadora is my aunt, she doesn't love me. She isn't worried about me in the slightest. She only wants to use me, to use my power.

"Did you do this?" I ask again. "Did you set this up?"

She pretends to look hurt. "Why would I do that?"

"But how? Gage and Nathaniel …"

"Injected you with binding agent?" Isadora laughs. "Yes, well, there are ways around that." Isadora lifts my sleeve and shows me a tiny scar I never noticed before.

"What is that?" I ask.

"A tracker," Isadora answers. "It makes you accessible to those powerful enough to call you."

"Take it out."

"All in good time."

What a bitch.

Isadora smiles pleasantly, but there is nothing pleasant about her. "I've come to discuss the terms of our agreement," she says.

"Just tell me what you want so I can get out of here."

"Of course, Mercy," she coos. "I wouldn't want you to suffer for one minute longer than necessary."

I'm tempted to point out that my suffering shouldn't be necessary at all, let alone have time limits.

Isadora stands. She comes around behind me. Leaning in close, she says, "Remember our deal, little girl," she whispers in my ear. "You do as I say and no harm comes to your family. Break that promise and you'll suffer in ways you never thought possible."

"I know. Tell me what you want."

"I want you to kill The Assembled."

What? "*You* are The Assembled."

"Obviously, I'm not talking about me."

She's a lunatic. And it's beyond eerie to me that she and I want the same thing. The only part of Isadora's plan that differs from mine is she would like to exclude herself from the kill list. My intention was definitely to bring down The Assembled. But I can't let her know about my power, about how I reached into my mother's chest and started her heart. If she ever finds out, she'll be even more certain I can do what she asks. So I lie. "I can't. No one can. It's not possible."

Isadora pouts. She eyes my prison uniform and shrugs. "Well, then. I guess you're lucky gray is your color." She fiddles with the handle of her briefcase and slowly slides it off the table as if she's going to leave.

"Wait! Tell me why. Why do you want to kill The Assembled?"

Isadora retreats to the other side of the table. "You don't need to know my reasons. All you need to know is this is what I want. You may not believe me, Mercy, but you and I are on the same side. You just don't know it yet."

"You and I are not on the same side. I only agreed to help you to save the people I love."

"Yes. Exactly."

She's not telling me something. I can feel it.

"I don't know if I can kill The Assembled," I say.

"My sweet Mercy, it will be my utmost pleasure to watch you try." Isadora sits back down. She leans forward with her elbows on the table. Her green eyes pierce me with their stare. "I'm going to help you be all that you can be."

This does nothing to squelch my suspicion of her. Isadora opens and closes the briefcase. She pushes back from the table, comes around behind me, and jabs the back of my arm with something. It stings for a second. Isadora returns to her side of the table. She takes the briefcase in her hand and straightens her stance before she approaches the door and knocks. "Guard!"

The room around me sways. "What did you give me?" Merely speaking those five words leaves me gasping for breath.

Isadora smoothes her hair. "Just adding a little extra to the binding agent the guards gave you earlier. I need to make sure you stay put for now. Believe it or not, this is the safest place for you."

The guards are working for Isadora. That explains the piercing pain in my neck from before. Struggling to stay lucid, I say "Why are you doing this?"

"I like to think of it as protecting my assets."

"You won't get away with this," I say forcefully.

"I already have."

"Isadora, please."

The guard returns and allows Isadora to leave the room. Before she is out of my sight, she turns to the guard, she says, "You'll see that my client's injuries are attended to, or you'll be facing your own day in court. Got it?"

Chapter Four

Gage

Mercy lies motionless on the couch. Too much time has passed. Something is wrong. "We need to get her to the hospital," I tell Nathaniel.

Bracing myself for the argument that's sure to follow, I stand with my arms folded across my chest and glare at him sternly to show I'm resolved and not backing down. This is our best option. Without the warehouse, we don't have the equipment necessary to keep Mercy's body alive. She needs fluids and vitamins, a heart monitor, and whatever else Rae used. *Damn! Why hadn't I paid more attention?*

Nathaniel looks down at Mercy's body, then up at me. "You're right. We have to get her to the hospital, but we should call Ariana first."

"Do you want me to do that?"

"No, I'll do it." Nathaniel stalks off.

I crouch in front of Mercy's body and take her small hand in mine. Her skin is cool. "I'm going to find you," I whisper. "I'm going to bring you home."

Replacing her hand at her side, I reach behind her and pull down the blanket draped over the back of the couch. I wrap her snugly, hoping it will keep her warm.

It's taking Nathaniel too long to come back. I yell down the hall, "What's the hold up?" Though I don't want to, I leave Mercy's side in order to investigate. "Nathaniel! What did Ariana say?"

He isn't in his room or the kitchen or the backyard. Nathaniel is gone, and quite frankly, I don't know why I'm surprised. Of course he's gone. Nathaniel is reckless and brash, and it's in perfect keeping with his character to he would run off and exclude me from his plan. Anger surges inside of me. I let out an involuntary grunt of frustration.

"You sound like a pig," Nathaniel says from behind me.

Whipping around, I face him. "I thought you'd left."

"Yee of little faith."

"Where were you?"

"The garage," he answers. "I got the electric blanket out of the cabinet."

It's quite possible that I've underestimated him.

"What did Ariana say?" I ask him.

"She said to keep her warm, and that she'll be right over."

While we wait, Nathaniel covers Mercy with the electric blanket. Neither of us is going to say it out loud, but it's plain to see her skin is turning ashy. Nathaniel wipes her brow. The tenderness he displays disarms me.

The sound of a car pulling into the drive draws our attention. A momentary game of chicken occurs as neither one of us wants to be the one to leave Mercy. Unable to sit still, I lose, charging to the door and throwing it open. The frantic look on Ariana's face does little to steady my nerves.

"How is she?"

I step aside to let Ariana into the house. As she passes, I tell her, "We're keeping her warm, but I don't know if it's enough."

"Go out to the car. You'll find everything we need."

Nathaniel remains stationed at Mercy's side. I bolt to the car. The backseat looks like a medical supply store. It takes me three trips to unload it all.

We move Mercy to Nathaniel's bed. That wouldn't have been my first choice, but it doesn't seem right to argue. Nathaniel and I hang back while Ariana works. She starts an IV line in Mercy's right forearm, which connects to a bag of fluid. Within minutes, Mercy's color improves. A faint blush pinks her cheeks, and I let out a sigh of relief.

Ariana ushers us out of the room. "What happened exactly?" she asks, her voice spiked with irritation.

"Like I told you on the phone," Nathaniel begins, "we had a visit from her evil twin."

"Now is not the time for your quips," Ariana snaps.

Tensions are too high. "We're all on the same side," I remind them.

The three of us make our way to the living room. We sit in a triangle formation. Nathaniel's hands are clenched while Ariana's posture is rigid.

"Mercy was upset," I explain. "She was going to jump, but we got to her in time."

"You gave her binding agent?" Ariana asked.

"Yes," Nathaniel answers.

"It didn't work," I say.

Ariana's brow wrinkles. "What do you mean?"

"Something went wrong," I continue. "Mercy was in pain. And then," I snap my fingers, "just like that, she was gone."

Ariana nods her head like she understands. She might, but I don't.

"What?" I ask her. "What is it?"

"Isadora."

"Are you sure?"

Nathaniel is off the couch and pacing. "This is bullshit. We have to do something!"

"Anything we do will only place Mercy in more danger," Ariana says. "Isadora was very clear about her terms. Mercy agreed to this."

Nathaniel's rage intensifies. "What are you suggesting? That we sit by and do nothing?" He seethes, taking two quick strides toward Ariana. "Mercy only made this asinine deal as a way to protect us. We owe her the same."

"You think I don't know that?" Ariana stands, and they are face to face. "I want to keep Mercy safe just as much as you do."

"Enough!" I yell.

Ariana points at Nathaniel. "Do not forget for one second

that the reason Mercy is in this mess is because of the two of you." She scowls. "You are going to keep yourselves in check. Do I make myself clear?"

Yes, she does.

We go to our separate corners. Ariana heads over to the wet bar and pours herself a drink. She sips it slowly.

"I still don't understand how this happened," Nathaniel says, breaking the silence.

Ariana finishes her drink. "It's an extraction serum."

Nathaniel's face falls. He hangs his head sorrowfully.

"That doesn't make sense," I say. "Wouldn't Isadora have to be in close proximity to inject Mercy?"

"Not if Mercy has a tracker." Ariana holds out her arm. Above her wrist is a nasty, jagged scar.

My eyes go wide. "This is unbelievable. Why would Isadora do that? Mercy already agreed to work with her. What does this mean exactly?"

"It means, little brother, that Mercy isn't coming back to us. Once Isadora has Mercy under her control, she'll inject her with binding agent, and Mercy won't be able to leave whatever body she's in until Isadora releases her."

Ariana excuses herself to sit with Mercy. With her out of the room, Nathaniel and I can talk freely. I open my mouth, but he shakes his head, and then nods to the front door. We walk outside.

Once we're in the yard I say, "She could be anywhere."

Nathaniel puts his hand on my shoulder. "She's stronger than any of us. She'll get through this."

"I can't stand not knowing," I tell him.

"Me either, but we'll figure something out."

"Can't you find her, like you did last time?"

Nathaniel stands with his hands on his hips. He scans the yard. "It's not like last time. She's in a live body. When that happens, it's like the signal is blocked. I can't read her at all." He sounds distressed, uncomfortable, and full of sorrow.

"We could go to Isadora's warehouse and confront her," I suggest, knowing that my idea is idiotic and borderline suicidal.

"That's exactly what she wants. If we go charging in there, threatening her, she'll have the excuse she needs to end us." Nathaniel exhales. "We're going to have to wait."

He's right. All we can do is wait and hope that Mercy isn't in any danger. But of course she is. She has to be. We never should've let her make this deal with Isadora. We should've fought, done anything besides let Mercy hand over her life.

Mercy was in no position to make such a decision. Not after what Isadora did to her. The scene is still etched into my consciousness. Mercy, strapped to the table, listless, as a rib was yanked from her body. I'd never felt so helpless in all my life. And it was the first time that I truly understood Nathaniel and how he felt about me. It was the first time I fully understood how I came to be in existence. I was created from a rib stolen from Nathaniel's body. And then I was sent by The Assembled to kill him, his own flesh and blood.

The Assembled are supposed to keep the peace between the human world and all that lay beyond. They aren't supposed to interfere. None of us are. Nathaniel and Ariana were supposed to help humans cross over after they died. They weren't supposed to have contact. But they broke that rule. They were banished, made human, and stripped of all their power. But what The Assembled didn't know was that they wouldn't live and die as humans. They would be something else entirely—Breachers.

I was created to stop them. It's the sole purpose of my existence. But it wasn't until that day, until I watched them take a rib from Mercy, that I fully comprehended the severity of it. We still haven't talked about it, and I doubt we ever will. Some words can't be spoken. Nathaniel and I are twins; we are connected in a way I can never explain, and I know now our connection stopped me from killing him. I've had plenty of opportunities, but there was always a reason to let him go.

Now Mercy has a twin to deal with, and if her antics from earlier are any indication as to what we're up against, we are in for some serious trouble.

Embarrassed doesn't even begin to cover how I feel about being duped. I let my emotions and my desire cloud my judgment. Is this what it means to be human? Am I completely vulnerable to my impulses?

I'm afraid of my answer.

Ariana bursts onto the front porch, interrupting my mental flogging.

"Mercy called!" she yells.

Nathaniel and I dart across the yard and back into the house.

Ariana stands with her arms wrapped around her torso. "She's in prison, but she doesn't know where. She can't jump. Isadora made sure of that."

Nathaniel walks toward Ariana. "She didn't tell you anything? Give you any clues as to where she might be?"

"She doesn't even know her name." At the end of her sentence, Ariana hiccups as tears began to flow. "This isn't the life I wanted for her." She sinks onto the couch, wipes her cheeks, and tries to compose herself.

Stepping forward, I say, "I know we haven't said this in so many words, but we're sorry for putting Mercy in this position. I … we … had no idea this would happen."

She glares at me. "Save your words, Hunter."

The insult stings more than I want to admit.

"We're going to need a computer," Nathaniel blurts out.

"I didn't know you were good with computers," I say to Nathaniel.

He grins—a look I've come to know well. "I'm not, but breaching a computer geek can't be that difficult."

My face falls. Of course. It always comes down to breaching. When did I become okay with this? When did I decide that our needs outweigh a human life?

"Gage," Nathaniel snaps. "Now is not the time for moral dilemmas. We need to get down to the courthouse so I can do some digging and find our girl."

The only part of that I hear is *our girl*. "Right," I finally say.

Ariana stays by Mercy's side while Nathaniel and I hightail it downtown. We should've discussed this, made some sort of plan before we go charging into the building, but that's not exactly how Nathaniel operates. We are in the car and at the courthouse in less than ten minutes. After illegally parking out front, we run up the steps and through the entrance.

The reception area is a rotunda of opulence: marble floors, cherry wood benches, busts and statues of true Roman quality, and all of it leads to the desk of a small man whose nametag reads Mitchell.

It won't be easy to distract him. Twitchy little man has darting eyes, and an eyebrow that appears permanently fixed in an arc. He isn't the only one to worry about either. The entire place is buzzing with activity. Isolating someone long enough for Nathaniel to breach will be difficult, but when Nathaniel is determined, nothing will get in his way.

I knock over Mitchell's cup of coffee. He lets a string of obscenities fly as he glares in my direction. Playing the part of the bumbling fool, I apologize and try to assist him, which, of course only makes things worse. He calls someone to watch his desk so he can clean himself off.

Nathaniel trails him into the men's restroom. I keep watch, and though I don't see what's going on inside, from the sound of it, the clerk is putting up a fight. The bathroom door opens, and Nathaniel, in Mitchell's body, walks out.

"I can't believe I let you do this again," I say. "We don't know anything about this guy, and we're just going to kill him!"

"Keep your voice down," Nathaniel warns me. "And keep your guilt in check. This is about Mercy."

How can I argue with that?

Nathaniel takes his place at Mitchell's desk and buzzes me through. I hover as he fiddles with the computer. Computers aren't exactly my forte. I always relied on Jinx. He was a whiz at all things technical. I highly doubt that Nathaniel holds a candle to Jinx's technical knowledge, but he seems to be navigating through this system with ease.

"How do you know how to do this?" I ask.

"Actually, I learned this from Mercy," he answers.

"Mercy? I didn't know she was into computers."

"She's not," Nathaniel tells me. "But she did teach me something about breaching."

"What do you mean?"

"Mercy told me that she was aware of the soul of the body she took, like she was sharing the space as opposed to taking it over. It got me to thinking maybe that skill wasn't unique to Mercy. Maybe, when I took a body, I didn't want to have any connection to the host because I was trying to conquer it. Maybe, if I let myself, I could connect."

"And can you?"

"It would appear so." Nathaniel's fingers fly across the keyboard as he types in pass codes, allowing him access to the database.

I point to the screen. "What is that?"

"That is a list of visitors."

"Isadora."

"She used her own name." Nathaniel chortles.

"This could be a trap," I warn him.

"Of course it's a trap," Nathaniel agrees. "But at least we know where Mercy is now." Nathaniel punches in another code. "And we know who she is: Libby Reid, wife of alleged Vegas mob boss, Frankie Asters. She's twenty-five, a former Playmate, and mother of one-year-old son Alistair. She's been arrested in connection with her husband's murder."

I read over his shoulder. "It says here she's being held without bail at a maximum security prison outside of Las Vegas, Nevada."

Nathaniel looks up at me and smiles. "You know what this means, little brother."

"Road trip."

Chapter Five

Nathaniel

"We're leaving. Now." Isadora clutched Nathaniel's forearm, and together they transported from the human world to the other side.

When they landed on the bridge, Isadora walked away at such a clip that Nathaniel had to jog to keep up with her. They were nearly to the end before Nathaniel matched her stride for stride.

"I understand you're upset," he tried.

"You understand nothing!" she snapped. She stopped and faced Nathaniel. "Do you realize what you've done?"

"Isadora, please." Nathaniel reached for her. He held her hand in his, and kissed her palm softly. "I'm sorry."

Isadora shook her head slightly. "Sorry for what?" she whispered. "For breaking the rules? Or for hurting me?"

"Both," he answered honestly. "I'm sorry for both." Nathaniel *nestled her hand to his chest.*

"Who is she?"

Nathaniel averted his gaze.

Isadora leaned into Nathaniel. "Who is she?"

"Her name is Ellie."

"Was she worth it?"

"Isadora, don't."

Isadora pulled back, yanking her hand free. "Don't what? Be honest?"

"I said I'm sorry. What more do you want from me?"

"We could've had everything," she told him. "I loved you, Nathaniel. I wanted your love in return."

"I tried."

Fire blazed behind Isadora's eyes. "You tried? As if the thought of loving me is some menial chore?"

"That's not what I meant."

"I can't protect you from this. I have an obligation to tell them."

"You don't have to do that."

"You expect me to be complicit in your crimes? As if I owe you anything."

"My life means nothing to you? You know what will happen to me if they find out. Please. Isadora, I'm sorry that I couldn't give you what you wanted, be who you wanted, but this will get me killed."

"You've made your choice. You'll just have to live with your decision."

Nathaniel stood on the bridge and watched Isadora leave. Though she strode away determined, angry, Nathaniel held out hope that she wouldn't betray him. He leaned into the rail and watched the sun fade on the horizon. As he stood there, basking in streaks of orange and pink and shades of yellow, Nathaniel thought of Ellie. He'd made her a promise that he intended to keep; he would be there to guide her home. After all, if his life was all about helping humans, why was it so wrong for him to develop a relationship with Ellie?

He was lost in thought and unaware that someone had come up behind him. It wasn't until he felt a hand on his shoulder that he registered a presence.

"My sister is upset." Ariana spoke gently to Nathaniel. Yes, there was accusation in her tone, but there was also compassion.

"Am I in trouble?" In his voice was a hint of sarcasm, but his question was very serious.

"I'll speak with her," Ariana assured him.

Nathaniel straightened to his full height. "I need you to cover for me."

Ariana shook her head. "Nathaniel."

"There's something I have to do."

"What you need to do is your work." Ariana pulled an envelope from her pocket. "Your next assignment."

Nathaniel backed away. "Can't you, just this once, do it for me?"

Ariana's green eyes narrowed. A vertical line appeared between her eyebrows. "What are you up to?"

"There's this girl," Nathaniel started. "And she needs me."

Ariana huffed a short, stilted breath. "No."

"Just listen to me."

"No," Ariana said again. "Nathaniel, you know the rules. No interaction with humans until you see them on the bridge. You guide them across, and that's all. That's all."

"I know the rules, but—"

Ariana held up her hand. "No. There are no buts. The rules are absolute. You know this."

"The rules are stupid!" Nathaniel yelled. "What do The Assembled know? Nothing! They sit in their ivory tower, judge and jury over all. It's bullshit!"

Ariana looked around as though she was worried someone might overhear their conversation. "Lower your voice."

"Why? What more can they do to me?"

"You don't want to know the answer to that."

Nathaniel grabbed Ariana by the forearms. "You could talk to them." He spoke in hurried breaths as he said, "You are the most powerful of all the Guides. They'll listen to you. Make them see that interacting with humans is not a crime."

Ariana shook loose of Nathaniel's grip. "I will do no such thing."

"Why? Because you don't believe what I'm saying? Or because you don't want to risk your cushy little life here?"

"Watch your tone with me, Nathaniel. I am no one to be trifled with."

"That's what I'm saying. You can make them see. You have to make them see."

"No," Ariana said quietly. "I can't."

Nathaniel's expression softened. His shoulders eased when he saw Ariana's pained look. "What is it?"

"There's something you should know." Ariana threw her shoulders back as if she were bracing her whole body for the words she was about to speak. "They won't listen to me because I walked away from them. I gave up my right to be heard a long time ago."

"What are you saying?"

"I was once part of them. Now, I am not."

"I don't understand."

Ariana faced the sun. It illuminated her, making her skin glow. She closed her eyes momentarily, soaking it in. "It was a long time ago. Long before your arrival," she told him. "I made a choice, gave up my position."

"That doesn't mean they won't listen to you."

"It does." Ariana shoved the envelope against his chest. "We have but one job to do, Nathaniel. And I am instructing you to do yours. Do you understand me?" she asked with meaning behind her words.

Nathaniel took the envelope. He waited for Ariana to leave before he opened it. Inside, on a piece of parchment paper, he read the name of his next assignment: Eleanor Jane Levinson.

Chapter Six

Mercy

After Isadora leaves, I beg the guard for a phone call. He relents, I'm assuming, because he's still under Isadora's threat for not treating my wrist. When my mother answers, I break down crying. Part of me might be Mercy, badass Breacher, but most of me is still Mercy, sixteen-year-old kid who is scared out of her mind and wants her mom.

There isn't much I can tell her. I don't know where I am or even who I am. I was so stunned by Isadora's visit that I didn't ask any pertinent questions. Of course, it never occurred to me that she'd leave me in here. I honestly thought she was going to break me out. I really need to stop underestimating her capability for evil.

My mom assures me that Gage and Nathaniel will locate me. At least I can take comfort in that. But I don't know how long it will take for them to get to me. And once they get here, how do they plan on getting me out? The idea of an attempted jailbreak is not appealing.

When I finish the brief conversation with my mother, the guard has to pry the phone out of my hand. I don't want to let go of that connection to her, and I really don't want to go back to my cell. Luckily, we take a detour to the infirmary first.

The infirmary is white, sterile, with no frills, and nothing that can be used as a weapon. I am handcuffed to the side rail of the bed while I wait for the doctor. The guard is no more than four feet away at all times.

"Libby Reid," the doctor says as she walks into the room. "I'm Dr. Kelly."

This means I am Libby Reid.

She wears a lab coat, brown trousers from a distant decade, and shoes that were never fashionable. Lyla would definitely disapprove of her fashion choices. But there is something cheery about Dr. Kelly. Her hair is neatly curled, and her round face greets me with a pleasant smile.

Dr. Kelly washes and dries her hands before meticulously assessing my broken wrist. "That looks nasty," she remarks. "I'll be able to set it for you, but I won't be able to give you anything for the pain."

"Why not?"

"It says in your file that you've had problems with substance abuse."

Awesome.

"We'll have you in and out of surgery in about an hour," she says.

"Surgery?"

"It's a compound fracture, dear. It's going to take some pins to put it back together."

I've never had surgery before, and I'm not looking forward to it now. I really, really, really want my mom. "But you'll be able to put me to sleep for that part, right? I mean, I won't be able to feel anything."

She pats my shoulder. It isn't exactly loving, but it's something. Dr. Kelly tells me to lie flat on the table while the nurse preps me for surgery. I'm not allowed to change my clothes, or even go to the bathroom first. The guard never even takes the handcuffs off, which, to me, seems excessive. I'm going to be unconscious in a few minutes. Do I really need to be restrained?

The IV needle hurts. The nurse instructs me to count back from one hundred, but I can't remember saying anything after ninety-eight. When I open my eyes again, I'm sitting in the backseat of a car.

Nathaniel drives while Gage rides shotgun. They aren't listening to music or chatting. They're focused on the road ahead. From behind, they're identical twins—same posture, same dark hair, same stiff shoulders. But there are subtle differences I notice. Nathaniel's right earlobe is slightly longer than his left. And he has three moles in a cluster near the base of his neck. Gage's skin is creamy, pinkish, without a blemish, mark, or scar. His dark hair is in need of a trim, but other than that, there's nothing flawed about him.

"Nathaniel," I speak his name, hoping that he'll hear me. He doesn't. I figure I'm dreaming anyway. It's a good dream. I'm glad to be near them.

Scooting forward, I edge closer to Nathaniel. I touch his hand, which is locked in a death grip on the emergency brake. I can't feel him, not really, because, of course, I'm not there, but I pretend for a moment that I can feel heat between us.

As if I am controlling the dream, Nathaniel looks down at his hand.

"What is it?" Gage asks him.

Nathaniel shakes his head. "Nothing."

Lacing my fingers through his, I give his hand a little squeeze. His thumb brushes against my skin. If only this were real.

"I'm sorry this happened," I say.

"What?" Nathaniel asks.

"I didn't say anything," Gage responds.

Hopeful, I ask, "Nathaniel, can you hear me?"

Nathaniel looks up into the rearview mirror. But he doesn't see me. There's no sign of recognition on his face. "Did you hear that?"

Gage scans the backseat. "Hear what? What's with you?"

Nathaniel shakes his head again. He puts both hands on the wheel, and instantly, I feel cold. "I thought I heard Mercy's voice," he tells Gage. "I'm going crazy. This drive is taking forever."

Gage checks his phone. "It's only a few more hours. We're nearly there."

Leaning my head against the seat, I close my eyes. When I open them again, I'm back in the infirmary.

"There you are," Dr. Kelly peers over me. "How're you feeling?"

"Sleepy," I mutter.

"That'll wear off." She checks my wrist. "Surgery went well, and it shouldn't even take that long to heal. You can go back to lockup with your cast, but you'll have to stay in solitary."

I picture the dark, damp cell and shake my head back and forth. "Please don't make me go back there."

"Not in my control, hon." She fiddles with my chart and scribbles some notes. "I'll see you back here in a few days."

She leaves the room. Still groggy and sluggish, I am made to stand while two guards shackle my ankles together. Even after surgery, while doped up, I am still a threat to them. It makes me wonder what this Libby Reid person must've done to deserve such treatment. Maybe she's a mass killer or worse, a baby killer. She does drugs, and she has to be violent if they're worried about her every move.

The solitary cell isn't the same hole they left me in before. This room is clean and near the guard's station. Instead of bars there's a heavy metal door with a slit in the middle and a tiny Plexiglas window at the top. There's only one bed, and I'm relieved not to have to climb onto a bunk. I sink into the paper-thin mattress, cradling my arm as I go. It doesn't hurt yet, but I know the anesthetics will wear off eventually. I close my eyes and sleep.

Pounding on the door wakes me. Sitting up too quickly, I cringe as pain shoots from my wrist, through my shoulder, all the way to my neck.

The door opens, and a female guard enters. She lifts me from the bed and helps me down the corridor, but not before she chains my ankles together. Amazing how quickly I am learning to shuffle.

I'm not the only one being filtered into the large room. It seems as though the entire prison is on the same schedule. "What's happening?" I ask. She points to a sign on the wall that reads *Cafeteria*.

The room is crowded. Tables are full of hungry, disgruntled prisoners rotting in their own effluvium. Not even the smell of industrial strength gravy is enough to mask it. Masses of bodies in poorly ventilated areas would be enough, but these are the bodies of women who've given up entirely. They've succumbed to their surroundings and melded to it, become the walls, the floors, the unwashed toilets. The stench is everywhere and all around me, and if I don't get out there soon, I'll be scarred for life.

I slide my tray along the aluminum railing and wait for various treats to be plopped into their designated spots. White stuff, green stuff, and gray stuff with sauce serve as today's fare. For dessert, Jell-O shimmies and wiggles in a small bowl. As I slowly make my way to an empty table, I realize I have to be hungry at this point, but I can't eat. My stomach bunches, and sweat breaks out across the back of my neck. The trembling in my hands makes it nearly impossible to hold a fork.

A small woman sits down next to me. She has stringy black hair and inky, smudged tattoos along her arm. I can't guess her age. She looks like one of those people who appears young from behind, but then they turn around and they're the Crypt Keeper. Her fingernails are short and shredded; her cuticles dotted with hangnails and dried blood from where she's bitten too hard into her skin.

"You're new." She speaks with a smoker's voice, low and raspy.

"What happened to your arm?"

"I fell off the bunk." It's partly true. I don't need to tell her that when I fell I was lunging for my cellmate who was strangling herself to death.

"They give you anything?" she asks. I shake my head. "Bastards. So, what then, meth? Cocaine? Oxy?"

Confused, I push around the inedible food as I ask, "What?"

"Your drug of choice? What's your poison?"

I don't want to be having this conversation. Coming up with the quickest lie I can think of, I simply say, "Pills."

"There's probably stuff going around, if you're looking."

"I'm not."

"Going cold turkey." She cackles. "That's one way to go." She eats her lunch and stays quiet for the rest of the meal.

Relieved to be left alone, I try a few bites of the food-like products. There is no flavor to any of it, but I choke it down anyway. Like a dog in a kennel, I know that if I don't eat my food when they put it out for me, I don't eat at all.

The woman sitting next to me starts to laugh. She giggles like a schoolgirl, which sounds so strange coming from her ragged, worn body. People are turning around and looking at her as she titters into her napkin, rocks back and forth, and shakes her head.

I can't help myself when I ask, "What's so funny?"

Composing herself, she drops her napkin and wipes her hands along her thighs. "You have no idea, do you?"

"What are you talking about?"

"Mercy, it's me."

At the sound of my name, I swivel until she and I are

practically nose to nose. "Who are you?"

She clucks her tongue. "You don't even recognize your own sister. And here I thought we were going to be such great friends."

"You're ..." I can't finish my own thought. *My sister!* I knew, at some point, she and I were going to meet, but I didn't think it would happen here. It's not as though I thought it would be some special occasion where we exchanged tearful hugs like those people who are reunited on talk shows or anything, but I didn't exactly picture this either.

"Justice," she says. "Get it? Mercy, Justice. Isadora thinks she's so clever. I can't believe she left you here. You must've really pissed her off."

"I guess."

"Well, I'm ready to get out of this body. It smells, and hello, manicure much?" She flexes her hands and gives her nails a disapproving look.

"You can't do that here."

"Can't do what?"

"You can't breach out in the open like this. People will notice."

"People are stupid." She cranes her neck and looks around. "I mean, look at these women. They're unwashed, reeking of shame and self-pity. I did that girl a favor earlier." Justice mimes a chokehold around her neck.

My eyes go wide with horror. "That was you!"

She smiles sheepishly then laughs. "Dramatic, I know. Not my idea at all. I think Isadora wanted to scare you. I told her she should just explain what she's trying to do. I, for one, am all for it. And you are just like me, so I know you'll be all for it too."

I am nothing like you. "Be all for what?"

"Sorry, sis. I'm not allowed to say, and I'm not about to piss off Auntie Is. I like my freedom, if you know what I mean."

"So what am I supposed to do now?"

"I believe your rescuers are on their way. Nice job with them, by the way. Yum-my." She breaks the word in two and holds the last syllable like she's singing a musical note. "I may have had a little fun at Gage's expense, but I couldn't help it. I only went over there to introduce myself, but then he was standing there in his towel and, well, you know the rest."

I don't, actually, but I can guess.

"So, I'm gonna go," she announces. "We'll catch up on the outside. Be safe, sis, and watch out for that one over there." She points. "She looks lonely."

"You can't just leave me here," I say.

"Would you honestly trust me to help you?" she asks.

"No."

"That's what I thought."

Seconds later, the body of the woman sitting next to me slumps over, facedown, in her tray of half-eaten food.

***

Day two.

Day three.

Day four.

Still no sign of Nathaniel and Gage. I am going mad. The routine of it all, the schedule, is both comforting and maddening. Sleep, eat, shower, walk, read. On day five, I break from the routine. I have an appointment to see Dr. Kelly.

Sometime after breakfast the guard comes to get me, and by then, I don't even need to be told what to do. I assume the position and wait to be shackled before heading to the infirmary. The guard stands against the wall after she secures me to the bed. And then we wait.

Dr. Kelly is late. The guard checks her watch. "Don't move," she says to me in a voice that tells me she means business, and then she slips out into the hall.

Moments later Dr. Kelly hurries into the room and closes the door behind her. "We don't have much time," she tells me. "Take this." She removes a gun from her jacket pocket and shoves it into my hand.

"What are you doing?"

"Mercy," she says, glaring at me. "Catch on. I don't know how long the guard is going to stay down."

"Nathaniel?" It's almost too good to be true.

"Yes, it's me. Now hurry up."

"You want me to shoot myself?"

He, as Dr. Kelly, strides toward me. "No, I want you to shoot this body. You'll be fine."

"But can't you just get me out like last time?"

He shakes his head. "Isadora's binding agent is too strong. There's only one way to separate you from this body. You're going to have to kill it."

"Her, you mean. I'm going to have to kill *her*." My voice is small and unsure.

"Don't do that to yourself." The voice is that of Dr. Kelly, but the tone—that's all Nathaniel.

Lowering my gaze to the floor, I shake my head. It isn't like I know this Libby person, and she's obviously done something to get herself sent to prison, but does that mean I have the right to end her life? In my heart, I know the answer is no.

Dr. Kelly's hands are on my thighs, and I look up to meet Nathaniel peering at me from behind her eyes. He takes the gun from me. "Gage is waiting for you in the parking lot." He points the gun at the side of my head. "Close your eyes." I do. "Concentrate on Gage. One, two, three …"

Chapter Seven

Gage

Pacing in the parking lot, I try to remain calm. Nathaniel is inside doing his thing, killing humans, saving the day, while once again, I stand by and wait. Is this what my life has come to? Waiting? Holding the reigns of the white horse on which Nathaniel rides? It can't be true, and yet, it is. Nathaniel is the hero because he can breach. He can slip into any situation, manipulate it, and control it until things go his way.

Although I'm envious of him and angry at my own impotence for battle situations, I'm also grateful that he's on my side. It's important to keep Mercy safe, and if that means leaning on Nathaniel for assistance, so be it.

We've been in Las Vegas for three and a half days, but it took some time to figure out how to get Mercy out of prison. We had to do surveillance, scope out the situation. Prison is not a place to go barging into without forethought. Unfortunately, this meant leaving Mercy in jail while we prepared. Neither of us was comfortable with the idea, but what other choice did we have?

Like most of Vegas, the jail is surrounded by desert. Dust balls roll by frequently, and it's hot enough to fry an egg on the pavement. Sweat drips down my shirt and gathers along my waistband. There isn't a stray dog, let alone a stray car, for miles. No one comes to this prison unless they have to, and lucky for us, Dr. Karen Kelly has to.

We followed her from the prison to a small neighborhood in an area called Henderson. It's a subdivision with neatly rowed houses in varying hues of ecru shaded by palm trees. Dr. Kelly owns a two-story home complete with manicured lawn and dark-bottom pool. She lives alone—another piece of luck—and she apparently doesn't entertain many guests.

Nathaniel and I waited by her garbage cans as she made her way out her front door to the car. Poor woman never saw us coming. Once Nathaniel was inside her body, we drove her car to the prison.

"You okay in there?" I asked him.

"She has indigestion," he answered.

Before Nathaniel went inside, we rehashed the final part of our plan—how I was to wait outside for Mercy while Nathaniel went inside. Waiting for Mercy is at least some kind of consolation, but it will be Nathaniel she sees first. Of course, he'll be in Dr. Kelly's body, so maybe it won't be the most romantic moment.

I really have to stop this whole jealousy thing. It's ridiculous to be thinking such things at a time like this.

Suddenly, I am knocked backward by a strong gust. It takes me a second to realize that it isn't wind. I have Mercy in my arms.

"Gage." She breathes heavily. "It worked. I made it."

"Are you all right?" I ask, checking her over. She seems to be in one piece, though she's slightly faded, like a ghost of herself. It must be taking a lot of energy for her to project herself like this.

I wrap my arm around the apparition of her body. "Come on. Let's get you to the car." She rests her head against my chest. The palm of her hand is pressed to my heart.

"Wait," she tells me. "Just give me a sec."

I'll give her all the time in the world if she lets me.

I fear Mercy is starting to pull away, but she's just readjusting so she can look at me. "Jail sucks."

Laughter escapes from both of us, but Mercy's facade quickly fades, and she begins to cry.

"What's wrong?"

"Everything."

Nathaniel runs toward us. "Come on. We have to move." Hustling, I keep my arm around Mercy's shoulders as we make our way to the car.

"You drive," Nathaniel says as he throws the keys at me. He scoops Mercy into his arms and immediately she seems whole.

Reluctantly, I climb into the driver's seat while Nathaniel helps Mercy into the back. I try not to watch them in the rearview mirror as I speed away from the prison, but I can't help stealing a glance. Nathaniel holds Mercy to his chest, and she curls against him in the same way that only moments ago she'd leaned on me.

I drive like a maniac. Nathaniel admonishes me more than

once, but I remind him that we're making a getaway. The road ahead is blurry as I race along, my foot slammed against the gas pedal. Dust, dirt, Death Valley, it all flashes by at lightning speed while my mind tortures me with thoughts of Mercy. She's safe— that's a good thing—but she's in the arms of my brother, and that is not.

Day turns to night, and the hours wear on, and still Mercy sleeps. I can see the tension in Nathaniel's face, in the set of his jaw, and the narrowing of his eyes. He's worried.

"She's just tired," I say to him.

He grunts. "It's more than that."

"And you know what it is?"

Nathaniel glances down at Mercy. I refocus on the road, not wanting to watch him gaze so tenderly at her.

"She's scared," he whispers.

"Of course she's scared. Wouldn't you be if you found yourself in jail?"

"That's not it," he says. "I mean, that's not all of it. She's doubting herself, worrying that she'll fail, and that we'll all die."

Mercy has the world riding on her shoulders. A few months ago, she was an ordinary girl with a father and friends who loved her. She was blissfully unaware of her true origins until Nathaniel and I disrupted her life. We thought we were saving her from her mother, but we were so horribly wrong about that. And once we drew attention to Mercy, we basically put a huge target on her back. This little jail incident proves just how easily Isadora can get to her. Nathaniel's conclusion has to be correct—Mercy is frightened.

We ride in silence and the night drags on. It isn't until we are a few short miles from home that Mercy stirs. I swerve, sending Nathaniel and Mercy careening into the door.

"Dammit, Gage!" Nathaniel chastises. "Can you at least pretend to be a good driver?"

With white knuckles and clenched teeth, I ease the car into the driveway at Mercy's house. Killing the engine, I sit there for a minute, unable to exit the car right away. Nathaniel, on the other hand, has a task, and so he moves swiftly, hauling Mercy out of the car and up the front walk.

Ariana is waiting for us. She stands by as Nathaniel carries Mercy to her bedroom.

"She's been out this whole time," Nathaniel informs her.

Ariana looks over Mercy's body. "It's the binding agent," she tells us. "It shocked her system to be released so suddenly. She'll be fine soon."

"You're sure?" I ask.

"Yes. Put her in the chair," Ariana instructs.

Nathaniel gently sets Mercy down on the overstuffed chair in the corner. He seems reluctant to leave her. Squatting in front of her, he closes his eyes and holds them tightly shut. Mercy's head dips to the side. Nathaniel rests his forehead against her knee. The intimate moment is not meant to be shared, so I turn on my heels and stalk down the hall. I can feel Ariana right behind me.

"Gage." She touches my shoulder. "Thank you for bringing my daughter home to me."

"You're welcome."

"Let's have some tea," she offers.

I follow her into the kitchen and can't help but notice how different it looks. The first time I was in this kitchen, it felt empty. It looked as though they were only borrowing it for a short while. But now, the kitchen is full of life. Curtains hang over the small window that faces the backyard. The windowsill is dressed with potted plants. The counters are clean, as they had been before, but there are plenty of signs of use. A recipe book lays open with sticky notes protruding from its pages. There's a new spice rack along the far wall with lively colored jars in various stages of fullness. Mercy mentioned that Ariana loved to cook, and it's clear she's reclaimed her territory.

Ariana sets the kettle on the stove and motions for me to sit. Minutes later, the table is set, and she's pouring my first helping of the best tea I've ever had.

"You look concerned," she says.

"Of course."

"Tell me."

I take a sip of my tea and replace the cup on the saucer. "I'm uncomfortable being human."

Ariana's green eyes widen. She wasn't expecting me to be so candid. "You'll never really be human, Gage."

"I certainly feel human."

"You mean helpless."

Ashamed that she's read me so clearly, I lower my head.

She pats my hand. "You're not helpless, Gage. You brought Mercy home."

I look up and speak the words I've been swallowing the entire drive, "Nathaniel could've done that by himself."

Ariana drinks her tea and eyes me sympathetically. "There's more than one hero in every story."

"Why are you being so kind to me? After everything I've done to put you in this position?"

Ariana sets the cup down, flattens her hands against her thighs, and leans back in her chair. "This isn't your fault. I know I blamed you before, but that's because I needed to be angry with someone for what The Assembled has done. But in truth, we are all their victims. I see that you're trying to make things right."

"I am."

"I know. But you also love my daughter. And whether you're human or not, I'm not ready to lose her again."

Confused, I ask, "Lose her?"

"You'd have to be a mother to understand completely. Breacher or not, Mercy is my child, and I missed much of her life. I've only just gotten her back, and now, there's more people with claims on her heart."

"I wouldn't be so bold as to claim her heart."

"But you wouldn't be so foolish to deny it either."

"No." I take a quick sip of my tea. "But I don't think I'm the one you need to worry about."

Ariana rises from the table. She pads across the small space and refills the teapot with water. As she brings it to the table, she says, "I only ask one thing." She tips the pot of warm water into my cup. "Please be smart, Gage. Don't let whatever you feel for her put her in danger."

"I won't."

"This isn't an easy promise to make. To keep her safe, you

may have to walk away."

For a brief moment, I picture myself saying good-bye to Mercy, and instantly I feel tightening in my chest, as though something is wrenching my heart. But despite what I feel, I still know the right thing to do. "I won't put her in danger, for anything or anyone, I swear."

Ariana nods and goes to check on Mercy. Unable to sit still a moment longer, I wander out into the backyard. It too has been altered since my last visit. The grass is sharply mowed without a weed in sight. Though it's dark, I can still make out the flowers that are newly planted. Once this backyard was stagnant and nearly desolate, and now, there are signs of life everywhere. I follow the stone path that meanders through the garden and clip my toe on the edge of a piece that protrudes slightly from the dirt.

It isn't an ordinary stone. In it are Mercy's childhood handprints. I wonder why I never noticed it before. Squatting, I trace the outline of the tiny hand with my index finger. I picture Mercy as a little girl, full of wonder, with soft brown hair curling slightly at the tip, bright brown eyes, and naturally rosy cheeks.

When she'd made this print, she'd been blissfully unaware of who she really was, and I can't help but wonder if she'd like to go back. *Of course she would.* Who would want this life? Mercy is supposed to be studying and hanging out with friends. She certainly isn't supposed to be lying unconscious in the other room, expelled from her body.

The sound of footsteps behind me draws me into a standing position. When I turn, the rosy-cheeked girl I've been imagining is before me. Only this time, I know it's not really Mercy. It's her twin. "You've got nerve coming here."

She slides her hands into the back pocket of her jeans. "I only came to talk, I swear."

"You need to leave."

Mercy's carbon copy shrugs. "So you're going to hold a grudge forever? I mean, it's not like you shoved me off or anything."

"I thought you were Mercy."

"If you say so." She steps cautiously in my direction. "I know you hate me or whatever, but I didn't ask for this."

"If you came here for my pity, you can forget it." I start for the house.

She reaches out and grabs my arm. "Gage, please. I didn't come here for your pity. I came here to apologize."

Turning, I face her dead-on. "You're sorry?" I laugh, mocking the pained expression on her face. "That's pathetic! You fooled me once. Never again."

"I get why you're pissed, but I thought you of all people would understand."

"Why would you think that?"

"Because you know what this feels like. You and I are basically the same."

With three quick steps, we are practically nose to nose. "Don't ever compare yourself to me." Backing away, she sincerely looks hurt. But I don't care. "We have nothing in common."

She scowls. "Um, we have everything in common. And you're an idiot not to see it. Did I ask to be created? Nope! Did you? Nope! Are we both pawns in someone else's game? Yep!"

"But you're still working for her!"

"Duh! Of course I am. You just don't understand what she's trying to do."

"She's trying to kill Mercy."

She giggles "You think Isadora wants to kill Mercy? Yeah, right. That's never going to happen. What Isadora wants is for Mercy to join her against them."

"Against who?"

"Sorry, sweets. I've already said too much. I really only came here to say I'm sorry."

"And why would you do that?"

"Because I like you. You're sweet, and while I don't have a ton of experience to tell me otherwise, I'm pretty sure you're one of the hottest kissers on the planet."

My cheeks burn and redden at the mention of our make-out session. It was intense and wonderful, but that's only because I thought I was kissing Mercy. *Right?*

"I'm never going to believe anything you say," I say spitefully.

"Suit yourself." She shrugs. "But it doesn't have to be this way, you know. Isadora is going to get what she wants. You won't be able to stop her. I was only hoping that you'd be smart and stay out of the way so that you're around when it's all over."

"You sound awfully confident for someone who's only a copy of someone else."

She throws her head back and laughs. "I like how you keep forgetting how you and I were created. I'm from Mercy, just like you're from Nathaniel. We're the same whether you like it or not."

"You need to leave."

She walks toward me and puts her hands on my chest. Flinching, I almost back away, but for some reason, I don't. Maybe it's her eyes, how they remind me of Mercy's, or maybe it's just that she surprised me, but either way, here we are, inches from each other.

"I really am sorry about the other day," she says with deep sincerity and conviction. "I took advantage of you, and I shouldn't have."

Releasing me, she starts across the lawn. I watch, mouth agape, unable to formulate words or even a cohesive thought.

Before she's out of sight, she whips around. "I'm Justice, by the way." And then she's gone.

I stand there a moment longer, trying to process everything that just happened. There's no way I believe what she's trying to tell me. We are not the same. Justice was created from Mercy, like I was created from Nathaniel, so yes, in that way, we are similar, but that's where it ends.

When I was a Hunter, what I did, I did for the greater good. I was made for a purpose, and I fulfilled that purpose until it all came crashing down around me. It isn't the same for Justice. She has no honor, no sense of duty. I don't know what her intentions are, but I know enough to understand it isn't good. She made that plain when she pretended to be Mercy.

While walking back into the house, I fully plan to tell Ariana and Nathaniel that Justice paid me another visit, but the sight of Mercy standing in the kitchen stops me in my tracks.

She closes the distance between us and throws her arms

around my neck. I bury my face in her hair and hug her tight. When we finally break apart, I say, "I'm so glad you're all right."

"Thank you for getting me out of there, for bringing me home."

"Of course. And you feel okay now? You look like you're back to your old self."

She wraps her arms around herself. "Yeah, I think so. The whole thing still kind of trips me out though, you know? I don't know if I'll ever get used to being able to leave my body."

"I can't even imagine."

Mercy tilts her head to the left as a mischievous grin stretches her lips. "If you want, I could show you."

"What do you mean you can show me?" I ask, dismayed.

"How to be a Breacher. I can teach you, and then you can be just like me."

A horrifying thought occurs to me. This can't be Mercy standing in front of me. It's Justice. That's the only explanation. Charging forward, I grab her by the arms. "I told you to leave!"

"Gage, let go. You're hurting me."

"I will not let you mess with my mind like this. Get out! Now!"

Nathaniel rushes into the room. "What's going on?"

"I'm throwing her out of the house," I tell him.

Nathaniel looks around. "Throwing who?"

"Justice. Who else?"

"Gage, look around. There's no one here."

Chapter Eight

Nathaniel

*O*n the last day of Ellie's life, Nathaniel appeared at her bedside, the parchment paper with her name on it secured in the breast pocket of his coat.

Her entire family was there as well. Her mother's face was partly absorbed by a handkerchief though it hardly stifled her multitude of tears. Ellie's father put his large hands on his wife's shoulders, and hung his head.

In the bed, Ellie lay eerily still. Her once supple skin was sallow. Her stringy hair splayed against the pillow. Her breaths were shallow and far apart.

"Ellie," Nathaniel whispered into her ear. "It's time."

Her eyelids fluttered, but they did not open.

"Don't worry," Nathaniel assured her. "It won't hurt. Just follow the sound of my voice."

A light visible to only Nathaniel began to glow around Ellie's body. The glow transformed itself into the shape of Ellie. She stood next to Nathaniel, still bathed in light, looking down upon her body with a sorrowful expression.

"I look so sick," she commented.

"Not to me."

Of course he wasn't referring to her lifeless form. He was talking about her soul, the one that stood next to him, luminous and healthy. He'd never seen a lovelier face, a face he wanted to touch and hold between his hands. Feeling bold, Nathaniel linked his hand with Ellie's.

"Will they be all right?" she asked him. "I feel awful leaving them like this."

To look upon them now, sobbing and holding one another, Nathaniel knew it would be difficult to convince Ellie that yes, in time, her family would learn to function without her. "They'll miss you," Nathaniel told her. "They'll be sad for a long time, but then they'll move on. They won't forget you, but the pain will subside."

"I promised to take Will to the lake this summer and teach him how to swim."

"He'll go. And when he does, he'll think of you."

"I hope so." Ellie turned to face Nathaniel. "There's so much I wanted to see and do," she said, her voice drenched in regret.

"You can see anything you want."

"Will it be the paradise I always imagined?"

Nathaniel stroked Ellie's cheek with his free hand. "It will be everything and more."

She smiled up at him. "Take me home."

Still holding hands, they walked together toward the front door. Ellie looked back over her shoulder one last time. When she faced Nathaniel again, she nodded, signaling that she was ready.

The stepped from the cottage into a light so blinding both Nathaniel and Ellie had to squint. His eyesight adjusted quickly. She, not being used to such brightness, shielded her eyes with her hand.

Nathaniel had felt this sensation hundreds of times, yet he never tired of it. The warmth radiated from his face down to his toes and enveloped him as though he was being drenched in the most comforting feeling imaginable. He let it soothe him, not wanting it to end, and he saw Ellie doing the same. Her chin tipped up, her eyes closed, a genuine smile stretched across her face.

"It's wonderful," she remarked.

"It is," Nathaniel agreed.

"I feel … It's indescribable."

"And this is just the beginning."

Beyond the light lay a path of stamped dirt bordered with gray stone. The path wound its way through the most vividly stunning garden conceived. Every kind of plant life was represented, from the traditional to the exotic. Roses mixed with gardenias and sunflowers and a thousand other variations Nathaniel couldn't possibly name. Trees rooted together forming an immense canopy of shade. Every color burst to life without a single blemish or dead leaf in sight. It was truly an immaculate Garden of Eden.

"Is this heaven?" she asked.

"This is the path to the bridge."

"So we can't stay here?"

"We can for a while, if you like."

"I would like that very much."

Nathaniel led her off the path and through the garden. Before them, another walkway appeared as if the garden knew where they wanted to go. They stopped when they came to a stream. The water was dark but remarkably clear so they could see all the life that existed beneath the surface.

Ellie giggled as fish jumped in and out of the water. "What fun they must be having," she said.

"And you? Are you having fun?"

"Is it wrong if I say I am?"

"Of course not. Why would it be?"

Ellie pulled away from Nathaniel and walked a little farther down the stream. When he caught up with her, she said, "I feel guilty."

"About what?"

"It's just that I'm in the presence of all this beauty while my family suffers."

This statement only made her dearer to Nathaniel. Her soul was the purest kind. She was loving, sweet, and gentle. He wanted to give her the world.

"What's this?" Ellie asked, stopping suddenly.

Nathaniel couldn't contain his delight. His eyes danced as he watched her survey the picnic laid out for her. Atop a red-checked blanket sat a flawlessly woven basket, open, exposing a treasure trove of food. Their places were set, complete with the finest bone china and crystal goblets. "Shall we?"

"You've thought of everything, haven't you?"

"I try."

"Do you do this for everyone?"

Nathaniel held out a tray of fruit for Ellie to choose from. "I try to make the transition as easy as possible," he said. "But you should know that I have never dined with anyone before."

"Why not?"

"Technically, this is against the rules," Nathaniel said, watching her reaction carefully.

Ellie brushed her fingers across her lips. "I'm sorry. We should go."

"No." Nathaniel reached out and touched her arm. "Please stay."

"I don't want to get you in trouble."

"It's worth it," Nathaniel said boldly.

Ellie lowered her gaze. "You make me blush when you say things like that."

"Does it frighten you?"

"No," she said, lifting her eyes to look directly at him.

"Ellie," Nathaniel leaned in, his lips inches from hers. "We don't have much time."

"Will I see you again? After today?"

Nathaniel hesitated. "I ..." He failed to put words together.

Ellie touched her lips to his. It wasn't a kiss exactly. It was more like her lips came to rest against his momentarily. Nathaniel was too stunned to move at first, but then something stirred inside him, something powerful. Desire, wanting—these were words he'd heard before, but he'd never understood their meaning until that moment.

His hand moved to the side of her face as he kissed her deeply. She tasted of berries and sugar and love, or at least what he imagined love would taste like.

Gingerly, he laid her back on the blanket and hovered above her.

She never once took her eyes off him.

"You are the most beautiful creature in creation," he said.

She pulled him closer. "I wish it could always be like this."

"Me too."

"I thought I only dreamed of you, Nathaniel. To see you here now, to be with you in this way, this is heaven."

Nathaniel kissed her passionately, and she responded in kind. It was a kiss to last for an eternity, but Nathaniel knew time was running out. They had to be looking for him by now. He'd broken all the rules. He'd pay for this.

"Ellie," Nathaniel whispered against her neck. "I love you."

"Well, isn't that sweet," said a familiar and unkind voice.

Nathaniel's eyes popped open, and his head snapped up. It was not Ellie who had spoken those words. It was Isadora. She was standing only a few feet away from them, arms angrily folded across her chest, her eyes full of hate, her teeth clamped together.

Scrambling to his feet, Nathaniel pleaded, "Isadora, please. I can explain."

"Who are you?" Ellie asked. Her beautiful face was crimson, a mixture of anger and embarrassment.

"I am the end," Isadora warned.

The picnic disappeared instantly. The ground hardened in Isadora's presence as if it too was bracing against the onslaught that was to come. The vibrant colors dimmed, and the leaves shriveled.

"What's happening?" Ellie asked, clamoring to Nathaniel's side.

"Everything will be okay," he told Ellie.

Isadora's glare hardened. "These are not reassurances you can give, Nathaniel."

"What does she mean?" Panic seeped through Ellie's voice. *"What is she saying?"*

"I will protect you," Nathaniel said to Ellie. *"I swear."*

"You can try," Isadora mocked.

Nathaniel yanked Ellie's hand roughly. They rushed out of the garden and down the path. He walked too quickly, and Ellie had to scurry to keep up. Isadora was no longer with them, but her presence lingered. The air was still while an unmistakably ominous feeling wafted overhead.

When they reached the bridge Nathaniel stopped short. Ellie slammed into him.

He held her by the shoulders. *"Find the light, Ellie. Run for the light, no matter what."*

"Nathaniel, I'm scared."

"I'm sorry. I ruined everything."

A low, rumbling sound broke through the air.

"What's happening?" Ellie asked, her entire body trembling beneath his touch.

There was no time to answer. He grabbed her hand and they bolted across the bridge. The light at the end was small but visible. Nathaniel dragged Ellie along. They had to get to the other side before the light vanished entirely.

"Hurry!" Nathaniel barked.

The light continued to fade. Nathaniel knew they weren't going to reach it in time, but that only propelled him to run faster. When they finally reached the other side, the light was gone.

"Dammit!" Nathaniel cursed.

"Nathaniel?" Ellie backed up quickly, stumbled, and fell.

Nathaniel turned to see the source of her fear. Isadora, flanked by two very large men, stalked toward them.

"Nathaniel Black," Isadora uttered authoritatively. "By order of The Assembled, you are hereby charged and will be sentenced for your crimes."

"Isadora, stop," Nathaniel ordered.

"Take him." Isadora stood watch as the two hulking figures moved toward Nathaniel.

They easily overpowered him, but he didn't put up much of a fight. Nathaniel knew he'd done wrong, but he planned to plead his case, to make them understand. He also had the piece of paper with Ellie's name on it. He was certain it would be his ticket out of this mess.

Isadora prowled toward Ellie. "Stand," she commanded.

Ellie scrambled to her feet.

"Eleanor Jane Levinson." Isadora's voice was authoritative and cold. "The light has closed. I'm afraid I have no choice."

Nathaniel roared, struggling against the arms that held him. "Isadora! Don't do this!"

Ellie looked to Nathaniel, her expression pleading. Her eyes were wide and brimmed with tears; her lips trembled.

"It should've been explained to you more clearly." Isadora almost sounded sympathetic as she placed her hand on Ellie's shoulder. "When a soul denies the light, there is only one choice left." Isadora paused for effect. "Purgatory."

"No." Ellie's legs faltered beneath her. "Please."

"Isadora," Nathaniel tried. "Punish me if you must, but let her go."

"Let her go?" Isadora asked innocently. "As you wish."

Isadora released her grip on Ellie just as a gray swirl of dust kicked up around her. Ellie tried desperately to swat the mist that encircled her, but within seconds she was centered in the storm. A sickening scream exploded from her lips. The gray dust pierced her eyes, her ears, her mouth, shooting through her until her entire body was punctured with holes.

And then she was gone.

Chapter Nine

Mercy

I wake with a start. Gasping, I try to catch my breath. My mother is at my side.

"It's okay, baby." She takes my hand in hers. "You're home. You're safe."

She's right. I'm home. I'm in my room. My bookcase and all my neatly arranged books are just as I left them. The blue jacket I forgot to hang is across my desk chair. And in my bed is my body.

I sit up straight, but I feel like slush, like the pieces of me are soupy and strained and fighting to stay together. I flicker in and out, worrying that without a foothold I'm going to be swept from the room at any moment. I need to get back in my body.

Slowly, I stand. My feet don't quite connect with the floor, but I move forward anyway, concentrating intensely on the task at hand. My mother walks with me to the bed and together we look down at my body.

"I'm sorry," my mom says, her voice racked with guilt. "If I could change things for you, I would."

I look upon her beautiful face and her green, crystal-like eyes. We reach for each other and embrace. Though I can feel her, it's only slightly. I long to hold her with my true self.

"Do you want me to help you?" she asks.

Confidently, I smile at her. "I've got it."

Turning to face my body, I inhale deeply to steady my nerves. I climb onto my bed and maneuver myself until I'm lying on my body. Sinking into my skin, I meld into each fold, each curve, until every finger and toe is within my reach. Then I open my eyes and see my mother.

"Hello, again," she says sweetly.

"Mom." It feels good to hear her name cross my lips, my actual lips.

"Relax a minute and I'll unhook you."

I stay still while she quickly flits around removing all the needles and wires from my skin. I try not to wince, not wanting her to know I'm uncomfortable.

When she finishes, she returns to my side and helps me into a sitting position. She keeps looking at me with the same concerned expression, almost like she's waiting for me to cry out or ask for help, but I'm not about to show her any weakness. If I do she'll only feel worse.

My muscles are tired, and they don't want to cooperate, but I bend them to my will, and walk to the family room. Nathaniel and Gage are seated on the couch. They turn at the same time and look at me expectantly, like they are waiting for confirmation that I'm okay.

"Hey," I say, giving them both a pathetic half wave.

Nathaniel is up in one swift motion. He stands before me, assessing. He cups my face in his hands. Then he kisses me squarely on the forehead, pressing his lips there for a full five seconds. In truth, I don't want him to pull away. I want to be in his arms.

Gage loiters in the background. His unsure face nearly breaks my heart, and I know I have to make the first move. When I reach him, I hesitate for only a second before I wrap my arms around his waist. Shrinking against him, I close my eyes and listen to the sound of his heart. Its rapid beat betrays him, and I know that he's anxious, nervous, and relieved. Quickly, he kisses the top of my head, and then he releases me.

I sit in my dad's favorite chair and inhale his lingering scent. "Where's Dad?" I ask my mom.

"He's at a conference." My expression sours. "He didn't want to go, Mercy, but I basically forced him. He was driving himself crazy with worry, but he'll be back tomorrow," she says. "Can I get you some tea?"

I nod.

Before she leaves the room, my mother gives me a hug and a kiss on the cheek. I don't mind the affection from any of them. Being back in my body, I crave their touch. It's good to feel whole again.

Gage and Nathaniel, like two caged animals waiting to pounce, stare at me.

"What?" I finally ask them.

"Sorry," Gage speaks first. "It's just good to see you sitting there." He shifts uncomfortably and clasps his hands together. "I feel like it's my fault this happened to you."

"Don't do that to yourself. It wasn't you. It was this." I show them the scar on my wrist, the one from my tracking device.

"I know, but, still …"

"I had the weirdest dream about you," I say to Gage. As soon as the words are out of my mouth I see Nathaniel's jaw clamp closed. He doesn't like that I'm dreaming of Gage.

"What did you dream?" Gage asks.

"We were in my kitchen, and I was trying to convince you to become a Breacher. Weird, right?"

Gage fidgets and flashes a look to Nathaniel.

"What?" I ask.

Gage and Nathaniel trade knowing glances, which only makes me more nervous.

"What?" I ask again.

"I don't know how to say this," Gage says slowly, "but it wasn't a dream."

I scoot to the front of the chair. "What do you mean?"

Nathaniel holds his hand up, signaling for Gage not to say anything, and then he turns his attention to me. "When you were in jail, did you have a dream about me and Gage driving to rescue you?"

Heat rushes to my face, and my pulse quickens. "Yes," I tell him. "I was in the backseat."

"And you leaned forward and held my hand," he says, completing my thought.

"How is this possible?" I look to him for answers. "How do you know what I'm dreaming?"

"I don't think you're dreaming," Nathaniel answers. "I think you're projecting."

"Projecting?" I ask, worried.

"Sending your thoughts to us, in a way," Nathaniel says. "That's how I felt you in the car."

"And you?" I ask Gage. "Was I really with you in the kitchen? Did I really say those things to you?" I clamp my hand over my mouth, horribly ashamed of myself. And then I can't sit still any longer. I'm out of the chair and pacing back and forth. My legs are tired and achy, but adrenaline keeps me going. I can't contain the questions that tumble from my mouth. "Why is this happening? *How* is this happening? Did Isadora do this?"

Nathaniel stops me. With his hands on my shoulders, he looks into my eyes. "Mercy, don't crack up on me now, okay?"

I break free of his grasp and slump into the chair. My hair falls every which way, so I grab it and shove it back. "I'm sorry. It's just a lot to take, considering."

"Considering what?" Gage asks.

I tell them about my meeting with Isadora, how she came to the jail and told me that she wants me to kill The Assembled. By the time I finish, they're both stunned into silence.

"I don't understand," Gage finally says. "She *is* The Assembled. Why would she want them dead?"

"Isn't it obvious?" Nathaniel leans his elbows onto his knees. "Isadora wants to be the supreme ruler."

"She can't do that!" Gage shouts.

My mother returns, carrying a tray with a silver tea setting. Her face freezes. She can sense the tension. "What's going on now?"

"We have a problem," Gage tells her.

"Gage, don't," Nathaniel warns.

Gage is not swayed. "Isadora wants Mercy to kill The Assembled."

The tray my mother is carrying spills and clatters to the ground. She winces as scalding water splashes against her skin. Hurrying, I go to her and guide her to the kitchen sink where I run the cold water. She holds her hand under the stream and grimaces.

"There's a first-aid kit in the hall closet," I yell to both Nathaniel and Gage. "Get it." To my mom, I say, "Are you all right? Do we need to go to the hospital?"

"I'm fine, honey. It's not that bad," she answers.

But I don't believe her. I can see it in her eyes. There's something she isn't telling me. "What is it? Is it your hand?"

She looks away. Nathaniel and Gage enter the kitchen. Gage escorts my mother to the table and begins dressing her wound.

I clean up the mess. Nathaniel helps. We pick up the pieces and walk back and forth to the kitchen for paper towels and eventually the mop and bucket to wipe the hardwood floor clean.

We finish and rejoin Gage and my mother in the kitchen. They're huddled together whispering. They break apart at the sight of us.

I wash my hands in the sink, and when I turn around, all three of them are staring at me. I'm sure it's out of concern, but I can't stand it. I can't stand being studied and worried over and treated like I'm a bomb about to explode. Anxious and irritated,

I need to move. "I'm going for a walk."

"I'm not sure you should be out there," my mother says to me.

"Isadora won't try anything just yet." I pause by the front door. "And there's no air in here. If you need me, I'll be at Lyla's."

"Let me walk you," Nathaniel offers.

Oh, how I would love to say no, but I know he'll follow me anyway. "Fine," I say through clenched teeth.

"Don't stay out too long," my mother tells me.

"Wouldn't dream of it." I know I'm being snotty, but I'm tired and fed up, which I undoubtedly convey when the screen door slams behind me.

Nathaniel and I walk, me with my hands jammed into my pockets, him stealing glances of me every few steps. Nothing about my neighborhood has changed, and yet everything is different. I don't see tiny houses owned by neighbors anymore. I see unsuspecting victims who don't know they live dangerously close to Breachers.

"You're awfully quiet." Nathaniel's arm brushes against mine.

I ignore him.

"Are you angry with me?" he asks.

Still I keep quiet.

"Mercy, stop." He pivots until he's facing me, forcing me to halt. "Don't be shut me out."

I fold my arms across my chest and cock my hip to one side. Apparently, all the time I spent being Lyla has rubbed off on me because this stance is all her.

Nathaniel sticks out his lower lip like a child, and despite myself, I laugh.

"That's better," he says.

Stalling, I look around at my neighborhood, at the house across the street where the Jensens live. Lyla and I loved trick-or-treating at their house because they gave out full-size candy bars. The memory saddens me. It serves as a reminder that I'm not the same girl anymore. I'm not Mercy Clare, local girl who lost her mother. I'm Mercy Clare, Breacher and God knows what else.

Nathaniel brushes a stray hair from my face. "I can see the wheels turning in there. Tell me. Let me help."

Relenting, I say, "You're all afraid of me."

His brow wrinkles as his eyebrows nearly knit together. "That's what this is about?"

"Did you see the look on my mother's face?"

"She's worried, Mercy. She's not afraid of you."

I kick the sidewalk with the toe of my shoe. "She should be."

"And why is that?"

"Nathaniel, the truth is, I don't know what I'm doing." I can tell he's about to put up an argument, but I hold up my hand to stop him. "Don't," I say. "Don't try to convince me otherwise."

He throws his palms up. "I wasn't going to."

"Thanks." I backhand him on the arm.

He rubs the spot I swatted. "All I was going to say is that we'll figure this out together." He slips his hand around mine, lacing our fingers together. "You're not alone. You have me." Nathaniel pulls me to him. He holds my head to his shoulder, kisses my hair. Nathaniel massages the back of my neck, and it feels good. I sigh with relief.

And then I feel that pull, the one I always feel when I'm

around him. Being in close proximity with Nathaniel awakens my body in ways that make me blush. I imagine his full, soft lips against mine as he kisses me gently at first, and then increases his urgency. I picture him kissing my throat and all along my neck as his fingers weave themselves into my hair. And then it's my hands that are on him—on his chest, his back, dipping below his belt line to feel the curve of his torso.

I have to stop. I step back from Nathaniel and clear my thoughts.

Nathaniel's expression gives me pause. He looks ravenous and shocked all at the same time. He's breathing hard. He wipes his mouth with his hand.

And that's when I know.

"Oh my God." I can barely look at him. *Kill me. Kill me now.* "You saw that, didn't you? What I was thinking, just now, you saw it?"

"Mercy, I—"

I cut him off. "Don't." Humiliated, I turn away.

"Is that how you feel about me?" he asks, his voice cautious and hopeful. "Mercy," he says as he faces me once again, "is that how you feel about me?"

He's waiting for me to answer. His eyes are full of love, full of wanting. I haven't seen that look on his face since Isadora yanked out my rib. It was then that I knew that Nathaniel loved me, and now, with that look, he's telling me again.

But I'm too afraid return his love.

"No," I say firmly.

His forehead creases as he frowns. "No?"

"I'm sorry."

"You're lying."

Did I show him that too? No, I can see that I didn't. The unsure look on his face tells me as much. He's accusing me out of desperation.

"I have to go," I say.

And then I run like hell.

I don't stop until I'm bursting into Lyla's house. The door bangs into the wall when I throw it open.

"Mercy!" Kate, Lyla's older sister, admonishes me. "Are you trying to break the door down?"

Kate is on the couch watching reality TV. She's wearing her standard uniform—yoga pants, rock band T-shirt. Her dark hair hangs limply, looking slightly greasy and in need of a good washing.

Breathless from running, I try to compose myself. "Sorry," I say as I gently close the door.

"Lyla's in her room with Jay. I'd knock first if I were you."

"Gotcha."

Since I vacated Lyla's body, their house has returned to its normal, disheveled state. Magazines cover the coffee table; shoes are piled by the front door. As I pass the kitchen, I see dishes that need to be done and garbage that needs to be taken out. There's a pot on the stove that's caked with congealed macaroni and cheese. I never thought any good could come from my being in Lyla's body, but the state of their house tells me otherwise.

I knock on Lyla's door.

"Very funny, Kate. We're not doing anything," Lyla calls from the other side.

"Ly, it's me," I yell through the door.

The door opens. Lyla greets me dressed in leggings and a button-down shirt, which she's cinched with a wide black belt to extenuate her gorgeous curves. Her long hair is twisted into a knot on top of her head. She's wearing her signature cat-eye makeup with red lips. My ensemble, jeans and a plain T-shirt, pales in comparison to hers.

"Have Mercy!" She squeals as she hugs me. "You're back!"

"You knew I was gone?"

"Hello! I'm your best friend in the whole world. You think you can disappear out of my life for days, and I'm not going to notice? No way."

She stands aside so I can enter her room. Jay, her boyfriend, and one of my best friends, is sprawled across her bed.

Lyla sits down next to him, and Jay circles his hands around her waist. Immediately, I become a third wheel.

"Seriously, did I interrupt anything? Because I can go."

"Don't be stupid. Kate's just in a mood. We were only listening to music."

"*I* was listening to music," Jay corrects her. "Lyla was trying on everything in her closet and boring me to death with a game of keep this, toss that."

"That explains the mess," I say as I scan at Lyla's room.

It's nothing like I left it. Feeling guilty for being in Lyla's body and not knowing how to fix it, I cleaned and cleaned and cleaned Lyla's room. I washed her sheets, hung all of her clothes, organized her shoes, belts, and other accessories. By the time I finished, there were actual surfaces to her furniture. Such is no longer the case.

I shove stuff aside so I have room to sit on the floor in front of the dresser. I lean against it and wait for Lyla's barrage of questions I know are coming.

"So, jail? You weren't like, somebody's bitch, were you?" Lyla starts.

"Very sensitive of you, and no, I wasn't," I inform her. "But jail was a total nightmare. Isadora—"

"That's your mom's sister, right?" Jay asks.

"Right. She injected me with this binding agent stuff, and I couldn't jump to get out of there."

Lyla's face registers shock. "Oh my God."

"Yeah, she sucks. Oh, and so does my *sister*, by the way."

Jay's curly mop of hair is so long it nearly covers his eyes. "Sister?"

"Sister. Her name is Justice, and she looks frighteningly like me, so look out. She already managed to fool Gage."

"What'd she do?" Lyla asks.

"Let's just say it was PG-13, and I'd rather not get into it."

"Got it."

"Anyway," I continue, "Nathaniel and Gage got me out, obviously, but now I have a bigger problem."

Jay eyes me skeptically. "Bigger than your evil twin and aunt manipulating your paranormal life and trying to kill everyone you know?"

"Yeah, it's girl stuff."

Jay throws up his hands. "I'm out."

He shuffles off the bed. I reach out and grab his leg. "Actually, can you stay? I'd like to hear your thoughts. Plus, I have to tell you something else about me."

"Okay, I'll stay." Jay retraces his steps and takes his place behind Lyla.

"So, what's this thing you're going to tell us about you? Are you really Spider- Man, or can you fly like Superman?" Lyla laughs.

"I wish." I laugh with her. This is exactly why I need Lyla right now. It's impossible for her to take anything too seriously. "Apparently, I can send my thoughts to people's minds."

Both Jay and Lyla squint like they can't see me clearly.

"And what exactly does that mean?" Jay asks.

"Well, I thought I was dreaming, but I wasn't. I was thinking about someone, and imagining myself with them, and, it turns out, I really was, but I wasn't because I was only doing it with my mind."

"You know," Lyla crosses her legs like a kindergartener, "there's not a single part of that, that doesn't need explaining."

I sigh and say, "When I was in jail, I thought I was having this dream about Nathaniel and Gage coming to save me. I was in the backseat of their car. They couldn't see me or hear me, but I reached out and touched Nathaniel's hand." I pause for a second to see if they are following along. They seem to be, so I continue, saying, "Nathaniel retold that whole scene to me. He thought *he* was imagining it. And then there was this thing with Gage. I appeared to him in my kitchen, and apparently I told him I could make him a Breacher."

Lyla leans back into Jay. "Whoa."

"I know this sounds insane." I can barely look at them. "But it gets worse."

"Worse?" Jay asks.

I nod my head in shame. "So much worse. Just now, I was walking over here with Nathaniel. I can't explain it, but something happens to me when I'm around him. And I pictured us, you know, kissing or whatever, and he saw the whole thing."

"What do you mean he *saw* it?" Lyla asks.

"I was thinking it, but it's like I was thinking out loud, projecting it, almost like a movie."

"That's so cool!" Lyla squeals.

"It's not *cool*. Those thoughts were private, super private, and now Nathaniel knows them."

"What did he say after he saw it, or whatever?" Jay asks.

"He asked me if I was showing how I really felt about him."

"And what did you say?" Lyla asks.

"I told him no. And then I ran." As soon as I hear myself retell the last part, and I see the looks on their faces, I know I've done the wrong thing. "Oh God. I'm an idiot." I bury my head in my knees.

Lyla climbs off the bed and sits by me. She puts her arms around my shoulders. "You're not an idiot. And I'm sure we can do some damage control. Just tell him you were freaked out, say you're sorry, and then everything will be fine."

"It's not that simple, Ly."

"Why not? Nathaniel is hot. And he's so obviously into you."

"But she has to consider Gage," Jay points out. "She can't just go off with Nathaniel and leave Gage in the dust."

"Exactly!" I say, echoing Jay's sentiment. "If I choose Nathaniel I'll lose Gage. I won't do that."

"Mercy." Lyla's tone conveys a tinge of disbelief. "What do you mean you won't? You have to choose between them eventually."

"Why? Why do I have to choose? I don't want anyone to get hurt."

"You're probably already hurting them," Jay says. He sits at the edge of the bed, his long legs slumped over the side. "I saw you with them, Mercy. I know how they feel about you. Not telling them anything in return must be killing them."

I groan and lean into Lyla's comforting embrace. "This is awful. I need both of them to fight Isadora. I can't have them hating each other."

"Haven't they hated each other for most of their lives?" Jay asks.

"Yes," I answer. "But they're working together now. They're getting along. I don't want to ruin that."

"I don't think you have much of choice," Lyla says. "I mean, you already kind of told Nathaniel by showing him whatever you showed him, right?" She leans in and whispers, "You can give me all of those yummy details later."

"Ly! That's beside the point."

"No, that's the whole point," she says, scooting away so she can face me. "You've never really liked anyone before, and now you have these two gorgeous guys fighting over you."

"I also have my psychotic aunt and twin sister to think about. This isn't the time for boys and hormones."

Lyla shrugs. "Hey, all I'm saying is that if you're going to start the fight of your life, you might as well do it with love on your side."

Chapter Ten

Gage

Moments after Nathaniel and Mercy exit, I say good-bye to Ariana and leave. The night sky is dotted with stars, and a great white moon guides my way. I hear sounds I've never noticed before—doors closing, dogs barking, cars driving, leaves rustling through the trees. It's as if the world is a whole new place. This is my human world, and sooner or later I'm going to have to find my place in it.

When Isadora sliced the mark from my arm, I didn't know what it would mean to be human, and I remember thinking briefly that I might like a real life. It might be okay to fall in love, have a family, get a job—all the things that humans do. And when I pictured that future, I saw Mercy by my side. But watching her with Nathaniel, I know any hope I had of us being together is drifting farther and farther away.

The idea that Mercy is projecting her thoughts worries me. Her ability to breach is not limited taking someone's body. She is able to control someone's mind. She may not understand what's happening to her right now, but she will eventually, and the temptation to use her gift for ill gain might be too great for her to handle. It might overwhelm her, and what am I supposed to do then?

The sky is black by the time I reach my house. I hustle up the steps, and when I cross the threshold, Nathaniel is waiting for me. He's sitting in *the* chair, the one Mercy picked out a garage sale. It's purple and soft, made of velvet-like material. Nathaniel sits in a kingly manner, leaning back, his left ankle propped on his right knee.

"Where's Mercy?" I ask him.

As if waking from deep thought, Nathaniel casts a brief glance in my direction, and then he looks away. "Lyla's house."

There's something in his tone that makes me wonder what he's not telling me.

"Did something happen?"

Nathaniel leans forward, resting his forearms against his thighs. "You could say that."

Hurriedly, I walk around the couch and sit down. I know that whatever he's about to say requires being seated. I wait for a few moments, but when Nathaniel remains silent, impatience wins out. "Are you going to tell me what happened, or are you going to make me guess?"

"I'm not quite sure what to tell you." His expression hardens. "Actually, I *can't* tell you."

"Why not?"

"Because Mercy wouldn't want me to."

What the hell does that mean? "If there's something happening with Mercy, I should know. We're on the same side, Nathaniel— hers. Don't keep secrets from me."

Nathaniel rolls his eyes. "Relax, drama queen. You don't need to know the details, but we do need to discuss Mercy's latest mutation."

"Mutation? So, she's an X-Men now?"

"Don't be an ass, Gage. That's my job." Nathaniel stands, walks to the wet bar, and pours himself a drink. He offers me one, but I wave him off.

"Mercy's powers are evolving," he says. "She's changing."

"I know."

"You do?" Nathaniel seems surprised I agree with him.

"Yeah. I've been thinking about this. And I think we have to ask ourselves what we're going to do if she can't control it?"

"There is no, *if,* little brother. She can't control this."

"So what are we going to do?"

Nathaniel knocks back the rest of his drink. "Ever the Hunter. Always ready to swoop in and save the day."

"Forget it." This is pointless. Nathaniel and I are incapable of having a real conversation. "I'm going to bed."

"Wait." Nathaniel sets the now empty tumbler on the coffee table.

"What?"

"I don't know how to help her." He clears his throat. "And the truth is, I'm afraid we're going to lose her to this thing, whatever she's becoming."

I have no answer for him. I don't try to stop him when he leaves the room.

I go to bed, and I sleep in my clothes.

The next morning I wake when the sun pours through the window like a searchlight scorching my eyes. Rolling over, I throw the pillow over my head and try to go back to sleep.

"Gage?" I hear Mercy calling me from the other side of the door. "Are you awake?" Flashbacks of my encounter with Justice surge through my brain.

Not again. I slide to the edge of the bed, propel myself toward the door, and thrust it open. "You've got a lot of nerve trying this again."

At first she looks confused, a tiny wrinkle creases her forehead. Then she smiles. "I'm not Justice, I swear." She holds her hands up, surrendering.

"Prove it."

"Seriously?"

I wait.

"Fine," she relents. "We met in the library at school. You were stalking me, and then, when I nearly passed out, you helped me to the nurse's office."

I fold my arms and step back. "I wasn't stalking you."

"Yeah, you were," she says as she shoves past me. Her nose wrinkles in disgust. "Okay, so I know you're new to this whole human thing, but here's a tip, crack a window every once in a while. It smells like funk in here."

I pad over to the window and slide it open. "I'm going to assume you didn't come by just to tell me my housekeeping skills suck, so what's up?"

Mercy runs her fingers through her auburn hair. "You have to help me fix this."

"Fix what?"

"This." She holds out her trembling hands for me to see. "I feel jittery and exposed. My heart is beating a mile a minute. My skin is itchy. My hands won't stop shaking. Something is wrong with me."

"Come here."

She walks toward me. I hold her hands in mine. But it's only for a second, and then she pulls away. "Gage, I have to tell you something. Something important."

"You can tell me anything."

She takes a deep breath. "I didn't tell you this before because I didn't want to scare you, but now I feel like I have to."

"Okay." I sit on the mattress and wait for what's coming.

She rakes her lips over her teeth before she begins. "When my mother and I were being held by Isadora something happened. And at first I didn't think anyone besides us knew about it, but now I realize Isadora must know. She knows what I did, and that's how she knows I can kill The Assembled."

I can tell by the way her voice shakes that she's scared to tell me the rest. "What happened?"

"I was in a cell with my mother, and she was dead. I couldn't do CPR because I didn't have a body." She stands with her hands on her hips. "I don't know what made me try what I did, but it worked."

She's being evasive on purpose. "What worked?"

Mercy is shaking. I want to pull her to me and comfort her, but I stay where I am.

She exhales sharply. "It was like breaching except I didn't go all the way. I just reached in and held her heart and squeezed it with my hand until I brought her back to life."

I try to process what she's telling me.

Continuing, she says, "I didn't think Isadora knew, but she must. She knows, and that's why she wants me to kill The Assembled. And here I was being all smug, thinking I'm going to take down The Assembled because no one knows what I can do." Her voice nears hysteria. "But she knows! She's known this whole time."

I think back to when Isadora released Mercy. Mercy came back to us determined to kill The Assembled. Nathaniel and I were convinced she wouldn't actually be able to do it, but now I'm not so sure.

"We'll think of something," I say, trying to sound reassuring. "I swear. I won't let Isadora use you."

Mercy bites her lips. Her eyes are brimming with tears. She wipes them with the back of her hand. "I shouldn't be this person. It's not right."

"Mercy."

"Every time I breach a body, or Nathaniel breaches a body, there's a reason. And I always let the reason outweigh the fact we're killing innocent people. And now with this new power I realize I'm getting stronger. What if it gets to be too much? What if I end up no better than Isadora?"

"Mercy, that will never happen. You aren't like Isadora. You're good."

"Yeah, now. But who knows what I'll become." She sits down

next to me on the bed. "Gage, will you do something for me?"

"Of course, I'd do anything for you."

She turns and looks at me, her beautiful eyes soften around the edges. "You and I both know this is wrong, and the only reason you're not willing to admit it is because you lost your Hunter's mark." She takes my hand and entwines it with hers. "If you were still you, the old you, you'd know what the right thing is."

I don't like where this is going. "What are you saying?"

"There's only one solution. I have to fight The Assembled. And I have to lose."

No freaking way! "Mercy, I can't—" I pull my hand from her grasp.

"Please. Hear me out. The Assembled takes care of me. Then you take care of Isadora. It solves all of our problems."

I stand. "No."

"Why not?" she asks, incredulously.

"*Why not?* You can't honestly be asking me that."

She buries her hands in her hair, her fingers knotting and twisting. "You said you would help me."

"You trapped me! I had no idea what I was agreeing to. There's no way I'm going to let you die. I know you're having a hard time, but we'll find a way out."

"I can't control it. This thing," she picks at her shirt, like her powers are a skin she feels like shedding, "breaching people's bodies, and now, people's minds. This isn't how I want to live my life. If I fight The Assembled and win, Isadora will never stop. She'll never stop!"

I kneel before her and scoop her hands into mine. "I can't do this for you. I'm sorry."

"Because you love me."

It isn't what I expect her to say. I'm so thrown that my brain freezes.

She tosses my hands away and stands. I nearly topple over backward, but I'm able to catch myself at the last second.

"Sometimes," she says, her voice quiet and sad, "I miss the Hunter." Mercy crosses over to the door, opens it, and slams it behind her.

I start to chase, and then stop myself. "Dammit!" I kick the door, leaving a dusty boot print in the white paint.

What Mercy is asking me to do is absurd. It's out of the question. She's being irrational. She's scared and talking crazy. That's all there is to it. In time, with a little perspective, she'll see things aren't nearly as bleak as she imagines. She'll see that we can fix this, that we can find a way to help her.

Frustrated and, according to Mercy, rank, I take a shower. The hot water pelts my tired body. I linger under the stream until the water runs cold. Afterward, I towel off and head back to my room to put on fresh clothes. I choose a pair of jeans and a thermal shirt. It isn't cold outside—I'm dressed too warmly, but after the last twenty-four hours, I feel like I need insulation.

I hear the front door open and close. I stomp down the hall and find Nathaniel in the front room.

"Where have you been?" I ask, my tone biting.

Nathaniel smiles as if he's up to something. "I was coming up with a plan."

Why don't I find this comforting? "You have a plan?"

"Yep."

I gesture to the large envelope he's gripping tightly. "And it's in that?"

Nathaniel shakes the contents loose. Out slide two plastic cards. He hands me one.

"What the hell is this?"

"These are our high school ID cards."

"You're kidding, right?"

"We need to keep an eye on Mercy. This is how we're going to do it."

I study my ID card. "You do realize that no one is going to believe we're in high school."

"They bought it before when you were there," Nathaniel says.

"I never actually went to class. I just—"

"Stalked Mercy," Nathaniel says, cutting me off. "I remember."

"You're crazy if you think this will work," I tell him.

He shrugs. "I made us seniors."

Still gawking at the card, I sink into the couch cushions, boggling at the thought of homework and tests. This is idiotic. We really do look too old, but I guess we can give it a try. Of course we'll have to explain why we live alone without any parents. Then again, I'm not planning on making friends, so maybe no one will even notice.

Nathaniel does have the right idea, however. This is what Mercy needs—to get back to her old routine. And if something does happen, like she's forced out of her body, Nathaniel and I will be there.

Mercy made the deal with Isadora to keep us safe, and I'll be dammed if I don't do the same for her. True, I wish this task didn't involve high school, but I'm willing to go through with it for her. Mercy wants me to live my human life; she wants me to have real experiences. High school will certainly be a human experience.

Being a Hunter is all that I've ever known. We lived among the humans, but we fought the urge of humanity every day. We forced ourselves not to feel, not to let our emotions control us. The Assembled taught us that we were above humans, that we were evolved beyond them. But we were also there to protect them, to secure the balance of things. Humans live. Humans die. And for the most part, they know very little of the world that lay beyond. They aren't privy to that world until after death, until they shed their bodies and let go of their human needs.

Breachers are a black mark on humanity because they refuse to let go of the physical world. That's why the Hunters were created, to bring them to justice, to make them face their fate. I was happy to do so because I believed in the cause. I believed in the order of things. I still do. When my time as a human is over, I will cross over. On that point, I will not negotiate.

Immediately my conversation with Mercy comes screaming back to me. She's asking me for the exact same thing. She wants the chance to cross over. She doesn't want to go on forever. And selfishly, I denied her that. "Son of a bitch," I say softly.

Nathaniel narrows his eyes at me. "What?"

"I have to talk to Mercy."

"Why?"

"Because she asked me to do something, and I realize now that I can do it. I have to."

"Yeah, well, you can tell her tomorrow. Right now, we need to go shopping."

Who is this guy? And what has he done with Nathaniel?

Shopping consists of a trip to the mall. Apparently, Nathaniel doesn't hate this as much as I do. He drags me from store to store commenting that if he and I are going to "rule the school," I need a better wardrobe. He even decides I need a signature look, and, as ridiculous as that sounds, what he picks out for me I kind of like, though I will never admit it to him.

Before, I dressed to assimilate. But there was also something very military about it: boots, jeans, black T-shirts. That was pretty much my standard Hunter uniform. Sure, I occasionally topped it off with a leather jacket, but that was a gift from Rae.

My human style is apparently nerd-chic. Nathaniel and I practically empty the jeans section of the first department store we hit. I remind him that Lyla already picked out plenty of jeans for me, and his only reaction is to roll his eyes. Along with the jeans, he outfits me with several button-down shirts. 'Slim-fit' the tags read. To complete the ensemble, Nathaniel picks out a few vests.

"No one wears vests." I slide my arms through the openings and shrug the vest over my shoulders, examining myself in the dressing-room mirror.

"Be a trendsetter, little brother."

"I think you might be losing sight of why we're doing this."

"No, you are." He puts his hands on my shoulders. "Look,

Gage, I know we're in for the battle for our lives, and I know you don't give a shit about high school or any of this. But you can't let this opportunity pass you by. I know you. You won't become a Breacher like me. You'll live. You'll die. That's your plan."

I try to pull away from him, but he holds me steady.

"Don't even bother trying to convince me otherwise," he continues. "Like I said, I know you. And I've made my peace with your choice, believe me—I have. That's why I insist that you live every damn second to the fullest. Don't hold back. No regrets."

Nathaniel releases his grip and marches out of the room. His moment of clarity leaves me weak-kneed and bleary-eyed. The Nathaniel I know, the Breacher I chased for years on end— he isn't capable of such declarations. It occurs to me now that I'm not the only one undergoing a transformation. I've been so concerned with myself, and with Mercy, that I didn't notice the change in Nathaniel. And I should have.

That stunt Justice pulled—the swap when she pretended to be Mercy and came onto me in my bedroom—if that had happened a few months ago, Nathaniel would've gone for my throat. Yes, he threatened me afterward, but he kept his composure, and that alone should've tipped me off.

Of course, when Nathaniel learns what Mercy asked me to do, all bets will be off. He'll come after me with everything he has—of that I am certain. Preserving his own life may have been his top priority in the past, but that will take a backseat to preserving Mercy's. Nathaniel is in love with Mercy. When the time comes, he won't be able to let her go.

I decide to follow Nathaniel's advice. I'm going to take advantage of every moment and live life to the fullest. This means loving Mercy in whatever way she'll allow. If she doesn't love me back the way I would like, I'll have to live with that and accept her love in whatever form she's willing to give.

Once again dressed in my regular clothes, I gather my haul and meet Nathaniel. We pay for the clothes, spending way too much money. As we leave the store, Nathaniel seems more confident than ever. He's practically beaming. I'm not quite sure what he's so happy about. It isn't as if high school is an exciting prospect. And I don't actually believe we're going to be able to live normal lives. But I'm not about to spoil the mood. For now, we're two brothers on the night before school. Who knows who we'll be tomorrow.

Chapter Eleven

Nathaniel

*T*he scream that escaped Nathaniel was guttural and deep. He broke free from the two men holding him and lunged for Isadora. Catching her around the neck, he squeezed and squeezed. She clawed at his hands. "You evil, vindictive bitch!"

Her eyes bulged from her head as Nathaniel tightened his grip. The two men who had been holding him restrained him once again. Isadora shook her hair back and straightened her shoulders. She rubbed her neck.

"You had no right to do this, Isadora. She shouldn't have to pay for my choices."

"You should've thought about that before you risked everything." Isadora's glare was fierce.

"This isn't about my breaking the rules and you know it! This is vengeance."

"It's done." To the guards she said, "Take him away."

Nathaniel continued to curse her under his breath as he was led to the central building, the one where The Assembled regularly gathered. Though he'd been there before, he'd never been to this particular area. Past the main office, down a dark hall, into an elevator, and finally to what he could only assume was a basement, was a prison of sorts. The guards confined Nathaniel to a small room that held a cot, a desk, and a chair. "You can't leave me in here!" he yelled as the door was closed.

But apparently, they could leave him in there because that's exactly what they did. Days, perhaps even weeks, went by before the door opened again. And when it did, it was not whom he expected.

"Ariana. What are you doing here?"

"I came to see you, of course."

"Took you long enough," he huffed.

"I had to wait until it was safe." Ariana pulled out the chair and sat. "I've been under surveillance since your arrest."

"What do you know?"

"That there will be a trial of sorts, but mostly it's just a sentencing. They know you're guilty."

"Guilty of what?"

"Don't be a fool! You had contact with a human, developed a relationship with her. None of that is allowed."

"The distain in your voice reeks with hypocrisy."

"You won't be so flippant about this when you're sentenced, Nathaniel."

"What can they possibly do?"

"The Assembled have the ultimate authority. Do not underestimate them," Ariana warned.

"I exercised my free will, nothing more."

"You're being arrogant and stubborn as usual!" Ariana's cheeks flushed with anger.

"What would you have me do? Throw myself on their mercy? Beg like a dog?"

"That's exactly what I'm asking you to do. Save yourself before it's too late."

Nathaniel lowered his gaze to the floor. "I love her, Ariana. I won't make apologies for that."

"You risked so much for her." Ariana shook her head. "Was it worth it?"

A wistful look passed over Nathaniel's face. "Every second."

Chapter Twelve

Mercy

On the first day of school, my mom, my dad, and I sit around the table eating breakfast like a normal family. It reminds me of before all this started, back when I was nine and my mom was just my mom, my dad was still a college professor, and my greatest worry was the Friday spelling test. What I wouldn't give to go back to before everything got so complicated.

On my tenth birthday, when my mom disappeared and was presumed dead, I thought that life couldn't get any worse. I thought I'd been dealt the worst hand, and that there was nothing to do but fold. I was wrong, so very, very wrong. I would gladly change places with ten-year-old me. What lies ahead now is so daunting I can barely cope.

Since the *incident* with Nathaniel, I am hyperaware of every single thought I have. It's a relentless effort to guard my thoughts, so I find myself very often wanting to be alone. This, of course, sucks because I just got my family back. I would love to spend quality time with my mom and dad or with Jay and Lyla, but I can't until I learn to control what's going on in my head.

I am beyond paranoid about going back to school. I will have to become a complete loner in order to function. Of course, in general, it seems kind of stupid to be heading off to school when I have the task of killing The Assembled. And now that I'm all but certain Isadora knows I'm capable, I am stuck carrying out her task. I can't fake inability or she'll kill everyone I love.

Rock. Me. Hard place.

My mom covers my hand with hers. "You're a million miles away."

"Just thinking." I try to smile.

"Want to share some of those thoughts?" my dad asks.

"I was just thinking I hope I make it to prom." I can't believe I let those words slip out.

"Mercy," my dad says sympathetically, "you're going to have a long and wonderful life. You'll see."

The sound of Jay's truck honking brings us all back to reality. Today, at least, I'm going to pretend to be normal high school junior.

"Have a good day, sweetie." My mom stands and hugs me good-bye.

"I'll try."

I yank my backpack onto my shoulders and jog down the walk to Jay's truck. Lyla lowers the window and waves. "Mercy Clare, look at you! Is that a skirt you're wearing?"

I climb into the truck beside her. "Shut up, Ly."

"You look hot."

"Then all is right with the world," I say sarcastically.

Lyla fiddles with the stereo until she settles on a song. I keep the window down, feeling the cold breeze against my face. Everything about the ride to school is the same as it was before. We drive down the same streets. We pass the same houses. There's the street sign on the corner that's tilted slightly from where a car crashed into it last year. There's the one hideously painted house on the corner that looks like mint chocolate chip ice cream.

We stop for coffee, like we always do, so Lyla can load up on caffeine. Not being a fan of coffee, I wait in the truck while she and Jay go inside. I check my reflection in the mirror on the sun visor. Same wavy brown hair; same brown eyes. My outsides look the same, but I'm not the same girl I was before. I am a Breacher. No matter how hard I try, there's no denying who I've become.

Across the parking lot strides a girl who looks just like me. She flips her auburn hair over her shoulder and peers right at me, catching me gawking. To my horror, she bounces right up to the truck.

"Hey, sis." She rocks back and forth on her heels.

I sneer at her. "Don't call me that. I'm not your sister."

"Whatever you say," she winks, "sis."

"I realize this is super fun for you, but I have to get to school. Maybe you can come by and taunt me later."

"School?" She taps her lip with her finger. "Education is important, isn't it? And I certainly have some catching up to do. I guess I better hurry or I'll be late."

"No!" I open the door, forcing her back. Hopping out, I say, "You are not coming to my school." How had I not noticed her backpack? "This is too far."

"This is Isadora."

"Isadora planned this? Why?"

Justice shrugs her shoulders. "She thinks sisters should stick together."

Anger, red and hot, flushes my cheeks. "Like she stuck with my mother?"

"Ancient history."

"Like hell."

"Look, that's between them."

I roll my eyes. "Whatever."

"I didn't come here to fight."

"What do you want then?"

"Just to tell you that I'm not the enemy. And that I was hoping we could be friends."

"That's never going to happen."

"I'm sure you'll change your mind eventually," Justice says confidently. "See you at school, sis." She saunters off, leaving me stunned and slack-jawed.

Defeated, my shoulders slumping, I get back into the truck and wait for Lyla and Jay to return. When they do, I don't mention my little encounter. I know I can't hold off for long, but I decide to give them a few more minutes of ignorant bliss.

As soon as we pull into campus, I see the tribute that's been erected in honor of Mr. Andreas, and I'm instantly swept back to the moment in the alley when he put a gun in his mouth and pulled the trigger. Of course, it wasn't actually him—it was Nathaniel in his body. Regardless, the image of the back of his head exploding, the lumpy, gooey strawberry jam-like substance that scattered the sidewalk—it's all seared in my memory forever.

I hadn't even thought about the impact Mr. Andreas's death might have on the school. I missed the end of the school year and wasn't around for the aftermath. But I can picture it. I'm sure there was a memorial, counselors available to talk to grieving students, maybe even some sports team wore a black band on their jersey in honor of him.

Jay parks in the back lot. We hop out and head toward the quad. Nathaniel and Gage are waiting for us. They aren't even trying to be inconspicuous. Girls are staring—more like gawking. There are practically trails of drool all over the quad. Here I was hoping they would go unnoticed, but nothing is more newsworthy on a high-school campus than two new hot guys.

As I get closer to them, I see that Nathaniel is wearing a knowing grin, and immediately my cheeks flush with the memory of the last time he and I were together. I had hoped we could skip over it, pretend it didn't happen, but I can see now that it's impossible to keep my thoughts clear around him.

Nathaniel wriggles his eyebrows. "Hot guys?"

"Shut up."

Nathaniel's smile widens. Gage's expression is one of great displeasure.

Turning to Lyla and Jay, I say, "There's no way I can do this. I'm going home."

Lyla catches me by the elbow. "Hold up." She pulls me away

from the group, leaving Jay, Gage, and Nathaniel awkwardly huddled together.

"What?" I whine.

"Mercy Rose Clare. Listen to me. I have been your best friend since third grade. I know you, and I know what you've been through. And I know you can do this."

"Lyla, you don't understand." I gesture toward the buildings. "This is pointless."

"No. This is everything. This is your life. You're not what *they* say you are. You're whatever *you* say you are. Live your life. Go to school. Do your homework."

"What if I can't?"

"You took that binding agent stuff, right? So you won't breach?"

"Yes, but it's not just that."

"Then what is it?"

Where do I even start?

"Mercy," Lyla stares deeply into my eyes, "you've got this. Just be the girl I know and love."

My heart sinks. "I love you too, Lyla. So much. But I'm not that girl anymore."

"Maybe not," she nods, and then she grips my shoulders, "but you're going in anyway."

"Lyla!" I protest.

It's no use. She drags me back to the group. Nathaniel's smirk is gone. Gage still looks serious, maybe even a little more serious than he had before. Jay's face is full of sympathy. His mouth is smushed up, and he's trying not to stare at me.

"The bell is going to ring," Lyla announces. "Everyone have their schedules?" We all nod. "Good." She turns to me. "I'll see you at lunch."

Lyla and Jay walk off together.

"Try to behave yourself," Gage says to Nathaniel.

"I'll be a perfect angel," Nathaniel answers with heavy sarcasm.

Gage gives Nathaniel one last look of warning before stalking off.

Nathaniel extends his elbow as if to escort me. "Shall we?"

Shaking my head, I say, "Why are you enjoying this so much?"

He takes a deep breath and exhales. "I'm living. You should give it a try sometime."

The bell rings. Nathaniel waits for me to make my move. Rolling my eyes, I slide my arm through his. Turns out, Nathaniel and I have most of the same classes. Apparently, my leash doesn't go very far.

As we stroll through the halls, there are looks and even whispers. Nathaniel either doesn't notice or doesn't care. I'm guessing it's the latter. But I figure, if he can do it, I can do it. Let them stare. Let them talk about me behind my back. Whatever. It doesn't matter anyway. What's a little gossip compared to what I've been through already?

Our first class of the day is literature, which is usually my favorite, but today, I'm not feeling it. Bored, I tap my pen against the desk while the teacher, Mrs. Clark, drones on about all the great authors we'll be reading this school year. The other me, the old me, would've been taking copious notes and hanging on every word, but the new me, the Breacher me, hopes she'll stop talking and let us off without any homework.

"I think I've said enough for today," Mrs. Clark says suddenly. "You can hang out for the rest of the class period. Oh, and no homework tonight. Enjoy the first day of school!"

The class sits in stunned silence for a few seconds, waiting for the punch line, perhaps, but then Mrs. Clark settles at her desk and fires up her laptop. The chatter starts up immediately.

Nathaniel swivels in my direction. He cocks his eyebrow. "Do we have you to thank for this?"

"What do you mean?"

"Our teacher's sudden brain hemorrhage."

"Please, like I could ever really—" *No!*

"Don't panic. We don't know for sure this was you." He looks around the room. "But there's one way to find out."

He yanks me from my seat and leads me down the aisle.

"What are you doing?" I ask, knowing all eyes are on us.

"Testing a theory." A few steps before we reach her desk, Nathaniel puts his hands on my shoulders. "Whatever I say, just agree with me. Push your thoughts to her. Got it?"

He pulls my arm, but I don't budge. "I don't think we should be doing this."

"Mercy, trust me. The sooner we find out how far your little gift goes, the better."

I know what we're about to do is irrefutably asinine, and yet, I plod ahead.

"Mrs. Clark?" She barely looks up from her computer when

Nathaniel speaks. "Mercy and I are going to go to make-out, okay?"

"What?" I blurt.

Mrs. Clark glances up from her computer. "Mercy?"

I try not to picture it, try not to envision Nathaniel and I together, but once the thought is in my head, it's like I can't think of anything else. His mouth. His hands. *Shut up, brain!*

"You two kids have fun," Mrs. Clark says, and then she goes back to typing.

Nathaniel lets out a tiny laugh. "Thanks, Mrs. Clark. We will." He takes my hand and guides me out of the classroom.

He is nearly giddy by the time we reach the quad.

"Why are you so happy?" I ask him.

Nathaniel wraps his arms around my waist. "Do you know what this means?"

"That I've reached a new level of creepy?"

His enthusiasm wanes. "Must you always go straight for the negative?"

"How in the world is this positive, Nathaniel? I can manipulate minds. This isn't a good quality. This is a very, very bad thing."

He steps back and folds his arms across his chest. "What if it works on Isadora?"

I hadn't considered that.

Nathaniel rolls up on his toes and wiggles his eyebrows. "It's good, isn't it?"

"There's no way it'll work. Isadora isn't human."

"Well, Ms. Clare, it's your lucky day because neither am I." He holds his arms out wide, daring me.

"I'm not doing it."

"You really don't know how to have any fun, do you?"

"Fun? You think this is fun?"

"I'm offering you the chance to take full advantage of me. Something tells me any other girl would jump given the opportunity."

"Wow," I scoff. "How do you carry that big head of yours around? Your neck must be exhausted." I pivot, facing away from him. "I mean, really, I don't even know how you're standing here right now, you know with the weight of your ego pressing down on you like that. It must feel like an elephant on your back."

"Mercy."

"Do you ever have back pain? Or feel like you just can't hold yourself up anymore?"

"Mercy. Stop."

Spinning around, I find him on all fours, gasping for breath. He's trying to hold on, but I can see the effort is excruciating.

"Oh my God! What's wrong?"

"I … Being … Crushed …"

"Holy shit! I was kidding." Dropping to the ground, I cradle him against me. "I was kidding. I was kidding," I say over and over.

Nathaniel groans and rolls onto his side. His head lands in my lap.

I stroke his hair, which feels like feathers against my fingers. "You're not being crushed. You're fine. You're fine."

Nathaniel breathes heavily. He flops onto his back and stares up at me. "Yeah, it works."

"I'm so sorry. Are you all right?"

He tenses and then sighs heavily. "Just give me a sec."

"I didn't mean to hurt you."

"I know."

"This was your idea."

"I know that too." He stretches.

"Are you sure you're okay?"

His head is still in my lap; thick, dark lashes shroud his eyes. His lips are parted slightly, and his breathing is slowing, evening out. His lips …

Shoving him off, I get to my feet. "We're going back to class."

Nathaniel stands and dusts himself off. "Whatever you say, boss."

Chapter Thirteen

Gage

The bell rings, and class dismisses. According to my schedule, it's lunchtime. As soon as I realize this, a rumble of hunger erupts in my stomach—yet another thing about being human that frustrates me. The human form is rather delicate and requires constant maintenance. There's so much that needs to be clipped and trimmed and shaved, not to mention washed and groomed. It's a wonder humans accomplish anything.

As I walk to the cafeteria, I realize I need to take care of another human function. I find the nearest bathroom, push open the door, and step into a dimly lit, very smelly room. I make my way to the trough, and am about to unzip my jeans, when the door slams open behind me.

Nathaniel stumbles forward. He's unbalanced, breathing heavy, and sweating.

Quickly, I zip up.

He crashes into me. "Can't breathe," he gasps.

I've never seen him like this before, so weak, so unstable. "What's wrong?"

"Need ... Body ... Help ..." Nathaniel wheezes.

It takes me a second, but then I register his words. Nathaniel is losing his grip on this world. And if he doesn't find a body to breach soon ...

"Use me," I suggest, throwing out the first idea that comes to me.

In his weakened state, he still manages to shoot me an annoyed expression. "Kill ... You ... Idiot ..."

He's right. If he takes my body, he'll kill me. Nathaniel isn't like Mercy. He isn't able to slip easily in and out of bodies. He has to kill his host in order to extricate himself.

The door opens again, and a skinny kid enters. He takes one look at me and Nathaniel and starts backing away. Nathaniel, with me in tow, moves toward the kid. I know what he's going to do, and I know I should stop him.

"Nathaniel, you can't," I try.

"No ... Choice ..."

Nathaniel plows into the kid, grabs him by the shirt, and shuffles him into the wall. The kid is terrified. His mouth is agape with horror, but no sound emanates. His head shakes back and forth. His eyes are wide and vibrating.

Nathaniel lurches back and throws himself forward as if he were about to head butt the kid, but before he connects, he shatters into a million tiny pieces. There's a shrieking sound. I don't know if it's coming from the kid or the force of Nathaniel, but it doesn't matter. Within seconds, it's over. Nathaniel is gone, and the kid is slinking to the floor. His body gyrates, flops like a fish out of water, and then goes disturbingly still. If I didn't know better, I'd think the kid was dead. But I do know better.

The kid stands and braces himself against a sink. "That was close," he says.

When he turns around, it's almost as if I can see Nathaniel glaring back at me through his eyes. They're more determined and focus than they should be for a kid his age.

"I don't want to stay in this body for long," Nathaniel grumbles.

"Well, you can't kill him in the boy's bathroom."

Nathaniel cocks his head slightly. "Yes, I know," he says snidely.

"How could you let this happen? We're at school!"

"Oh, I see. It's not my taking bodies that irks you, it's my timing."

"Don't be a dick."

"Bite me."

"Why didn't you tell me it was this bad?"

Nathaniel glowers at me. "We've had other things to worry about. And I thought I was charged from the last time, from that nerdy guy at the courthouse."

"So, what happened?"

"It must've been Mercy," Nathaniel says.

Eycing him, I ask, "What do you mean?"

"We tried a little mind control experiment this morning. It

must've taken more out of me than I thought."

"I can't believe you did this," I seethe. "This is Mercy's school. You can't just go around leaving a trail of bodies."

Nathaniel mumbles something unintelligible, and exits the bathroom. Trailing behind, I follow him down the hall. We're in the clear for the most part. Only a few students linger at their lockers, but the majority have filed out for lunch.

"This kid is incredibly awkward," Nathaniel complains. "It's like there's no muscle at all, just sinewy cartilage held together by pasty skin. Next time remind me to bag a football player, someone with more bulk," Nathaniel rubs his chin, "or at least someone who's gone through puberty."

Sharply, I turn and latch onto Nathaniel's shirt. Dragging him to the lockers, he bangs his head as I tighten my grip. "Listen to me, Nathaniel. You are not ever breaching another kid at this school. I realize you may not understand this, but murder is *bad*. And the more bodies, the more questions. We can't have that. Do I make myself clear?"

Nathaniel loosens my grip and shoves me back. "Keep your hands off me," he says in his most threatening voice.

"Or what?"

"Don't tempt me."

"Have you seen you? Take your best shot."

Nathaniel looks down at his spindly arms and chicken legs, rolls his eyes, and presses on down the hall.

"Toby!" Someone is shouting behind us. "Toby! Wait up!"

In slow-motion horror, I turn and see Mercy jogging toward us. Nathaniel and I exchange quick, paranoid glances.

"I've been looking for you," Mercy says as she catches up to us.

Nathaniel remains mum.

"Hey, Gage," she says to me.

I greet her with a nod.

"What's going on, guys?" she asks, her voice full of suspicion.

"We're just headed to lunch," I say.

"We?" she says, disbelieving. "You two know each other?"

"We're partners for a project," Toby pipes in.

Mercy concentrates her dubious stare on Toby. "Really? A freshman paired with a senior?"

Again, Nathaniel and I trade knowing looks.

Mercy is not fooled. Her eyes narrow to slits. "Where's Nathaniel?"

I can't help myself. I sneak a quick peek at Toby, hoping Mercy doesn't notice, but it's too late. She knows.

"No!" She gasps and shakes her head back and forth. "You didn't."

Our cover blown, there is no use denying the truth. "Mercy, he had to."

Furious, she turns on Nathaniel. "What do you mean you *had* to?"

"Please calm down," Nathaniel says.

"Don't tell me what to do!" Mercy shouts. "Do you have any idea what you've done?"

"I know this situation isn't ideal," Nathaniel tries to explain, "but—"

"Stop. I can't even look at you right now." Facing me, she

says, "You have to fix this. Fix this now."

"We are in the process of doing just that," I assure her. "But we can't have any bodies here—"

"No. You don't understand. You can't kill Toby!" Mercy's voice borders on panic.

"You can't expect me to stay like this," Nathaniel says.

Mercy addresses Nathaniel. "You cannot under any circumstances kill Toby. I won't let you."

Nathaniel, taken aback, asks, "Why the hell not?"

"Because Toby is Jay's little brother!"

Ka-boom.

I close my eyes to shut out her words. I don't want to hear what she just said. It's too horrible.

"You never mentioned Jay's brother." Nathaniel stands to his full Toby height. It isn't much, but it has the desired effect. We all know he's livid.

"I didn't know you were going to go around breaching people at school," Mercy snaps. "He's Jay's half-brother. He's only been living here for a few weeks."

"This is unbelievable!" Nathaniel punches the nearest locker. "Son of a bitch!" He rubs his hand. "That actually hurt."

Mercy holds her head in her hands. "What are we going to do?"

"You know what I have to do," Nathaniel answers.

"No." Mercy leers at Nathaniel. "You can't."

"So you want me to live as this kid forever? That's your solution?" Nathaniel speaks as if this is the most ludicrous idea ever.

"Mercy, we can't," I say. "We have to get him out."

She's not swayed. "Why did you do this in the first place?"

"I had to." Nathaniel says, exasperated.

"Explain that to me, Nathaniel. Explain to me why you just *had* to breach!"

The leftover kids, the ones linger at their lockers, are starting to gawk at us.

"We should move this discussion somewhere else," I say to them.

Mercy and Nathaniel survey the hall. They see what I see—that we're drawing too much attention to ourselves. It is definitely time to go.

We make our way out to the unsuspecting quad. Students mill about in groups of varying sizes. We barely turn a head as we cross the lawn and near the parking lot. We are almost home free.

"Mercy!"

"Shit," Mercy mutters. "Shit. Shit. Shit."

Jay strides toward us. "We've been waiting for you. Aren't you coming to lunch?" Jay plants a jab on Toby's shoulder. "What up, Freshman? Shouldn't you be in class? Your lunch isn't until next period."

"Um, yeah," Mercy stammers. "We were just, um ..."

"I was just going," Nathaniel says quickly.

"Good. Wouldn't want you to get busted on day one." Jay shoves him. "Save that for at least day two."

Nathaniel turns and leaves.

"You guys coming?" Jay asks.

"Actually, I need to meet up with my brother," I say.

"Yeah, um …" Apparently Mercy is still at a loss for words. "I'll be right there," she says to Jay.

"Okay." Jay lopes toward the cafeteria, leaving Mercy and I alone.

"What do we do now?" Mercy asks, her voice urgent.

"I'll go find Nathaniel. You go to lunch with your friends."

She nods along, but I can tell she's hesitant.

"It'll be okay, Mercy. We'll figure something out."

Her glare on full, she says, "You better."

I watch her walk away, her gait tight and purposeful. She's beyond agitated, which makes me worry about her. Even though she doesn't want to admit it, we all know Mercy is unpredictable. We've learned to control her breaching by injecting her with binding agent, but that doesn't mean she's stable. There's nothing we can do about her ability to breach minds. There's no binding agent for that. Who knows if she'll go off half-cocked and hurt someone while angry.

Mercy will never be able to forgive herself if that happens. Of course she's not going to forgive Nathaniel or me if we don't find a way to get Nathaniel out of Toby's body. I know she wants me to find a solution to the problem, but I don't know of one. Even with all of Rae's fancy extraction equipment, the end result is always the same: the host body dies.

This is bad. This is so very, very bad.

As I hunt for Nathaniel, I rack my brain. This is an impossible task. In all my time as a Hunter, I've never known of any Breacher other than Mercy who can vacate a body without killing it. If I still had my team, we might be able to put our heads together and come up with something, but they're gone. I'm on my own.

An idea strikes me, but it's a long shot for sure. There might be something at the warehouse, or what's left of the warehouse. Rae was always doing research. Maybe she came up with something. Of course, if she had, she would have told me, but that doesn't mean it isn't worth having a look.

It doesn't take long to find Nathaniel, and when I do, I fill him in on my idea. He's up for it, but he's unhappy about having to remain inside Toby.

"We only have a few hours of school left," I remind him. "We can go then."

"Fine," Nathaniel reluctantly agrees. "But if we don't find anything, you know what I'm going to do. I can't stay like this."

"You shouldn't have done it in the first place," I say.

"The alternative is death, Gage."

I don't need the reminder. I know very well what happens to Nathaniel if he's not attached to a body. And as angry as I am that he got us into this mess, I don't want him to die.

Chapter Fourteen

Nathaniel

*T*here was a trial of sorts, and Nathaniel was sentenced for his crimes: banishment, forced to live as a human.

"You won't get away with this!" he screamed when the verdict was read. He shouted to Isadora, "How can you just sit there! Do something!"

Isadora refused to look at Nathaniel. She appeared bereaved, as if she was the victim.

"You made your choice, Nathaniel," said Lucas Church, leader of The Assembled. "There is nothing left to be done."

Broken, desperate, all signs of arrogance vanished, Nathaniel momentarily slipped out of the guard's grasp. He rushed to Isadora and threw himself at her feet. "Please, Isadora. Please. I'm begging you. Don't let them do this to me."

Isadora refused to look at Nathaniel. A single tear dribbled along *her cheek. "I'm sorry," she said.*

Nathaniel arched back, struck by her words. Was she sincere? She certainly appeared pained, but why would she feel sorrow when she set this all in motion?

The guards grabbed Nathaniel and hauled him from the room. He didn't look back at Isadora. He never wanted to see her face again.

They dumped Nathaniel in his cell, and there he rotted for a very long time. One day, the guards came for him. They led him to the bridge. The entirety of The Assembled gathered to watch his march into oblivion. Isadora was there, dressed in white, looking regal, beautiful, as if she were made of marble. Ariana stood at Isadora's side, the look on her face making it evident that she was forced to be there.

"Nathaniel Black," Lucas Church bellowed. "Once you cross the bridge, you will never again be allowed back. You will live as a human and die as a human. Do you have any final words?"

"Yeah." Nathaniel broke free from the guard's handle. "Fuck you."

Nathaniel stared into the distance, into the unknown, unsure of what he would find. He marched proudly, never once glancing back. He didn't want to see all that he was leaving behind. He tried not to think of what brought him to this fate, but it couldn't be helped. He thought of Ellie and her kind, warm smile. He thought of her eyes, her lips. He tried to hold onto those thoughts, but then as if being slammed into a brick wall, he saw her being swallowed into Purgatory, and his throat tightened. A tear dribbled and swam the length of his cheek.

Though he'd made this walk countless times before, he'd never done so knowing he wouldn't return. When he crossed the threshold, the world darkened as the path behind him closed.

He landed on a dirt road with nothing, not a penny to his name. Almost instantly, he was bombarded with humanity. It was Winter, something that had never been anything to him before except the name of a season. Nathaniel hadn't known what it meant to be chilled, but he knew then. He shivered and drew his jacket around him.

Suddenly, he felt another new and strange sensation—hunger. His stomach protested and whined like a petulant child. He needed food, but he had no way to get it. As soon as that realization hit him, he was flooded with other human emotions: fear, worry, anger, regret. They swarmed and overwhelmed him and nearly brought him to his knees.

Nathaniel sought refuge on a park bench. It seemed the perfect place to wallow in self-pity. He sat staring off into the distance and contemplating his life choices. Nathaniel knew his situation was dire, and as night fell, he began to give himself over to despair.

From behind, he felt an abrupt shove. He was flung forward onto the ground. He'd never fallen or been in pain before, and at first, he couldn't even register what was happening to him. So many parts of his body pinged and burned.

"Gimme your money," his attacker commanded.

Nathaniel rolled onto his back just as a shoe met his rib cage. He cried out, but the cry was quickly stifled as he was mounted and frisked. Coming up empty, his attacker, angry and cruel, pummeled him. Fists, feet, it was all a blur of black spots and bright flashes as Nathaniel clung to consciousness. The only thing that kept the blackness at bay was the pain; pain that flared from everywhere, impossible to ignore, impossible to shut out.

The assault didn't last long, but the repercussions stuck around for weeks, even months after. Days passed before Nathaniel could take a solid, deep breath without wincing. The bruises on his face healed after a few weeks, but the body bruises took much longer to fade. In that time, Nathaniel wandered and learned.

He learned which areas to stick to and which to avoid. He found a fascinating establishment known as a soup kitchen where he could occasionally feast on semi-edible food. What Nathaniel observed quickly was that humans ignored other humans for the most part. No one stopped to bother him, to ask him why he slept on the street or why his clothes were torn. No one cared.

It was this ambivalence to their own kind that Nathaniel zeroed in on, even relied upon. He quickly went from prey to predator. When he wanted new clothes, he stole them. When he needed money, he mugged someone. He was clever, cunning, and quick. And, fairly quickly, he was able to amass a savings.

The savings earned him a room at a boarding house. Finally, a real bed. True, it was lumpy, dirty, and bug-ridden, but it was his. With an address to go with his name, gaining employment was much easier. Of course Nathaniel had no work experience, but he knew how to pay attention and use people to his own advantage. He landed a job was washing dishes at the fanciest restaurant in town.

At the start, the job merely fueled his rage. He saw patrons in fine clothes with wads of money come and go from the restaurant, and the jealousy he felt toward them was all-consuming. He was so much better than them! He knew about the universe, about what lay beyond, and he knew that none of this—the money, the clothes, the cars—meant anything in the end. He laughed at their futile efforts to stockpile wealth and rolled his eyes at their idle chatter.

But then he decided to beat them at their game. He'd come so far already, pulled himself up from nothing, why not see how far he could go? After all, he only had this one lifetime. Why not make the most of it?

With even more money saved, Nathaniel upgraded from the boarding house to an apartment. He worked his way from dishwasher to line cook. There he honed his skills, learning to chop and simmer, sauté and poach. And soon, he was promoted to sous chef.

Food, the basic human necessity, became Nathaniel's mistress, his only love. He adored everything about food: the smells, the flavors, the textures, the colors. He immersed himself in all its glory.

After a few years as a human, Nathaniel opened his very own restaurant, one he overhauled and completely restored. The restaurant was a huge success with a line around the block almost every night. He catered to the finest of people, city officials, bankers—people whom, only a short while before, never noticed his existence.

Nathaniel had done it. He'd made something of himself. He'd even purchased a grand home on the wealthiest avenue and decorated it lavishly. He had a staff of twenty, and he never wanted for anything.

One day, while surveying his accomplishments, something dawned on him.

He was happy.

The sentence leveled against him was meant to punish, to torture, but that was not what had happened. Nathaniel appreciated what he had, having lost his anger and resentment somewhere along the way.

He had made a life for himself, and it brought him joy, something he never expected to experience. Yes, he was mortal, and yes, he still often thought of Ellie and it would set his heart to pang, but for the most part, he was sincerely happy.

***

At age eighty-two, Nathaniel Black lay prone in a hospital bed dying, surrounded by no one. He never married, never attached himself to anyone, therefore there weren't mourners by his bedside. No one to hold his hand, to wish him safe passage on his journey into death. And that was just fine with Nathaniel. He didn't need comfort or reassurance through this process. He knew exactly where he was headed. He was going home. He'd paid for his crime, and he was ready to be released from his human form and returned to the other side.

Nathaniel coughed and sputtered. Bright red spots flecked his blanket. The nurse assigned to him wiped his chin. Time was most certainly running out. Closing his eyes, Nathaniel dreamed of hearing his Guide's voice, of crossing the bridge into the light. He knew he'd be there without Ellie—that she'd always be in Purgatory—and for that, he still felt crushingly guilty. But Nathaniel held out hope that there would be some way to rescue her, to plead her case for her. Certainly Isadora couldn't still be holding a grudge against him. And if she was, he was ready to do whatever to appease her. He'd be with her, rule with her, whatever she wanted as long as Ellie was released from her certain hell.

Breaths were sparse and ragged as Nathaniel felt the end nearing. For a split second, he thought he sensed someone's presence. He thought his Guide had arrived to take him, but then the strangest thing happened. Searing pain ripped through his body like a tidal wave of aguish. Literally feeling the flesh peel from his bones, Nathaniel tried to cry out, but no sound came from his mouth. He breathed hard and rapid as he splintered into a million pieces. More than ever before Nathaniel wanted to die. Anything to stop the torture.

The pain changed directions suddenly, and instead of being pulled, Nathaniel felt every molecule, every piece of tissue and flesh, slam back together. Waves of nausea rocked him, and he knew he couldn't take much more of this. Through the darkness, light appeared, and Nathaniel prayed this was it. He prayed for his end.

Nathaniel's feet hit the floor with a thud. He panted and tried to regain control of himself, but it was a struggle. The moment he opened his eyes, he saw the horrified expression on the nurse's face. Petrified and silently screaming, the nurse backed away. Nathaniel sprang at her, instinct and urge controlling his every movement. He wanted to silence her, to keep her from calling for help. Just as he thought he'd choked the life out of her, Nathaniel felt himself splinter again. This time he shattered like broken glass. The pieces were nearly impossible to control, but Nathaniel managed to pull them together. He directed every piece to one point, and they collided, diving straight down the nurse's throat.

He glued himself to the walls of skin around him. It was uncomfortable and strange, and every inch of him felt battered and beaten when he finally opened his eyes. Stretching his neck and flexing his fingers, Nathaniel was uniquely whole once again, no longer in pain, but rather charged, electrified, rejuvenated.

Looking down in the bed, Nathaniel saw the human form he'd once occupied. The monitors were quiet. Nathaniel was definitely dead, but it wasn't the death he was expecting. He was cheated out of the light, tricked somehow. There was no Guide there to meet him, no one to assist him over the bridge. He was alone in the room, trapped in the body of a nurse. Nathaniel looked straight forward, knowing he was being watched, knowing there was no way The Assembled was going to let his death pass as if it were nothing. To piss them off, he winked and smiled toward the heavens. Screw them, he thought. They won't get the last word this time.

His bravado, however, was short-lived.

Almost immediately Nathaniel was accosted. He was stripped of his human form and returned to the bridge. Lucas Church stood there waiting, two hulking figures at his side.

"Impressive." Lucas clapped his hands.

"You did this to me," Nathaniel seethed.

"I did nothing of the sort." Lucas smiled wickedly. "But what fun we're going to have, Nathaniel. What fun, indeed." Lucas said to the man on his left, "Bring me the girl."

Minutes later, the man returned dragging a frightened and disheveled Ariana with him.

"What's going on?" Nathaniel asked.

"My children." Lucas shook his head like a disappointed father. "My dear children. It seems as though you have been rather naughty."

"Ariana is innocent!" Nathaniel yelled. "Leave her alone."

From his breast pocket Lucas Church pulled a piece of parchment paper. Nathaniel's heart sunk. "Is she now?" Lucas clucked his tongue.

Nathaniel glanced at Ariana, his eyes full of question. Ariana shook her head slowly, and Nathaniel realized the truth. Ariana had given him Ellie's name. She'd broken the rules for him. And she was going to pay.

"Now," Lucas church slid the paper in his pocket, "what shall I do with my new toys?"

"Let us die," Ariana begged.

"Heavens no!" Lucas clutched his chest as if he couldn't bear the thought. "You are much too talented for death. I propose an arrangement. You do as I say, and at the end of your term, I will give you what you so greatly desire: a human life and a human death."

Nathaniel and Ariana exchanged looks. They resignation in Ariana's face nearly brought tears to Nathaniel's eyes.

"What do you want us to do?" Nathaniel asked.

***

Late one night, after completing yet another one of Lucas's gruesome requests, Ariana and Nathaniel sat huddled together around a campfire.

"We can't continue like this," Ariana said. "The bloodshed. The wars. I never would've agreed if I'd known what Lucas had planned."

"We had no choice," Nathaniel reminded her. He thought back to the day on the bridge when Lucas threatened their lives. He remembered how helpless they both were. What other option did they have but to comply?

"He's using us, Nathaniel. Don't you see? He's trying to control us because we have talents he doesn't."

Nathaniel balked at her words. "You consider taking human lives talent?"

"We can occupy human bodies. No one before us has ever achieved such a feat. Lucas is frightened of us. He's keeping us as slaves so we don't overthrow him."

"You're speaking nonsense," Nathaniel said.

But something about Ariana's words rang true. Lucas himself admitted that he hadn't planned for them to take other bodies. Maybe Ariana was right. Maybe Lucas was afraid of them.

"I'm going to run," Ariana said boldly.

"You will do no such thing."

"I have to try. I can't carry on like this."

"Just a little while longer, Ari," Nathaniel tried to sound reassuring. "You'll see. Lucas will release us. He gave us his word."

They didn't speak for the rest of the night. Nathaniel tried to sleep, but he was restless. Ariana's words rattled in his brain. He knew her pain because he felt it too. He didn't want to kill anymore. He didn't want to jump from one body to the next, mercilessly bringing destruction wherever they went. He wanted it to end. But he couldn't think of another way. Lucas was too powerful, and if they denied him, he would make them suffer in unimaginable ways.

They carried on the next day, and for years after. They murdered, they slaughtered, they committed unspeakable acts, and not once did Lucas give any indication he would set them free. Finally, Nathaniel agreed they had to run. This was no way to exist.

Chapter Fifteen

Mercy

For the rest of the school day I stress. How could Nathaniel be so reckless? So stupid! Thinking back I should've expected this from him. He's selfish, self-serving, arrogant, and rash. Of course he breached the first body available!

And then I remember a story Nathaniel told me about how he and I are different. He is not rooted here because he is not human. He has to fight to stay here. He has to breach in order to stay alive. *Damn!* I want to hold on to my anger. I want to hate him for what he did to Toby, but suddenly there's sympathy mixed with hatred.

I can't even imagine what Jay is going to say or do when he finds out about Toby. Jay barely understood my being in Lyla's body, but he knew it was an accident, so he forgave me. But when I breached Kate's body out of necessity, he was furious with me. He won't understand this. And why should he? Breaching goes against all the rules. Who are we to decide which life is more valuable than the other? Yes, Nathaniel would've died if he hadn't taken a body, but does that mean that Toby should die instead?

The last bell sounds. The first day of school is over. Quickly, I dart to my locker where I find Gage waiting for me. "Where's Nathaniel?"

"Waiting in the car," he answers.

I gather what I need, all the while thinking, *does any of this really matter?* Honestly, what is the point of homework and tests and projects and grades when there are so many other more important things to worry about? Isadora and my evil twin are still out there running wild. Nathaniel is inside Toby's body. Who really cares if I pass calculus?

Gage and I walk without talking to the car. As expected, Nathaniel is there. It's strange seeing him this way. Nathaniel and Toby could not be more different. Toby is skinny, bony, all sharp edges and knobby knees. Nathaniel is sharp too, but because he looks as though he was carved. Nathaniel is beautiful, like a sculpture. Toby kind of looks like the leftover scraps.

I get into the passenger seat, and Gage drives. The tension in the car is palpable, and like low-lying fog it hovers and nearly strangles us all. Gage's grip on the steering wheel is death-like. My teeth are so clenched I'm giving myself a headache, and every few minutes Nathaniel mumbles something under his breath that I can't make out.

As we drive I think about Nathaniel's current predicament, and a sickening thought occurs to me. "Does my mother do this?" I ask no one in particular.

Nathaniel makes eye contact with me in the rearview mirror. "Do what?"

I don't want to say ask out loud because it's too awful. So I think it. I think it loudly.

"Yes," Nathaniel answers my silent query, "she has to breach in order to live."

She never told me.

Nathaniel's eyes soften. "She didn't want you to know."

At first I'm not sure if Gage understands our conversation, but when he flashes me a look of pity, I know he's following along.

We really need to find a solution to this. I can't stomach the idea of Nathaniel, let alone my mother, randomly killing people just so they can stay here.

I sit on my hands to keep them from shaking.

"We'll figure something out," Gage says. He sounds confident, but I'm pretty sure he's trying to convince himself as much as he's trying to convince me.

"What makes you think we'll be able to get into the warehouse?" I ask. "Isn't Isadora camped right next door?"

"She was. I'm hoping she's vacated by now," Gage says.

"And if she hasn't?"

"We fight," Nathaniel says plainly.

I turn around so I can face him. "You're going to fight?"

"I'll do what I have to do."

"You can't let anything happen to Toby," I say sternly.

"So you've said." Nathaniel's irritation is evident by his snarky tone and the way he looks out the window as if he's done talking to me.

Gage parks the car a couple of blocks away from the warehouse. "Nathaniel," he starts, "I'd tell you to stay here, but my guess is you're not going to listen to me."

"You've got that right," Nathaniel says, and then he exits the car.

As we approach the warehouse, Gage goes into soldier mode. His shoulders are pulled back, and his eyes dart every which way. I can hear my heartbeat in my ears as adrenaline pumps through my system.

Gage gives us a signal to stay quiet and close to the building. Like ninjas, we slip into the ruined warehouse. As soon as we're through the doors, I'm reminded of the first time I came here. It wasn't that long ago, only a few months, that Gage gave me the grand tour. It looks nothing like it did back then. For one, it's only a smoke-damaged shell of what it was before. It smells like rotting wood and stale water and rusted metal. Everything in sight is twisted, blackened, and stained. It must be killing Gage to see it this way. This was his home. This was where he lived with his team.

This is where his team was murdered.

I try not to think about that as we make our way to the library. The first time I saw this room I was more than impressed with its expanse of books, its large wooden tables, and its keeper, Zee. Zee wasn't a typical librarian. For one, he looked like he belonged on the football field. He was huge in stature with muscles upon muscles. Nothing about him read as bookish or nerdy. I barely knew him and yet, it makes me incredibly sad to be in this room without him.

"What are we looking for exactly?" I ask Gage.

"Anything."

Not exactly helpful, but I don't bother asking follow-up questions. Instead, I turn left down the long stacks while Gage banks right and Nathaniel forges directly down the middle. I don't know what I'm looking for, and I don't know what I'm looking *at* either. This isn't exactly a normal library. Dewey Decimal does not exist here. Randomly, I pull books, flip them open, and cast them aside. Mostly what I find are encyclopedia-style books, volumes upon volumes of random information and histories gathered together and shortened into succinct paragraphs.

"Any luck?" Gage's voice carries over the stacks.

"No," I answer.

I can hear Gage's heavy footsteps coming toward me. "Rae was always studying Breachers, how they work, how to extract them. She spent hours in here researching. There has to be something useful."

"Have you ever tried before?" I ask.

"Tried what?"

"To extract a Breacher without killing the host?"

"Yes."

"It never worked, did it?"

"No."

We continue to search, pilfering shelves, skimming over words that barely register, and we come up empty time and time again. Gage's frustration oozes out of him by way of grunts and exasperated sighs. It's irritating.

"Find anything?" Nathaniel asks as he walks toward us.

"Nothing," Gage answers. "You?"

"I found some manuals." He holds up two books. "But I can't make heads or tails of them."

Gage and I follow Nathaniel out of the stacks. He slaps the books down on a table, and Gage pounces, whipping through the pages.

"These are definitely something," Gage says as he mulls over the books. "I'm just not sure what yet. Give me a few minutes."

Nathaniel and I back away from the table while Gage gets to work. I don't know where to go, but I keep walking, knowing full well that Nathaniel is going to follow me. He stays half a step behind me, which is good because I'm not in the mood to face him just yet.

We reach the garage, and I expect to see it as it was once described to me, housing their cars, and Zee's expensive and prized Ducati, but it's empty, cleared out, and vacant. My footsteps echo against the cement floor.

"How long are you going to give me the silent treatment?" Nathaniel asks.

"A long time," I answer, realizing immediately that I've just broken the silence.

"You know I'm sorry," Nathaniel says. His words aren't forceful or mean. He isn't trying to convince me of *what* I know. He's asking me *if* I know.

I spin and face him. "I don't want Toby to die."

"I don't either."

"But you knew when you did this that he would."

"I knew that I needed a body. I held on as long as I could, Mercy, I swear."

"You shouldn't have."

"I would have died."

"Then maybe you should've died!"

Nathaniel's shock registers on Toby's face. His eyes are wide, his mouth hangs open, and his eyebrows are nearly to his hairline.

"I'm sorry." I rush to him. "I didn't mean it."

Nathaniel backs away. "You did."

"It's not like you think though, Nathaniel." I shake my head and try to figure out how to say what I want to say. "I don't want you to die. Of course, I don't want you to die. You're my ..." I swallow and start again. "You're my friend. I care about you."

"But ..."

"But this isn't right."

"I know that," Nathaniel says honestly. He inches toward me.

My lip quivers. I sniff and shake my head, trying to hold it together. Tears flow despite my efforts to deny them.

"Mercy?"

I wrap my arms around my waist. "I get it. I completely understand why you did it. And I can't honestly say I wouldn't have done the same." As soon as the truth is out, the shame crushes me. I want to sit, but there aren't any chairs.

Nathaniel pulls me to him. Toby's scrawny body becomes the thing I lean on.

"I hate myself for this," I sob into his shoulder. "I shouldn't be able to understand your decision. I shouldn't be able to empathize with you."

He runs his hands along my hair. "Please don't hate yourself, Mercy. None of this is your fault."

Sniffling, I step back. "It is though. All of this is happening because of me."

"That's a lot of guilt you're heaping on yourself."

"Am I not supposed to feel guilty?"

Nathaniel pulls his shoulders back. I know he's gearing up to give me some speech about how this is the way things are and we can't do anything about them and we have just as much right to life as Toby.

"I've never felt guilty," Nathaniel says.

"What?"

Nathaniel turns and walks a few feet away. I don't follow. "I always blamed them. The Assembled. I never thought of what I was doing to the humans."

"But you think about that now?" I ask, hopeful.

"No. I don't."

His answer stings.

Nathaniel charges at me. "I can't think about what I'm doing to them. Maybe I could've before, but not now. Now I don't have a choice. I can't—"

I'm tempted to ask him what he was about to say, but I think I already know. He was going to say that he can't be without me, I can feel it.

"Mercy." Nathaniel's voice softens. "I'm sorry for what I did to your friend. I'm deeply and profoundly sorry to have caused you any pain or discomfort. I'm sorry for the guilt you're feeling.

But if I hadn't … I'm not ready to …"

"Leave me."

Maybe he'll lie. Maybe he won't confirm my suspicion.

"No. I'm not ready to leave you."

"Nathaniel," I start, so not ready for this conversation. "I know what I showed you before with the whole kissing thing, so I won't lie to you and say that I haven't thought about it, about us—"

"Hey!" Gage calls to us as he crosses the floor. "I think I found something."

Chapter Sixteen

Gage

I've interrupted an intense moment—this I can clearly tell. I give them a beat to divulge what they've been so intently discussing, but they've both gone quiet. I can see that Mercy's been crying. Her eyes are rimmed pink, and the tip of her nose is red. I have a strong urge to console her and slap Nathaniel all at the same time, but I squash those feelings and get back to the matter at hand.

"What did you find?" Mercy finally asks.

"There's an anti-binding potion," I ask.

"Great. Let's do it," Nathaniel says.

"It's not that easy," I explain. "Ingredients are difficult to find."

"How difficult?" Nathaniel asks, an edge to his voice.

"Water from the river difficult," I say.

"That's not difficult," Nathaniel scoffs. "That's impossible!"

"What river?" Mercy asks.

"Nathaniel, we just need someone who can cross over," I say as if it's easy, which we both know it's not.

"What river?" Mercy asks again.

"I thought you said you'd actually found something useful."

"I have."

"Really? Go get it then. We'll just wait here." He checks his fake watch. "You'll be back in, what? Never?"

"Don't be an ass," I say to Nathaniel. "I'm only trying to help clean up the mess you made."

"Fuck you!"

"Stop!" Mercy yells. "Stop fighting! And tell me about the river."

"When you cross the bridge," I start.

"When you die," Nathaniel adds.

"As I was saying," I glare at Nathaniel and then turn my attention to Mercy, "when you cross the bridge from this life to the next, there's a river. It's the river of life. We need water from the river to extract Nathaniel and keep Toby alive."

"So, let's go," Mercy proposes.

"Aren't you listening?" Nathaniel says snidely. "The only way to cross the bridge is if you die. And once you cross, you can't get back. If you don't go into the light at the end of the bridge, you'll end up in Purgatory. That's the way it works."

"Maybe," I add.

"No." He waves me off. "Whatever you're thinking, just forget it."

"She might have a chance," I try. "We at least have to consider it."

"No." Nathaniel blazes toward me and forcefully grabs my shoulders. "Listen to me very carefully. There is absolutely no way she's doing this."

"What if I can?" Mercy asks.

"You can't," Nathaniel snaps.

"How do you know?" Mercy folds her arms indignantly across her chest.

Nathaniel releases me and faces Mercy. "Because I've seen it. I've seen what happens when you reject the light. You have no chance against it, Mercy. And I'm not going to let you try. Not for me. We'll figure out another way."

"What other way? We don't have any other way! Nathaniel, Jay is one of my best friends. I have to do this. For him." Mercy's expression changes. She reaches into her back pocket and removes her phone. "It's Jay." She shows us the screen. "He's looking for Toby."

"Tell him you don't know anything," Nathaniel advises Mercy.

"That's a lie," Mercy replies.

"That's your big concern here? Lying?"

"Don't say anything to Jay just yet, okay?" I say. "If you don't answer, you're not lying. You're just avoiding."

"Fine," Mercy reluctantly agrees.

The lights suddenly shut off. Mercy, Nathaniel, and I are standing in utter darkness.

"What's happening?" Mercy asks nervously.

I raise my finger to my lips. She quiets instantly and edges closer to me. We three form a circle, facing outward, bracing ourselves for whatever is coming. When nothing happens right away, I seize the opportunity to move to a safer location. "This way," I whisper.

Nathaniel and I flank Mercy as we inch quietly toward the exit. I'm hoping beyond hope that we can make it to back to the library before—

Shots ring out to our left. Nathaniel pushes Mercy along as we scramble. Each one of us assumes a defensive position as if that alone will protect us from the bullets. Footsteps, thundering footsteps, are coming toward us.

"Run!" I yell.

The shots continue as we race down the hall to the library. Of all the rooms in the building, it provides the most shelter, the most nooks and hiding places. Once they're safe, I can go on my own to the weapons room. I'm guessing it's probably been cleared out by now, but it's my only hope.

We reach the library unscathed. Nathaniel immediately topples the tables, making it more difficult for whoever is chasing us to charge into the room.

"Stay here. I'm going to try for the weapons room," I say forcefully. I don't want any argument from either of them.

Mercy grabs my arm and gives it a squeeze. "Be careful."

I nod. Looking to Nathaniel, I say, "If I don't make it back—"

"You'll make it back."

I dash off without another word, zigging and zagging through the maze of tables Nathaniel made. Near the entrance I pause, flatten myself against the wall, and listen. The coast appears to be clear. Cautiously, I slither out into the hall looking both left and right and over my shoulders in rapid succession. I snake along, low to the ground, silent as can be.

I'm hit from behind sharply, and I stumble forward, blinking the stars from my vision as I'm struck again. My knees and palms smack the pavement. I whirl around, and hop to my feet. Grabbing my assailant by the middle, I attempt to tackle him to the ground. He's surprised and thrown off balance at first, but he quickly recovers, plants his feet, and tosses me aside. I hustle to regain my footing, ducking and dodging as he takes aim with his pistol. I kick out and knock the gun from his hand. We dive, both of us clawing for it while still fighting each other. Wrestling and struggling, I clamor with all my might, trying to gain purchase. We grab the gun at the same time. It fires once, twice, and then the body against me goes still.

Now armed, I push the body off of me and run for the weapons room. My heart pounds wildly, adrenaline coursing through my human veins. Fighting as a Hunter is much different than this. Before I was controlled, prepared. Now I'm flailing, just trying to stay alive.

As expected, the weapons room is empty. How could it not be? Between the police and the fireman who trampled through here, I would expect nothing less. But they could only take what they could see, which means my hidden stash might still be safe. On the far wall is a glass case containing, ironically, a fire extinguisher. I smash the glass with my elbow, yank the extinguisher free, and throw it to the ground. I'm making too much noise.

I can hear someone approaching and I have to move fast. In the wall there's a panel, which I punch through. Behind the panel are two pistols and three knives. I grab one knife. An angry, meaty, bald man plunges into the room. I flip the knife in his direction. He ducks, but I aimed low, and it slices right through his ample gut. He doubles over, grunting, and I go on the offensive. I strike with a series of punches and kicks. Weakly, he tries to defend himself, but when I yank the knife from his belly, he uses both hands to try to stop the gush of blood. It's no use. Defeated, he sinks to his knees, but I am not finished yet. Rage I've never experienced before pulses through me. I finish him off by jabbing and twisting the knife into heart. He's dead almost instantly.

Winded but still amped, I grab the rest of the weapons. In the hall I'm met by a woman, about my height, with a slick, tight ponytail, and a scowl that would make anyone cower. She's aiming a delicate but deadly gun right at me. "Drop your weapons," she instructs.

I don't.

She tilts her head to the side slowly, clearly calculating her next move. "I said, drop your weapons."

"Who sent you?" I'm stalling. She knows it. I know it.

"I'm going to give you one last chance," she threatens.

Slowly, with great effort, I begin to crouch. She's watching me carefully, never altering her aim. Even if she isn't a great shot, she has me dead to rights. One at a time, I set each weapon down on the floor. As I'm about to release the last gun, I take my chances, raise it quickly, and get off one shot before my thigh explodes with pain. White-hot and burning, the fire spreads quickly up and down my leg. I drop my gun without thinking and latch onto my leg with both hands. It does nothing to alleviate the burning. My vision blurs. Tipping over, my right shoulder hits the ground, and I force myself to focus my eyes, force myself to gauge my surroundings. I see her feet in front of me. She's still standing, so I must've missed.

Pop! Pop! I squeeze my eyes shut, waiting for the light to take me. But nothing happens. Stealing a glance, I see the woman drop, her life extinguished by three or four gaping holes in her chest. Rolling to my left, I try to look over my shoulder, but the movement is too much. Blood rushes from my thigh and drips over my hands.

"Stay down," a female voice commands as she steps over me.

"Mercy?" I ask, confused as to how she found me, and where she got a gun.

"Not quite," she quips. She checks the hall, and when it's clear she squats in front of me.

"Justice?" I'm so confused. Everything is wrong. Everything is black and thick and heavy. "What are you doing here?"

"You can give me the third degree later. Right now we have to move."

Justice picks up my weapons off the floor. She slides one knife into each boot and sticks a gun inside the waistband of her pants so that it hugs her tailbone. She worms her arm under mine, shoulders my weight, and helps me to my feet. The effort is agony, and I want to collapse, but I stand, sort of.

"Where are the others?" she asks.

"Library." I nod in that direction.

"Hold this." She hands me a gun. "Fire at anything that moves, got it?"

Again, I nod.

It takes a century to reach the library, but Justice never once complains about the pace. We slip through the doors. With her foot, Justice rights a chair. She lowers me into it. "Give me your shirt." She holds her hand out, palm up, waiting.

I shrug off my jacket and ease the shirt over my head. Justice makes a substantial rip in the fabric. Then she tears the shirt into strips. Gingerly, she wraps one of the strips around my thigh. "Ready? This might hurt."

"Do it."

Justice yanks the ends of the fabric, and my leg screams. I grit my teeth as she makes the final knot.

"This won't hold for long," she tells me.

"Why are you helping me?"

"Questions later, Gage." She surveys the room. "Where are they?"

"They should be here," I tell her.

"Again, fire that thing at anything that comes through those doors. I'm going to look around."

Justice clicks off the safety on her gun and leaves me facing the door. My hand trembles, but I force myself to keep it as steady as possible. I don't know what's going on—I just know it's not good—and I hope I survive long enough to get some answers.

Minutes tick by and Justice still hasn't returned. It would be stupid to call out to her, but I'm tempted.

Just as I'm about to yell her name, I hear her. Her footsteps are labored, like they were when she was assisting me. I twist in my chair, gun still pointed at the door and take in the scene. Justice is dragging Toby. He is propped against her, one of his arms around her shoulder, the other limp at his side. One of her hands holds his arm over her shoulder; her other hand is around his waist. His head is bent and bobbing, and the toes of his shoes slide along the floor.

I want to help her, but in my condition, I can't. Panicked, I ask, "Is he alive?"

"He's breathing. Has a pulse." She eases his limp body into a chair next to me. "But he took a beating for sure." She pulls his hair back and shows me his lumpy, purple and black face.

"Jesus. Who did this?"

Ignoring my question, Justice takes her cell phone from her pocket. She makes a call. "It's me. I have Gage and Nathaniel. Mercy's gone."

Her words register, and now I can't help myself. I have to look for Mercy. I stand and instantly regret it. Justice eyes me, gives me a reproachful look, and I sit back down.

"Got it," she says and then she ends her call. "Help is on the way."

"Who did you call? What's going on? Who has Mercy?"

Justice paces back and forth.

"I asked you a question."

"I heard you," she snaps.

"You're not going to answer me?"

"No. I'm not." Justice marches to the door. "Stay put. I'll be back."

"Where are you going?"

My final question is met with the door closing behind her.

With great effort and searing pain, I scoot my chair closer to Nathaniel. I check for a pulse. It's there, but it's faint.

Mercy is gone. Nathaniel's host body is unconscious. I've been shot. Justice saved my life. In such a short time, everything has gone to hell.

I sit there stewing, unable to do anything but wait for Justice to return, which she does only moments later. With her are four hulking figures I recognize. "You called Isadora? That's who you were on the phone with? Are you insane?" I want to kill her! How could she bring Isadora of all people into this? Aren't things bad enough? I'm powerless to resist the hands that hoist me from the chair and assist me out of the building. One of the men carries Toby's motionless body. "Where are you taking me?" I ask Justice.

"Somewhere safe."

"If Isadora is involved in this, none of us are safe."

Justice isn't in the mood to argue with me, apparently, because she doesn't respond.

Just outside the warehouse, parked at the curb, a black town car waits for us.

To the man holding Toby, Justice says, "Drop the body somewhere visible. Call 911, and don't leave until you see they have him. Got it?"

I'm appalled. "You're just going to leave him somewhere? That's Nathaniel in there!"

"Go," Justice says to the one holding Toby. He takes off without looking back.

Justice stands directly in front of me. She places her palm on my bare chest. Her touch is surprisingly warm. "Gage," she begins with no trace of anger or malice, "Toby's been reported missing. The police are all over town looking for him. We'll make sure that they find him and take him to the hospital. This is what needs to happen."

She holds my jacket out to me like a peace offering. When I don't move, she throws it over my shoulders. Relenting, I slide my arms through the sleeves.

She's right. It's so wrong, but she's right. Toby's body is in trouble. Mercy would want me to make sure he gets the help he needs. I know this, but I still don't feel right about letting Nathaniel out of my sight, not when I've already lost Mercy.

Two men assist me into the backseat of the car. Each movement is agony, but I hold it together as best as I can. Justice slides in next to me. The two men get into the front, leaving one still on the sidewalk.

"He's not coming?" I ask. I don't know why I'm care. Mostly, I'm just curious, and I'll take all the information I can get.

"Clean up," Justice says as if it's the most normal thing in the world.

"Right."

I know she won't give me any more information. She won't tell me where we're going or why she's helping me, so I don't bother to ask. I keep my thoughts fixated on Mercy and how once again I've managed to let her down. I should've been there to protect her. I never should've left her alone with Nathaniel, who was in no position to defend her, obviously.

The car stops. When I realize where we are, I suppose I should've known all along this is where we were headed: The Sheraton Grand Hotel. It wasn't that long ago that Nathaniel and I came here looking for Mercy's mother. And since Ariana is Isadora's sister, it's only fitting that they should choose the same hideout.

Getting out of the car is as torturous as I imagined it would be, but at least Justice's makeshift tourniquet seems to be holding. I'm not bleeding profusely anymore.

We make our way through the lobby with little fanfare. I understand now what makes a hotel such a great escape. People are too busy with themselves to notice what's going on right under their noses. Once we reach the penthouse suite, Justice knocks, and we are let in immediately.

The scene inside is more than startling. "What the ..."

I expected to see Isadora. I did not expect Ariana and Mercy's father, Eric, to be standing next to her.

Chapter Seventeen

Nathaniel

*T*hey fled. And they were quickly caught. Nathaniel was returned to his cell where he remained in isolation for weeks. The waiting was driving him insane.

Eventually, Lucas's men came for him. They dragged Nathaniel along the corridor to a room he'd never seen before. It looked very much like a hospital room, with lots of medical equipment and people dressed in white scrubs. Nathaniel bucked and fought as the guards threw him onto a table situated at the center of the room. They strapped him down, immobilizing him entirely.

"What's happening?" Nathaniel wailed.

Workers hustled about. Nathaniel's shirt was cut free from his body, exposing his chest. He thrashed, but it was no use. He was trapped.

Lucas appeared at his side. He placed his hand on Nathaniel's *forehead. "It's distressing to see you like this, my son. But you've brought this on yourself."*

"Let me go!" Nathaniel yelled, but Lucas walked away.

Someone else approached Nathaniel's side. His face was partially covered by a mask. In his hand, he held a scalpel.

"No!" Nathaniel squirmed. "No!"

The blade pierced his side, and Nathaniel let out a roar that nearly shook the heavens. The pain was excruciating. Nathaniel blinked in and out of consciousness as his insides were violated. He opened his eyes again just in time to see a rib, his rib, being wrapped in muslin and hurried from the room. Unable to go on, Nathaniel shut his eyes and prayed for death.

"Nathaniel!" His body shook. "Nathaniel, wake up."

He peeled open one eye. "Isadora?"

"Can you move?"

Nathaniel tried. He rolled onto his left side, used his hand for support, faltered, and crashed down on the table.

Isadora slid her arm under Nathaniel's body. She cradled him and lifted him into a sitting position.

"Leave me," Nathaniel groaned.

"Listen to me," Isadora spoke quickly, frantically. "There's no time. You have to hurry."

Nathaniel sluggishly shook his head.

"Please," Isadora begged. "I've opened the path. But you have to go now."

"Why?" Nathaniel asked. He couldn't understand, after everything she'd done, why she was helping him escape.

"It doesn't matter," she said hastily. "But I have to warn you. You

won't survive in this form, Nathaniel. You have to find a body."

"I am tired of human flesh."

"You've already died," Isadora said gravely. "And you didn't go into the light. In order to survive you must be in human form."

Nathaniel's shoulders slumped. He was too tired to fight, too tired to run.

A noise sounded from outside the room.

"They're coming." Isadora's voice was full of panic. "Go! Now!"

With great effort, Nathaniel obeyed. He slipped from the room with Isadora right behind him. Nathaniel didn't know how they made it all the way to the bridge undetected. He saw that Isadora was telling the truth. The path was indeed open. He could almost taste his freedom.

Nathaniel turned around to thank Isadora. But she was gone.

Chapter Eighteen

Mercy

My head is thick with fog. Pushing myself up into a sitting position, I wait for a wave of nausea to pass. I'm so used to being pulled from my body, but it appears this time my skin came with me. I'm whole. And that makes this so much worse than all the other times. Because whatever or whoever summoned me didn't need to pull me from my body to do so.

I'm in a vast room with concrete floors and aluminum walls. There would most certainly be an echo if I scream, but I decide not to test it out. Instead, I utter a simple, "Hello," and hope that someone hears me.

"Mercy." A voice booms from behind me. "So good of you to come."

I peel myself off the floor and wait for the muscles in my legs to adjust and hold me in place. "Oh yeah. Sure. You call. I come,"

I joke, but I have a feeling this guy doesn't understand comedy.

He's wearing what looks like a very expensive steel-gray suit; the fabric has a subtle shimmer. His shirt is white, his tie dark purple, and his shoes are freshly shined. He's at least six feet tall, if not taller, with shockingly white hair. Judging by the hair, I expect him to be old, but there's barely a wrinkle on his distinguished face. His eyes are gray, like his suit, and his lips are thin. They disappear when he smiles at me. The smile, I guess, is to put me at ease, but it has the opposite effect.

My nerves are tingling as he approaches with his arms out stretched. I think for a second that's he's going to hug me, but then he claps his hands together. "I do apologize for the suddenness of my summons. Come, sit." He gestures to a chair. "Do you drink tea?"

Befuddled, I ask, "Tea?"

"Yes, dear, tea. Little bags, dip them in water?"

"I'm familiar with the concept."

"Excellent." He squeezes my hand. "There's such civility to two people sitting down to tea, don't you think?"

"Sure."

I hadn't noticed before that a gorgeous table is set in the corner. Though it's small—a table for two—it has all the elegance of a grand dining table: white linen tablecloth, silver tea service, and the most beautiful bouquet of pastel flowers, which look professionally arranged, bloom from a silver vase.

With flourish he slides out the chair for me. No one has ever pulled out a chair for me, and I can't help but look over my shoulder at him. I'm waiting for him to stab me, gag me, or do something heinous, but he simply winks again and assists me in scooting my chair to the table.

Once I'm situated, he sits across from me. Unbuttoning his jacket reveals an old-fashioned pocket watch dangling on a chain. He flips it open as if checking the time and clasps it shut again. He snaps his fingers, and service begins. Waiters, dressed in the most formal of tuxedos, complete with starched shirts and tails, appear as if from nowhere and pour the tea. They offer me sugar, cream, lemon, all of which I decline. Next comes the sandwiches—cucumber and cream cheese with the crusts cut off. Using the silver tongs provided, I put two sandwiches on my plate. My host takes two as well.

He seems to be waiting for me to drink my tea. Either he has impeccable manners, ladies first and all, or my drink is laced with something. Nervously, I raise the delicate china teacup to my lips, but I can't make myself drink.

He laughs, his head falls back, and he claps his hands again. *What is with him and the clapping? Is he five?*

"I'm so sorry. Please forgive me," he says. Taking his napkin, he delicately wipes the corners of his mouth. When he's finished he puts his elbows on the table. He laces his fingers together into a prayer position. "Mercy, mercy me," he says, and then he laughs some more.

Impatience gets the better of me. The teacup rattles when I put it back down on the saucer. My head is starting to pound. "I think I've played this game long enough. Tell me who you are and what you want."

"You're just like her."

"Like who?"

"Your mother."

"You know my mother?"

He smiles, but it's not a creepy, all-knowing smile. It's something different, something unexpected. Kindness, maybe? "I know everything about your mother. After all, I raised her."

"You're my grandfather?"

"Oh, heavens no!" he scoffs. He drinks from his teacup like he's taking a shot of tequila. When he finishes, he replaces the cup, and the waiter immediately refills it for him. "Grandfather? Do I look like a grandfather?" He holds up his knife and examines his reflection.

"You said you raised her. I was only assuming."

"Of course you were, child." He wipes his mouth again with his napkin. "I'm her brother."

"I didn't know she had a brother."

"There's been no need to make my presence known until now. Don't be angry with me, Mercy. I'm here to help you."

"Help me with what?"

"I know all about your bargain with Isadora."

I sit ramrod straight. "What bargain?"

He squints. "I know that you agreed to do whatever she asked, and in return, she's going to leave your precious family alone."

"And you want to add yourself to the list or something?"

"You're so sweet to think of me." He sips his tea. "But I'm afraid it is you who will need protection from me."

Trying to remain calm, struggling to keep all my *oh shit*

comments to myself, I lean forward. It's a tactical and incredibly stupid way to demonstrate I'm not afraid of him. Probably would've convinced him if my hands weren't rattling. My voice quivers when I ask, "Why do I need protection from you?"

He smiles, but the sweetness is gone. This smile is menacing. "You've been asked to kill The Assembled." He sits back in his chair and crosses his legs. "I am The Assembled."

Recognition snaps into place. I remember him from the video Zee showed me of Nathaniel's trial. "You're Lucas Church."

"Pleased to meet you."

"But I thought The Assembled is a group of people, like the Supreme Court or something."

"Pay attention as this will be the most important history lesson you've ever been given. I am them. They are me. I created them."

"What does that mean exactly?"

He clucks his tongue. "And here I thought you were the smart one."

Frustrated with his games, I say with venom in my voice, "What is all this? What do you want from me?"

"You are trying to kill me, are you not?"

"I'm not trying to kill you." I don't realize until I've said it that it's true. Here he is, right in front of me, giving me the perfect opportunity to fulfill Isadora's request, and yet, I have no desire to end his life.

"No?" He's trying to sound surprised, but I know mockery when I hear it.

So I say with conviction, "No. I'm not."

"Interesting." His eyes dance as he speaks. "And why is that? Don't you worry about your friends? Your family? Your tasty triangle?"

"My what?"

"Gage and Nathaniel, of course."

"There isn't a triangle, not that it's any of your business. And yes, I am worried about all of them. There's no guarantee that Isadora will keep her end of the bargain."

"Very true," he concedes. "And what do you think of all your newfound powers?" he asks, abruptly changing the subject.

There's no way I'm talking about it with him. "I don't know what you're talking about," I say, wearing my best poker face.

Laughter erupts from him. "You do remind me so much of Ariana!" Clapping his hands, he says, "It's wonderful! Truly wonderful! My dear sister. It's like she's sitting right in front of me." He rises from the table and walks until he stands behind me. Sleekly, he pulls out my chair. "Walk with me."

I push back from the table and stand. As I do, a side door I didn't notice before opens revealing the most beautiful garden I've ever seen.

"Do you like it?" he asks, his voice hopeful.

"It's beautiful." Sidling away from him, I run my hand along a violet flower. The beauty of this place is distracting, and I feel as though I could lose myself entirely. Before that happens, I ask, "Who are you exactly? I know you're The Assembled, but I know there's more to you than that."

"And how do you know?"

How do I know? "I can sense it, somehow."

He smiles proudly. "I am The Creator. I created this world," he gestures to the scenery around us, "just as I created yours."

The pieces of what he's telling me start to form a picture. "You created man. *You* did that. You're the reason we all exist." As I say the words aloud, I'm not sure I believe them.

He nods.

"So where did you come from? Who created you?"

"I was alone," he says simply, as if that explains everything. "When I opened my eyes for the first time, there was nothing and no one. I did not hunger or have thirst. I only had the need to create, to make worlds and species. Think of a child with limitless capabilities, endless imagination. Whatever I designed appeared. It was easy. It was fun. I was completely sated in my work. I had no wants of any kind for a very long time. But then one day, I grew lonely. I craved companionship. I guess you could say I wanted a touch of the humanity I created.

"Your mother was my first. We were quite the pair," he says fondly. "But she wanted a sister. And so from her, I created Isadora. For a time, we three were very happy. I believed because they were part of me, they would be loyal to me. But I was wrong.

"Your mother rejected the life I so willingly gave her. Just as Nathaniel did. Things were spiraling out of control. Something needed to be done, so I created The Assembled, and I put Isadora in charge. Such messy business, the banishment of Nathaniel and your mother." Lucas strolls along casually with me at his heels. I hang on every word, soaking in this lesson. It's more than my mother or Gage or even Nathaniel have ever told me.

Lucas stops walking. He turns to me, looks me up and

down. "Even I could not have foreseen what came next," he says. "Breachers. Amazing creatures, really. Like rebellious teenagers. I have to admire their efforts, their will to live."

His story is fascinating, but it doesn't change the facts. "You did this to my mother. To your own sister. You made her what she is. What I am."

His eyes travel over me again as though he's drinking me in. It makes me want to add a few layers of clothing.

"*Isadora* did this to your mother," he says sharply. And then he smiles like he's delighted. "She really is a ruthless leader. I'd almost be in awe of her if she hadn't decided somewhere along the way to betray me. She means to put an end to me, and she has you to do her dirty work."

"I told you. I don't want to kill you."

"For now."

We continue to walk until we reach a river. My heart leaps into my throat because this has to be the river of life. This is the water I need to release Nathaniel from Toby's body. My entire body itches with wanting.

Suddenly, Lucas Church stops walking and faces me. Reflexively, I back up a step.

"In the end all of my children have disobeyed me, Mercy. I hope you're not a disappointment to me."

"What exactly are you asking me to do?"

"I'm asking you to join me. And if you say yes," he glances knowingly at the water, "I'll give you everything you've ever wanted."

The power to save Toby? Isadora off my back? This is more than tempting.

"Here's what you need to understand. Your mother and Isadora are working together. Oh, they had me fooled for such a very long time." He laughs as if he appreciates being tricked, as if he admires their cunning nature. "They were so convincing, you see."

"That's not possible. My mother hates Isadora for what she's done."

"Does she?" He presses his forefinger to his lips. "Let's think about this, shall we? What is it that your mother wanted more than anything?"

The words slip out of my mouth. "To be with my father."

"Ding! Ding! Ding!" He claps again. "How convenient then that she was banished, don't you think?"

My stomach falls to my feet as a horrifying thought flashes through my mind. *Nathaniel?*

"No, my sweet girl," he answers, hearing my thoughts. "Nathaniel was never aware of their pact."

I breathe a sigh of relief.

Lucas clasps his hands behind his back. "Just out of curiosity, why do you deny your feelings for him?"

"That's really none of your business."

"We disagree on that point, sweet girl. You see, that is of most interest to me."

"Why?"

"Because it's what sets you apart from the rest of them. Nathaniel, your mother, Isadora, they are driven mad by love. It is that single emotion that drives them. But you see past that, don't you? You see the danger in giving over to your emotions because you know what will happen if you do. You've seen what it's done to them, and that's not what you want. You don't want to go on forever. You want to live and die, to follow the design of things. My design."

He's right, but hearing him say it out loud makes me reconsider. "You make me sound heartless."

"On the contrary! Your heart is greater than one love. You see the big picture. You understand. It's selfish what they've done, Mercy. They've upset the balance. But you, you would never do that."

I don't know if he's right. He makes me sound noble when really I was mostly too freaked out to acknowledge my feelings. I never wanted to choose between Nathaniel and Gage. I never wanted a love triangle, as he called it. And I did want to die. I *do* want to die. Eventually. If I let myself love Nathaniel, if I let him have my heart, he won't let that happen. I thought I could count on Gage to help me, but even he denied me when I asked.

"What do you want me to do exactly?" I ask.

"It's not what I want, Mercy. It's what you want."

"Meaning?"

"All you have to do is die."

Chapter Nineteen

Gage

Instinctively, I back toward the door. This hotel room is not where I want to be. Seeing Isadora, Ariana, and Eric together is too much.

"Gage, wait." Isadora cautiously approaches. "Let me explain."

"I have nothing to say to you."

"Please." Ariana begs me with her eyes. "I can see that you're hurt. Sit down and we'll talk."

I wait for them to settle their positions before deciding where to sit. Never in a million years would I choose to sit with Isadora, so the spot next to her is out. My first choice would've been to sit near Ariana and Eric, but they're here with Isadora, which makes me question everything. I realize Justice is my best option, but that doesn't exactly sit well with me.

"I know this must seem strange to you," Ariana starts.

"Understatement of the year," I say flippantly.

"Isadora and I have been running for a long time, Gage. And we're tired of it."

What? "What?"

"There's so much to tell you, and we don't necessarily have time to explain it all right now, but you need to know that we are not your enemy."

"We? Meaning you and her together?" I jab my thumb in Isadora's direction. "*Her?* The one who sliced my Hunter's mark from my arm? Who had my entire team murdered?"

"Isadora is the one who saved me," Ariana says. "After you killed me, she put me back together. She gave me life. I owe her for that."

And now it makes sense. "I always wondered how you survived," I say. "Doesn't change what she did to Jinx. Or Rae. Or Zee. She tore a rib from Mercy's body for Christ's sake!"

Isadora's steely gaze weakens. "I wasn't acting on my behalf, Gage. I was following orders."

"Why the hell should I believe you?"

"Because she's telling the truth," Eric answers, speaking for the first time.

Hearing Eric plead for Isadora is too much. My stomach churns with acid. My whole world is flipping upside down. Again.

"I'm not the one who attacked you in the warehouse today, Gage. I'm not the one who took Mercy," Isadora says.

"Who did?"

"Lucas Church," Ariana answers.

"This is unbelievable." If I were able, I'd leap up to make my point, but I'm not, which I hope does not diminish the weight of my message. "Isadora is the one who caused all of this. And now you're on her side? Why?"

Justice puts her hand on my good leg. "Gage, please listen," she pleads.

I don't want trust Justice. She has done nothing but cause trouble.

Right up until the moment she saved my life.

"Fine." I lean back into the couch and fold my arms. "I'm listening."

"You know him as Lucas Church," Ariana explains. "But his real name is The Creator. He's the first, Gage, the first being." She makes a sweeping gesture with her hands. "He made all of this, me, you, everything. And in the beginning, it was wonderful." She sounds wistful, as if she's remembering a better time. "But then things changed, and the more they changed, the more Lucas tried to control it all. He commanded us to be faithful only to him." Ariana takes Eric's hand in hers. "But we wanted more. We wanted love of our own. We wanted freedom.

"And Lucas couldn't stand for that. But he's clever. He's never the one acting; he's the one pulling the strings. He created The Assembled to stop the Guides from interacting with humans. He could've let Nathaniel be with Ellie, but no, he couldn't have that. He couldn't tolerate Nathaniel defying his precious rules. And he couldn't kill Nathaniel himself because that would make him appear spiteful, so he had The Assembled punish him. He had Isadora, who loved Nathaniel the most, punish him."

I look to Isadora. Her green eyes are glassy. She appears, for the first time, almost vulnerable, almost human.

"And when that backfired," Ariana continues. "When Nathaniel turned into a Breacher, he created the Hunters. He made you, Nathaniel's own brother, hunt Nathaniel down like a dog in the street."

I don't want to believe this. I want to scream that none of this is possible except I already know some of it to be true. I already know that I was created to destroy Nathaniel. But I'm not ready to budge. I'm not ready to concede the point. "This doesn't excuse what Isadora's done," I say firmly.

"I did what I had to survive, Gage. I did what I could to keep Ariana and Nathaniel safe." Isadora's stare is unsettling. "I don't expect you to understand. And I'm not asking for forgiveness. But I am asking for your help."

"Why would I do that?"

"Because we're trying to save Mercy." Ariana crosses the small space and sits next to me. "Mercy is more powerful than any of us. You must know that by now. The things she can do." Ariana hesitates and looks over at Eric. "We finally have the upper hand. Mercy can stop him. She can put an end to all of this."

"So you're willing to risk her life, just not your own, is that it?"

"If what we believe is true, Mercy is more than capable of handling herself," Isadora says.

"What do you believe to be true?"

"I know Mercy told you about starting my heart, Gage," Ariana says.

A snort escapes me. "Mercy told me that Isadora knew about

that. She was frantic. Imagine how she'll feel when she finds out her own mother ratted her out."

Ariana leans forward. "It is my hope she'll understand once we explain everything to her."

"Good luck with that," I say sarcastically.

"I also know she has the power to project thought, to manipulate minds." Ariana drops this bomb and the room goes quiet.

I try not to register shock on my face, but I don't think I'm being very convincing. "How do you know that?"

"A mother knows her daughter."

I don't confirm her theory. I will not betray Mercy.

"Lucas knows everything Mercy can do," Isadora says, her voice urgent. "He fears her power. He knows it puts him in jeopardy. That's why he's coming after her. He's been playing us all along, waiting to see if her powers manifested. And now that they have, he's going to make his final move."

"And what's that?" I ask.

"He's going to convince her to kill us," Ariana says solemnly. "The same way he once convinced you."

I've always known she hated my Hunter side. How could she not? But now I understand a little more about her hatred. If what she says is true, if Lucas Church is the ultimate enemy, then I was once his errand boy. He filled my head with righteousness and purpose and sent me on a misguided mission.

"What do you want me to do?" I ask.

"We want you to convince Mercy not to listen to Lucas," Ariana says.

"I won't be able to do that," I tell her solemnly.

"And why not?" Isadora asks sharply.

"Because Mercy wants to die."

"That's ridiculous," Ariana declares.

"No," Eric rests his hand on Ariana's arm, "it's not. Think about it. Mercy wants what's right, Ari. And living forever? We both know that's not right."

Ariana hangs her head. We all fear what comes next. If Mercy sides with Lucas Church, we're all doomed.

My head is throbbing. My eyes are bleary, and it hurts every time I blink as if my eyelids are coated in sand. The bullet is no longer silent but rather burning. I want to lie down.

"I need to get the bullet out of Gage's leg," Justice says, as if she senses my discomfort.

Isadora and Ariana nod in agreement.

Justice rises off the couch. I want to follow her, but I can't make my leg move. Isadora signals for her henchmen to assist me, but Eric gets to me first. I'm uncomfortable, but I let him. He walks me to a bedroom and places me on the bed, my feet still on the floor.

He exits without saying anything, and Justice closes the door.

"Can you pull your leg up on the bed?" she asks.

I try and fail. "Apparently not."

She lifts my feet and swivels me around so that my whole body is on the bed. Next, she props pillows behind me and one under my injured leg. The last thing she does is untie the tourniquet she made from my shirt. "Comfortable?"

"As much as I can be." My tone is biting, and when I see the injured look on her face, I feel bad. She's only trying to help me.

"Thank you," I quickly add.

Justice arranges the supplies around me as I shrug out of my jacket. I feel somewhat self-conscious around her, shirtless and exposed like this, but she doesn't seem to notice. She's gathered cloth, bandages, an intimidating-looking syringe, a scalpel, a needle and thread, and pliers on a silver tray. I know better than to ask how she got all this. Isadora has her ways. And I'm guessing her band of goons has been in the position of needing a bullet or two removed.

"We need to get your pants off," she says sheepishly. "You know, for me to be able to ... um ..."

"Right," I say, trying not to sound embarrassed. I unzip my jeans, and I try to shimmy them off, but it hurts like holy hell.

"Here. Let me help you." Justice grips the ankles of my jeans and slowly tugs them off.

Now I'm really exposed, wearing nothing but boxers.

Justice stands over me, a syringe in her right hand. She flicks the plastic until the liquid rises and squirts from the tip. "I'm sorry," she says as she plunges the needle into my thigh.

I grimace as the burning spreads. The liquid feels both cold and hot, and I almost vomit all over the bed. After a few seconds the pain subsides and I feel pleasantly warm.

Justice makes a small incision around the wound, not too deep, but enough to brighten my skin with blood. When she's finished, she swaps the scalpel for the pliers. I feel pressure as she digs into my thigh and fishes out the bullet. It makes a plinking sound when she drops it on the tray. I pick it up and examine it. Strange how something so small and twisted can cause so much damage.

Justice uses the cloth to wipe my skin as best she can, applying pressure until the stream of blood shrinks to a trickle before she stitches me back together. When she's finished suturing, she wraps my leg with bandages. "There. You should be okay." Justice uncaps a pill bottle from the nightstand and holds out two white pills. "These will help with the pain."

"I don't need those."

"Okay, hero, whatever you say." She replaces the pills in the bottle, recaps it, and stashes it in a drawer.

I exhale heavily, suddenly exhausted.

"You can sleep," she says. "I won't let anything happen to you."

My eyes are already closed by the time I say, "I'm not that tired, actually."

She laughs quietly at my lie.

I know I'm falling asleep despite my efforts not to. "Why are you helping me?"

I can hear her moving around, avoiding my answer.

The bed dips. My eyelids are too heavy to open and confirm what I know, that Justice is lying next to me.

"Justice, why?" My voice is barely above a whisper.

"Go to sleep, Gage."

And I do.

My dreams are frantic, vivid, one piled up on top of the next, blended together, indiscernible, and frightening. In one dream, Nathaniel is dead, Mercy standing over him, his bloody heart in her hands. In another, Mercy and I are standing on the bridge, the light waiting on the other side, and she's telling me to go, but

I won't listen. And in my last dream, Mercy is dead, lying in my arms, her eyes closed, her lips parted, and I'm screaming her name.

I wake with a start, gulping for breath.

I feel a hand on my bare chest. "It's okay. You're okay."

I expect my eyelids to be hooded and heavy, but they open easily. "Nightmare."

Justice nods. She feels my forehead with the back of her hand. "You've been fitful. I keep thinking you have a fever, but you don't."

I move from under her touch. "I'm fine."

"Of course." Justice sits up and pulls her knees to her chest.

"I'm sorry," I say, though I don't know why I'm apologizing or what I'm apologizing for.

We're quiet for a few moments.

"What time is it?" I ask, breaking the silence.

Justice motions to the clock on the nightstand. "One fifteen."

I rake my hands across my face. "Where is everyone else?"

"Isadora is asleep, I imagine. Ariana and Eric left hours ago."

"No word on Mercy?"

It's barely noticeable, but Justice flinches at the mention of Mercy's name. She shakes her head.

"What about Nathaniel? Did they find Toby and take him to the hospital?"

"They did, but last I heard, he was still unconscious."

"Damn." I lean deeper into the pillow.

Justice uncoils and lies down, facing me. "How did you do it?"

"Do what?"

"You and Nathaniel were enemies. Now, you're like brothers."

I know what she's asking. She wants to know if that relationship is possible for her and Mercy. She wants to be sisters, not foes.

"You didn't exactly start off on the right foot," I say honestly. "I don't know if Mercy will ever see you as anything other than Isadora's pawn."

"Wow. That wasn't judgmental at all," Justice barks.

"I'm sorry. Just telling the truth."

"All right fine. So I did this all wrong. But you try getting dropped into this situation, sixteen, clueless, emotions all over the place, and see how well you do."

"A monkey could've done better than you." We both laugh at my stupid joke.

"Screw you." She playfully shoves me. "Honestly though, do you think Mercy will ever forgive me? I was only going along with Isadora because she said we couldn't let Lucas know we weren't on his side."

"None of this makes sense to me. Every time I think I know who we're fighting, we uncover a new layer of horror."

"I hope you're not still fighting me."

I can't give her an answer. I'm not ready to let my guard down completely.

"So you're saying," I angle myself toward her, "this whole time Isadora has been secretly on our side?"

"I don't know about *that*. But she is now."

"What about the whole jail thing? Was that Lucas or Isadora?"

"That was Isadora. See, with Mercy inside someone else's body, she's undetectable to Lucas. It's the perfecting hiding place. Of course Isadora knew you'd rescue her, but she was trying to buy some time, I think."

Once again, Nathaniel and I put Mercy in danger. I'm starting to wonder if we're ever going to do right by her. "So by making Isadora the ring leader," I prop my head in my hand, "Lucas has built this huge case against her. He wants Mercy to kill her."

"Pretty much."

"This is so messed up."

Justice lowers her gaze. "Gage," she starts. "I am sorry for my part in all this. I know I don't deserve your forgiveness or anything, and it's okay if you don't want to give it. I just need you to know that I'm sorry," her eyes flash to me, "and that I still think you're the hottest kisser on the planet."

My stomach stirs with heat as she continues to look wantingly at me. "Justice."

"I know. It isn't meant to be. Your heart belonging to Mercy and all. But what happens when you finally realize that Mercy's heart belongs to Nathaniel?"

I open my mouth to speak and quickly close it.

"I wasn't lying when I said you and I are alike," Justice says, sadness drenching her voice. "We're the copies of the original, the leftovers. There's no one fighting for you or me. And when this war ends, where will we be?"

Her words are like thorns twisting in my side.

Justice shifts and our knees are touching. "We're players in someone else's game. I know that. But I don't think you do."

I'm beginning to understand.

"I want what they have. I want a love of my own. I want you, Gage."

Alarms, bells, sirens—they're all blaring in my head, and I can't seem to get a grip on anything when Justice slides her hand up my bare chest. She places her fingers over my heart. "I want you," she says again.

What's right? What's wrong? What's smart? It all goes out the window with those three little words. *I want you.* And when Justice touches her lips to my throat, I lose all sense of myself. Because she's right. To have someone to call your own, that's what this is all about. It's about human connection. It's about love. Maybe I don't know what love really feels like, but I do know the pull of desire, the need to be touched and held and made to feel secure. I wanted all those things with Mercy. But Justice is right. Mercy's heart belongs to Nathaniel. And I don't want to deny it any longer.

Mercy has never declared her love for me. She's never told me plainly that she wants me and only me. What Justice is offering is right here in front of me. And though I don't know if I return her feelings quite as strongly, I can honestly say that when she's this near, what I see is the girl who came to my rescue, the girl who saved my life and healed my wounds and stayed by my side while I slept.

Justice blazes a trail of kisses along my collarbone. She scoots closer but is careful not to lean on my injured leg. I twist my fingers into her hair, and when I do, she looks up at me. My eyes are fixated on her lips, remembering what it was like last time. Yes, I thought she was Mercy then, but that doesn't change the sensation it left me with. This time, when I kiss her, I know she's Justice, and I'm delighted that knowing this doesn't abate the moment.

Human connection. There's nothing else quite like it.

Chapter Twenty

Nathaniel

*W*ith each day, Nathaniel felt weaker. He replayed Isadora's warning in his mind. He knew he had to find a body, and he had to find one fast. Nathaniel didn't want to be someone too young, but he didn't want someone too aged or fragile either. He needed someone established and settled, someone with money and resources, someone who would give him a comfortable existence. So he chose retired businessman, Ethan Wake. He was the perfect host. He lived alone, a widower with no children or family to speak of.

Before taking him over, Nathaniel did surveillance and memorized his routine. Ethan encountered very few visitors. He occasionally golfed, meeting a group of men at a country club where they would play a round, exchange barbs, and drink overpriced beer. Nathaniel could make do with that.

When the opportunity presented itself, one afternoon after

Ethan returned home, Nathaniel pounced. He charged up the path. Stumbling back, Ethan tried to flee, but it was no use. Nathaniel exploded into fragments. Swarming, the pieces flew together like a flock of birds, purposeful and true, and dove straight down Ethan's throat.

Once settled, Nathaniel eased into Ethan Wake's life. He established a daily routine of exercise, breakfast, some reading, running errands if needed, a light lunch and a sensible dinner. Nathaniel took special care of Ethan's body, not wanting to die prematurely.

Weeks turned into months, and Nathaniel continued to live, continued to worry that Lucas Church would find him. And just when he'd resigned himself to his new life, he heard someone pounding on his front door. He threw it open to find Ariana, dirty and scared. He ushered her into the house, gave her towels to dry herself and then clothes, which he found in Ethan's closet. Apparently Ethan had been reluctant to throw away his dead wife's things, lucky for them.

When she was dressed, and seemingly calmer, Nathaniel asked, "How did you find me?"

Ariana sneered. "I didn't lead them here, if that's what you're implying."

Nathaniel cleared his throat. "You understand why I have to be sure. You know what they did to me."

"You left me there," Ariana said, her voice teeming with rage. "I faced Lucas Church without you."

"I didn't know where you were, Ari," Nathaniel tried. "I had once chance to get out. I took it."

"How exactly did you escape?" she asked, her tone accusatory.

"Isadora," Nathaniel said plainly. "She let me go."

"Did she now?" Ariana sucked in a breath and exhaled slowly. "And why would she do that? After she betrayed her own sister."

Confused, Nathaniel asked, "What do you mean?"

"Who do you think told Lucas about Ellie? Who would possibly have something to gain by exposing us both?"

Ariana's accusations hung like thick smoke. Nathaniel didn't know what to make of it. What kind of game was Isadora playing?

"And now what are we supposed to do, Nathaniel?"

"Perhaps I can be of some assistance." A new voice in the room jolted both Nathaniel and Ariana to attention.

Nathaniel prepared himself for battle. "Show yourself!" he ordered.

"With pleasure." He strolled into the room dressed in the finest clothes: tailored suit, crisp shirt, shined shoes. His blonde hair was styled impeccably, and his white teeth shone behind his smile.

"Ellis!" Nathaniel said excitedly. He walked to him and they collapsed into an embrace. "It is so good to see you."

"And you as well," Ellis said fondly. "Though this isn't exactly you, is it?"

Nathaniel laughed uncomfortably, and then he said, "You've taken a great risk coming here."

"Which is why I don't have much time," Ellis said, his expression morphing from calm to intense. "I came to warn you," he looked to Ariana, "to warn you both. Hunters are coming."

"Hunters?" Nathaniel asked, unfamiliar with the term.

"A special task force," Ellis explained. "They only have one objective. Capture all Breachers."

"Breachers?" Nathaniel again needed clarification.

"That's your new classification," Ellis told him. "A being capable of taking bodies and thereby living forever."

"I never wanted this," Nathaniel pleaded his case.

"Regardless, it is what you've become, what you've both become. Breachers have been declared an abomination. The only outcome is death."

"Let them come," Ariana said, her tone loathsome and fierce. "We'll fight."

"You don't understand," Ellis spoke with caution. "Their leader was created from you." Ellis nodded toward Nathaniel. "From your rib. He is your equal in every way, Nathaniel. There will be no escaping him."

Nathaniel lowered his head and stood with his hands on his hips as he processed what Ellis was telling him.

"How much time do we have?" Ariana asked Ellis.

"A day or two at most. Their training is nearly complete."

"Thank you for the warning," Nathaniel said.

"Of course." Ellis nodded. "One more thing. You'll be more difficult to track in human form, not impossible, but difficult."

Nathaniel looked to Ariana, still in her original form. "We understand."

"I must go," Ellis said.

"Thank you, friend." Nathaniel and Ellis embraced again, and then, with the nod of his head, Ellis vanished.

"We need to move," Nathaniel told Ariana. "But I can't be on the run in this body. Someone is bound to miss him eventually."

"You heard what Ellis said, Nathaniel. We need to be in bodies."

"*Then we find a place, Ariana. We settle down somewhere. Together.*"

***

For nearly a year they hid in peace until Nathaniel's host body suddenly died. Expelled forth, Nathaniel was exposed and vulnerable. His only hope was to make it home to Ariana, gather their things, and get on the road before they were discovered.

Nathaniel climbed the steps to their apartment and froze. Out of the corner of his eye, he saw movement.

"*Stop right there!*" *a voice commanded.*

Nathaniel held his arms in the air.

"*Don't move,*" *the voice said again.*

Out of the shadows stepped someone who was nearly his exact replica: same dark hair, same dark eyes, though his eyes were slightly rounder, his nose slightly less angular. Pressing his luck, Nathaniel pivoted to face his other self. A silver blade trained right at him, Nathaniel said, "We finally meet."

"*I said don't move!*" *He raised the blade higher.*

"*Remarkable, isn't it?*" *Nathaniel asked, inching to his right. "The resemblance. It's like looking in a mirror."*

"*I said, don't move,*" *Nathaniel's other self instructed.*

Nathaniel continued to slowly, gingerly turn until he and his mirror image were face to face.

His other self warned, "Come any closer and I'll kill you right now."

Cocking his head to the side, Nathaniel said, "I don't think so."
Nathaniel sprang into action, knocking his twin off balance slightly.
They grappled. Nathaniel concentrated all his energy on the hand
holding the blade. Banging that hand against the railing, the knife
finally burst free and clashed to the ground. His look-a-like scrambled
to reclaim his weapon, but Nathaniel pounced, throwing him to
the ground. Nathaniel gained the upper hand, looping a chokehold
around his twin's neck.

Breathing hard, Nathaniel asked, "Name?"

"No."

Nathaniel tightened his grin, yanking back with all the force he
had, and asked again, "Name?"

"Gage."

"Until next time, Gage." Nathaniel constricted until Gage lost
consciousness. He could have killed him, but he didn't.

Swiftly, Nathaniel dragged the body into the apartment. He
propped Gage in a chair, tied him up, and left him there.

Chapter Twenty-One

Mercy

He wants me to die. Lucas Church wants me to die. I think I'm going to be sick.

"I need sit down." And suddenly, I am. We're back at the table, the tea service still laid out before us.

Lucas leans back in his chair. "You're uneasy with the idea?"

Glaring at him, I say, "You think?"

He looks mildly disappointed. "You know this is the right thing to do, Mercy. Or you wouldn't have thought of it yourself."

I don't know how he knows that I asked Gage to let me die. Maybe he saw my thoughts. It doesn't matter. What does matter is that dying seemed like the right thing to do when it was my idea and my idea alone. But the thought of dying presented by someone else, with their motives attached, well, that changes things.

"If I die, what happens to everyone else?" I ask.

He shifts in his chair, and for the first time, I sense that he is uncomfortable. "With all of you connected, your death would sever the line."

"Meaning?"

"Meaning four birds, one stone."

"Me, Mom, and Isadora? We'd all be gone?" It takes me a second to think of the fourth. "And Justice? She'll die too?"

"Yes."

"What about Gage and Nathaniel?"

He clears his throat and adjusts his tie, patting it against his stomach. "You'd have to take care of them the old fashioned way."

I shoot out of my chair, knocking it over as I go. "Do you know what you're asking me? You want me to kill my entire family, kill everyone I love, and for what?"

"You've said it yourself multiple times. Breachers shouldn't exist. No one should have this kind of power."

"I can talk to them. Give me a chance to fix things."

He shakes his head. "Where is Nathaniel right now?" He wears a knowing smile, one I'd like to knock clean off his face. "He took your friend, Toby, didn't he?" He tsks. "Poor, unsuspecting Toby, inhabited by a Breacher. And why? Why did this happen to innocent little Toby?"

"He had to. He didn't have a choice," I say through gritted teeth.

"That's where you're wrong."

"Nathaniel would've died!"

"Yes. He would have!" Lucas rises to his feet. "Such as he

should have years ago. Don't you see, Mercy? We have to set things right again. Together, you and I can end this reign of terror."

I don't know what to do. Just hours ago, I told Nathaniel he should've died, but that's because I was angry. I didn't *really* want him dead. The truth is I can't imagine my world without him. Yes, he irritates me and frustrates me and scares me to my core, but I—

I love him.

"I won't do this," I say, resolved. "Find someone else to be your puppet."

Lucas exhales through his nose and sits back down in his chair. "So you will be the biggest disappointment of all?"

"Just give us this lifetime, then we'll die," I offer.

"No," he says without hesitating. "This ends now." He crosses his legs and folds his hands neatly in his lap.

I gulp hard and say, "What happens now?"

"Run, little girl. Run home to mommy." He takes out his pocket watch, opens it, and then violently clamps it shut. "War is coming."

The last thing I see is him snapping his fingers.

Landing is unpleasant, to say the least. Of course it would've been too much for him to drop me anywhere near civilization. Instead, I end up in some dusty, dirty field. It takes me a moment to orient myself and realize that I'm near the causeway, the road that stretches between Sacramento and Davis. It's going to be a very long walk home.

Unfortunately for me, the solitude allows time for thought, and the inside of my head is the last place I want to be. Emotions, like popcorn kernels, sizzle and burst, and it's almost too crowded to tell one from the other. A kernel of guilt ends up on top of the pile.

I feel guilty for wanting Nathaniel and my mother to live. I know their lives are no more valuable than the ones they take. And yet, letting them go is unthinkable. I'd love to believe that we'll all make it across the bridge together, that we'll live on the other side together, but what if we can't? Nathaniel denied his light, and if he dies, he's headed straight for Purgatory. I don't honestly know if my mother is also Purgatory bound, but it must be true otherwise she wouldn't be holding onto this world so tight.

I'm screwed.

Around mile four, the guilt kernel is replaced with a kernel of defeat. When it pops I have to stop for a moment. I'm fairly certain I won't win in a fight against Lucas, and though I continue on, with each step I take I feel heavy, weighed down by what I know will be a terrific loss when I try to go against him.

Eventually, I make it to a bus stop. Rain, which is rare in this region, starts coming down in sheets. I pull my thin flannel shirt across my chest as my whole body starts to prick and tingle from goose bumps.

Two buses pass, and neither stop. I'm starting to feel as if defeat is going to stick around for a while. It's not just that I can't win against Lucas. Leaving there without the water from the river means I have no way to safely pull Nathaniel from Toby's body. Toby's death will end my friendship with Jay and Lyla, effectively severing my last touchstone to humanity.

Rain slithers down my back. At this point I'm soaked completely through. *Is this really my first day back at* school? I told Lyla school was a stupid idea. I should've stayed away, gone off to some cave like Superman's Fortress of Solitude and stayed there forever. It would have been safer for everyone if I'd just disappeared.

Finally, a bus slows and stops in front of me. I climb aboard, drop change into the machine, and move toward the back. I pick an empty seat as the driver closes the door and pulls away from the curb.

I don't know where I'm going, so I ride around until I come up with a plan. Going home seems appealing. I like the idea of curling up in my bed, sleeping, and hoping that when I wake this will all have been a nightmare. But I know I can't hide, not while Nathaniel is still inside Toby's body.

"Such a shame," says the woman across the aisle from me. She's scrolling through her phone and shaking her head.

"Excuse me?"

"They found the missing boy. Says here he's in a coma." She holds the phone out for me to see.

Toby. My throat clenches. "What else does it say?"

"Not much. Just that he's been taken to Sutter General."

I need to get to the hospital. Jay and Lyla will, of course, be there, and they will definitely be wondering where I am.

Luckily, there's a bus stop not far from Sutter General. I only have to walk a few blocks, which isn't so bad. And at least it stopped raining. Visiting hours are over by the time I arrive. There's no one at the information desk, so I'm searching blindly.

It takes me a while, but I finally find Jay, Lyla, and Jay's mother hunkered down in the exact same waiting room where this all started. As soon I see it, I flash back to waking up in Lyla's body. I remember how it felt to literally want to claw her skin off, and how I had to stand around and listen to the doctors tell my dad that I died. For obvious reasons, I do not like this room.

As soon as Jay sees me he pops out of his chair and crushes me into a hug. "Where have you been?" he asks, his breath against my hair. "You're soaking wet."

"It's a long story," I say as he releases me.

Lyla is next. Her hug is only slightly less reserved. "We've been calling you for hours." Her tone is both concerned and agitated. I know she probably has questions, but I can't answer of them now. Not without her hating me for life.

"I'm sorry. I got here as soon as I could." Lyla eyes me suspiciously, so I quickly ask, "How's Toby?"

"Still unconscious," Jay answers.

Jay's mom dabs her eyes with a tissue. She's clearly distraught. I can hardly look at her. I worry she'll see right through me and know I'm the reason her son is in a coma.

"Can I see him?" I ask.

"They won't let you in," Lyla says a bit harshly. "Family only."

"Oh. Okay," I say. "Do you guys need anything?"

"I need coffee." Lyla steps toward the exit.

"I'm good," Jay says to me. "You guys go."

I nod. "Okay. We'll be right back."

Lyla leads the way to the coffee machine just down the hall. The selection of drinks looks appetizing in no way.

"I can't believe you're going to drink this," I say, stymied.

She loads the machine with change and punches out her order. "Yeah, well, desperate times," she says, her tone clipped.

We watch the small paper cup fill with sludge. When it's nearly brimming over, Lyla snatches it. "Bottoms up," she says and then she takes a tiny sip.

"I'm sorry I couldn't get here sooner."

She narrows her crystal blue eyes at me. "So what's really going on?"

"What do you mean?" I ask, trying to sound casual.

"Seriously?"

"Lyla, I honestly—"

"Don't. Don't lie to me. I know you were with Toby earlier. Jay told me."

"Yeah, I saw him at school, but—"

"You're lying!" Lyla says too loudly. The nurse at the nearby station glares at us. "You know I can tell when you're lying."

"Lyla, I can't ... I don't ... I never meant for Toby ..."

Nodding, she purses her lips. "You know what? Don't tell me. Just fix it." She steps toward me, and I flinch. "This is Jay's brother we're talking about."

"I'm sorry." I don't know what else to say.

"I'm going back," Lyla says.

"Okay." I start to follow her.

"Go home, Mercy." Lyla's look of disgust is like a knife to the gut. "You don't belong here."

Too stunned to move, I watch her walk away. My stomach twists in knots, tangling itself and crushing me from the inside out. Tears trickle down my cheek. Using the back of my hand, I swipe them away and sniff, but it's no use. They come in waves. Unable to hold myself up, I slide along the wall until I'm on the floor. Cradling my knees against my chest, I cry for Toby, for Jay and Lyla, and for all that I've lost.

I wish I didn't feel sorry for myself, that I could solely think of others and all the grief I've caused them, but I can't help it. I didn't ask for any of this. It was thrust upon me, and now I'm left to deal with it all.

The person I want to talk to most is Nathaniel. I feel lonely and lost without him, and I have no idea what to do with that thought, so I stuff it deep down and switch my thoughts to Gage. Gage is the planner; he's the Hunter. He'll at least have some idea what to do. All I need to do is find him.

Picking myself up off the floor and drying my face with my sleeve, I exit the hospital and walk to Gage's house. All the lights are off when I get there, which isn't a good sign. Yes, it's the middle of the night, but it's not like Gage will be sleeping through this. He's probably completely panicked at this point, which is why I expected the house to be completely illuminated with Gage wearing tracks in the carpet from pacing back and forth.

Since I'm the one who hid the spare key when they moved in, I find it quickly. The door sticks when I try to open it, so I have to nudge it with my shoulder. Nathaniel complained about the door when he and Gage first moved in. I explained quirks like a sticky door are part of the house's charm. He responded by rolling his eyes at me.

The house is quiet and empty. I don't bother flipping on

any lights as I wander aimlessly from room to room. Gage and Nathaniel haven't lived here long, but in that short time, they've managed to make it a home. A messy home, but still. The living room is comfortable and cozy. Shoes are under the coffee table; a blanket is tossed over the back of the couch. There's a plate with a half-eaten sandwich, a half-empty glass of water—so many signs of life.

Down the hall, I pass Nathaniel's room. My heart aches to go inside, but knowing he's not there, knowing if I go in there I'll be consumed with regret and loneliness, makes me keep walking. Gage's room feels less threatening, so I settle there. The bed is unmade, and it sags a bit when I sit on the corner. Gage's room is neatly arranged: bed, dresser, nightstand, big slouchy chair in the corner. His leather jacket is strewn across it.

I miss him. I miss them both. And I feel like I'm going to cry again, which makes me want to scream, so I scoot farther onto the bed, nestle into the pillows, and try to fall asleep before the tears start.

"Finding you on Gage's bed isn't exactly a dream of mine." Nathaniel is standing in the doorway, propped up against the frame, hands in the pockets, one foot crossed over the other.

"Nathaniel!" I fly off the bed and fling myself at him.

"Mercy." He breath is hot on my neck.

"How?" I ask, still wrapped tightly around him.

"I don't know," he says.

His hands work their way from my back to the sides of my face. I lean into his touch and close my eyes. My hands drop to his hips. I know exactly where this leading, and that I should slam hard on the breaks, but I can't make myself.

Opening my eyes to take him in, I say softly, "I'm sorry."

Confusion alters his expression. "For what?"

"For saying that you should've let yourself die. I never wanted … I didn't mean … " I can't finish my thought.

His lips brush against mine, and I know he forgives me.

"I thought you'd hate me forever," I say.

"I could never hate you."

"There's so much I need to tell you," I say as his fingers brush through my hair.

"We have all the time in the world."

"We don't. Nathaniel—"

His lips engulf my words. I stand on my tiptoes to reach him fully. He helps me along by picking me up and pressing me to him. Kissing leads to an explosion of light and color behind my eyes, and I forget all about the important things I wanted to say.

I'm not quite sure how we make it to Nathaniel's room. The windows are open, and the smell of rain wafts through the air. The persistent patter makes for the perfect background noise as we curl into each other on the bed. I've never been in such a compromising position before, and suddenly I'm very aware of myself. I want to be touching him the right way and responding to him correctly and I worry that I'm not enough until I hear him moan.

That one sound is like a green light. Once I hear it, engines rev, and the race is on. We fumble around buttons and buckles until we're skin to skin. His kisses against my bare shoulder curl my toes. But there's nothing more intoxicating than the swirl of his tongue in my mouth.

Nathaniel is beautiful. His collarbone, chest, abs—all of it is flawless. Despite this, he feels completely human beneath my touch. It makes my heart knock against my ribs every time he reacts to my touch. Nathaniel's breath is as labored as mine as we continue to consume one other.

Of course every girl imagines her first time, but other than knowing I'd have one, I've never given it much thought. I didn't think about the where or the who, only how embarrassing it would be to let someone see me naked. And though I'm sure Nathaniel is taking in every inch of me, I don't feel a hint of shame. In this moment I know that I am his and he is mine and we are everything to each other.

Sometime after, still tangled together, we drift off to sleep. And for the first time in a long time, I forget that my whole world is a disaster, and I simply live in this one, wonderful moment.

"Mercy."

I hear my name being called softly.

"Mercy."

My shoulder shakes.

Languidly, I open my eyes. Gage is standing over me. Startled, I sit up and grab sheets to cover myself, and that's when I see I'm fully clothed. I'm in Gage's bed, in Gage's room, and nothing makes sense.

"Gage?"

"Are you okay?" he asks me. "Have you been here all night?"

Daylight streams through the window.

"I guess." I swing my legs over the side of the bed. "Where's Nathaniel?"

Gage exhales. "Still in Toby's body. I stopped by the hospital on my way here. There's been no change."

"No." I shake my head. "I saw him."

"Nathaniel? When?"

"Last night." I try to swim through the confusion. "He was here." I gather myself together and race down the hall.

The door to Nathaniel's room is closed.

"No," I whisper. I open the door and step inside. The bed is neatly made, curtains drawn, windows closed. "No," I say again.

"Mercy? What's going on?"

"I don't know," I say frantically. "It felt so real. It had to be real."

But it wasn't.

I sink down onto Nathaniel's bed. Gage stands in front of me. I bury my face in my hands.

"Gage, do you take cream in your coffee?"

My head snaps up, and I see Justice standing in the doorway, two to-go cups of coffee in her hands.

"Oh. Hey, Mercy. I didn't know you were here."

If I was confused before, I'm downright befuddled now. Slowly, I stand. I look back and forth between them, and my head spins. "What's going on?" I ask Gage.

"We—," Justice starts.

"We?"

"Let me explain," Gage tries. "It's not what it looks like."

"It's *exactly* what it looks like," Justice mumbles.

My eyes nearly pop from my head. "What?"

Gage charges to the door, a slight limp to his gait, and ushers

Justice out of my line of vision. I can hear their voices, but I don't know what they're saying. A few moments later, I hear what I assume are Justice's annoyed footsteps followed by the door slamming.

When Gage returns, he is wearing a sheepish look. I didn't notice before that his jeans are ripped and he's not wearing a shirt under his leather jacket.

Folding my arms across my chest, I say, "You two seem quite cozy together. Are you friends now or something?"

"She saved my life."

Chapter Twenty-Two

Gage

"What happened?" Mercy asks. She's pissed. Her shoulders are rigid and her posture unyielding.

"I lost you at the warehouse," I start. "And then I got shot."

Mercy sucks in a breath, and her expression changes to concern. She may be angry, but at least she still feels compassion for me, and that's something.

"I'm fine. Now." I swallow and brace myself for the difficult part. "I mean, I'll heal, thanks to Justice. She got me out of there. And she's the one who made sure Toby got help."

"Why would she do that?" Mercy asks snidely.

"She's trying to make up for getting off to a rocky start with us."

"Rocky start?" Mercy laughs. The sound is unkind. "Is that what we're calling it?"

"She wants to make things right."

"Isadora made her from a rib she tore out of my body!" Mercy is livid, seething. "Or have you forgotten that already?"

"I haven't, actually. I was made the same way."

"That's different," Mercy says adamantly, but I can tell she doesn't really believe it. Her mouth is scrunched and her eyebrows are stitched together like she's trying to make an argument she knows she can't win.

"There's something I have to tell you," I say, knowing that I'm treading on thin ice. If seeing Justice set her off, what I'm about to say will send her over the edge. I clear my throat. "Justice took me to Isadora. Your mother was there."

Mercy looks ready to do battle. "Isadora has my mother?"

"It's not like that," I saying, trying to diffuse her anger. "They're working together." A strange look flashes across Mercy's face, one I can't quite read. "What is it?" I ask.

"Nothing," she says, but I don't believe her. "Just tell me what's going on."

"They told me about Lucas Church, how he's really the one behind all this, and how they've been running from him their whole lives."

Mercy leans forward and lowers her head.

I keep going. "They told me how he manipulated them, hunted them."

"Lucas Church didn't have me thrown in jail and practically tortured," Mercy says hatefully. "Isadora did."

"Only because she couldn't let him know that she wasn't on his side. Isadora has been Lucas's right hand this whole time, but she's tired of it. She's finally broken free."

"Gage." Mercy exhales deeply and shakes her head. "I already know all of this. I talked to Lucas."

"What? When?"

"He pulled me from the warehouse."

I know from her slumped shoulders and sad expression that whatever happened isn't good.

"It's such a long story," Mercy starts. "But here are the highlights. He wants me to kill all of you. He actually used the same argument I did to try and convince me, that Breachers shouldn't exist, that no one should have this much power. He said we have to reset the balance of things, that in order to make everything right, in order to make sure no more innocent people die, I have to be the one to end it all." Mercy runs her hands along her thighs. "Oh," she says like she's just remembering, "I didn't get the water to save Nathaniel, so he's stuck in Toby, apparently."

"If he wants us all dead, why doesn't he just do it himself?"

"I get the feeling he doesn't exactly like to get his hands dirty, so it won't be him that comes for us."

"Wait," I say, her words registering. "You didn't agree to kill us?"

Mercy scowls. "Do you really think that little of me? I was willing to sacrifice myself, not all of you. And because I won't he's going to have us killed."

"We can fight," I say, determined.

"What for?"

"What for? Did you really just ask that?"

"You don't understand." She pushes her hair back from her face. "He told me that my mother and Isadora were working together, that they've been working together this whole time. I didn't want to believe him," she points at me, "but you basically confirmed it. No, they didn't intend for Breachers to exist, that was an accident, but it doesn't change anything. Nathaniel and my mother are still killing people whenever they need a recharge. And because I'm not willing to stop them, I'm no better than they are. We're not the righteous in this situation, Gage. We're the damned. And we probably deserve whatever's coming to us."

"You're not damned."

"Aren't I?" Mercy laughs nervously. "I have two choices. I can kill my mother and Nathaniel and sentence them to Purgatory, or I can let them live, allowing countless others to die in their place. Sounds pretty dammed to me."

"We will find a way."

Mercy jumps to her feet. "Jesus Christ! Do you hear yourself? There is no good way out of this. We're all going to die, either by my hand or Lucas's. We can't win!"

I don't want to believe her. These can't be our only choices. There has to be something we can do, something we haven't thought of yet. My life can't be over before I've even begun to live it.

I never expected to be human, never would've chosen this life, but now that I have it, I'm not ready to let go. And I'm not willing to let Mercy give up so easily either. It wasn't that long ago that I believed just as she did—that Breachers shouldn't exist. But look at me now. I'm protecting them, helping them, looking for a way for them to carry on in this world. When did I change my mind? When did I decide that Breachers are worthy of life?

I don't know what's right anymore. All I know is that I don't want to die.

"I'm going home," Mercy says suddenly. "I'm tired, and I want a shower."

"I'll walk you," I offer.

"You don't have to."

"You said yourself Lucas is coming after us. Now is not the time to be splitting up."

"Fine."

Mercy doesn't wait for me. She's out the door before I have time to throw on some fresh clothes, grab my jacket and keys, and lock up the place. I have to jog to catch her on the sidewalk, which isn't easy considering my injury.

We fall into rhythm as we walk, matching each other stride for stride. I'm trying to keep my mind in the present, but I can't help but think of Justice, of all that happened the night before. I can still practically feel her lips against mine, feel the way our bodies fit together.

Tires squeal in the distance. Mercy and I both freeze.

"They're here," she says, her voice trembling. "Lucas's men. I can feel it. They're coming. We have to move." She tugs my arm, and we take off running.

Behind us, footsteps stomp the sidewalk. I steal a glance over my shoulder, and sure enough, there are two men chasing us, and they're gaining fast.

Mercy and I sprint. My wounded leg protests, but I ignore the stabbing sensation and keep moving. We make it to her street. I can see her house in the distance. If we can just get inside, we might have a chance.

When we get there, I race up the steps with Mercy on my heels and use my shoulder to shove the door open. It doesn't budge. "It's locked!"

"There's a key under the flowerpot!" Mercy drops to her knees and crawls to the row of pots. She flips each one over until she finds the one she's looking for. A silver key, outlined in dirt, is under the last pot. "Here." She tosses me the key, and I quickly jam it into the lock. "Gage! Hurry!"

The two men have made it to her yard. The door finally gives way just as shots explode through the air. We duck inside. Slamming the door behind us, I lock it. The front window shatters as a storm of bullets pelt the house leaving a gaping hole.

We drop to the floor. I crouch above Mercy, sheltering her with my body. What I wouldn't give for a gun or even knife right now. "Kitchen!" I yell, and Mercy nods understanding.

We crawl. Thank God Ariana likes to cook. There is an ample supply of scary-looking cutlery at our disposal. Bullets continue to rain down on the living room as we make our way back. Using the sofa as a shield, I set up and wait for my moment.

There's a brief pause in the firing, and that's when I stand and throw two knives in quick succession. I hear a moan and a body hit the ground. We are down to one attacker, and he's making use of the giant hole in the front of Mercy's house. Glass crunches under his feet as he enters the room.

Mercy throws her knife, but it flies past him. He smiles wickedly at us, aims, and fires. We flatten ourselves to the floor just in time. I can feel Mercy trembling beside me. She looks at me, terror in her eyes. I pull her against my chest and hold her there while we wait to be slaughtered.

"Mercy!" A voice calls from the front yard. "Mercy!"

"No, no, no," Mercy whispers against me as we both realize

the direness of the situation. Her father is here.

I have to move. Leaving Mercy, I leap from our hiding spot and hurl myself at the gunman who is pivoting toward Mercy's dad. I land on his back and wail on him with all my might. The gun fires once, twice, three times before I'm able to choke him to death.

He slips from my grasp and falls to the floor. I kick his gun away from his hand.

Screaming comes from all directions: in front of me, behind me—it's practically in surround sound.

Mercy's dad lies on the front porch, a puddle of blood pooling beneath him. His eyes are rolled back into his head, his mouth wide open. Ariana is leaning over him, pleading with him to wake up, but he's gone.

I look back at Mercy. She's holding her head and shaking it back and forth, her mouth wide open. I rush to her, lock her in my arms, and hold her against me. Her shoulders shake as she sobs heavily.

Suddenly, she stiffens, shoves me off and trudges, wobbling and unsteady, to where the body lies. Dropping to her knees, Mercy takes her father's hand and presses it to her cheek. "Please, Daddy. Please don't leave me."

Sirens wail in the distance. Someone must've called the police. I squat next to Mercy and put my hand on her shoulder, but I can't tell if she even knows I'm there.

Seconds later, several squad cars come to a screeching halt in front of the house. Police officers hustle toward us and yell for us to raise our hands. I comply, but Mercy and Ariana aren't paying any attention. The officers cautiously approach and assess the scene. One goes to Ariana and forcibly lifts her away from

Eric's body. Ariana fights against him until she's wrenched free.

Not wanting Mercy to suffer the same fate, I hold her by the shoulders and gradually pull her away. She doesn't struggle. I bring her to Ariana, and they cling to each other while officers begin to process the scene.

Once things have calmed down some, the questions begin. I tell them a version of the truth: how Mercy and I had just gotten home, how we sensed something was off, and that's when they started shooting at us. When they ask me why, I tell them I have no idea. There's no way they're ever going to piece this together, so let them try to fill the holes in my story.

The officers are extremely patient with both Mercy and Ariana. They want us to come down to the station, and though I try to protest, they basically tell us we have no choice.

We are ushered into the back of a squad car. It's a tight fit, but we manage. No one speaks. Occasionally Mercy sniffs, but Ariana is silent, which is more frightening than I want to admit.

On the way to the precinct, I text Justice to let her know what's happened, that Eric is dead. I don't wait for a reply before slipping the phone back into my pocket.

Once we reach the station, we have to wait to be let out of the car. We're taken separately for questioning. I worry about leaving Mercy. I don't know when she last took her binding agent, and I'm worried that if it's worn off she might jump.

I'm questioned again and again, and I repeat my story each time without varying the details in the slightest. When I'm finished, I'm let out into a holding area. I was hoping that Mercy would be there already, but she's not. I sit and wait.

"Gage?"

Justice standing in the doorway. The moment I see her, everything I've been holding back comes gushing to the surface. She runs at me and throws her arms around my neck, but it isn't so that I can hold her. She's holding me.

I have seen more death than I care to admit, but this is different. For the first time, I am experiencing loss, and I fear if I let go of Justice, I'm going to come apart at the seams. I don't know how to cope with any of this. I am so unbelievably unprepared to deal with the hole in my chest, the ache in my stomach, the tightness in my throat.

Life is fragile. This notion makes me worry about my own life, about Justice's life, about what it would be like to lose her. I'll never be able to handle that. Even though what I feel for her is new and, quite frankly, strange and maybe even wrong, I don't want it to end.

Her lips linger on my throat, and my heart suddenly beats from that place. I press my cheek to hers, soaking in her warmth. She kisses my jaw, my cheek, and finally my lips. I move my hands to the sides of her face and hold her lips to mine, wanting to stay that way, forgetting where we are and that people are probably watching.

Even though I'm immersed in Justice's kisses, I sense someone watching us. The hair on the back of my neck stands up, and I pull away from Justice just in time to lock eyes with Mercy.

Her mouth is agape. The look of disappointment, of betrayal, cuts deep. She shuffles backward, turns, and runs away.

"Mercy!

Chapter Twenty-Three

Nathaniel

*G*ripping *the steering wheel, Nathaniel drove into the night with Ariana in the passenger seat beside him. They'd hardly spoken in hours. Nathaniel spent the entire ride feeling stressed and guilty. It was his choice to let Gage live, and because he had he put Ariana's life in danger.*

"I'm sorry," Nathaniel finally said. "I should've killed him when I had the chance."

Ariana propped her elbow on the door. "It's not your fault."

"It is."

"You're forgetting, I have a sister of my own."

"He's not my brother," Nathaniel snapped.

"He is, Nathaniel. He was made from you just as Isadora was made from me. The connection is not so easily severed." Ariana shook her head. "I've wanted to strangle Isadora so many times, but I never could."

"She betrayed you," Nathaniel reminded her.

"Only because she is afraid of Lucas."

Nathaniel couldn't believe his ears. Was Ariana defending Isadora? Yes, she'd helped him escape, but did that make up for all of her crimes? "You don't really believe that, do you?"

"I have to." Ariana's green eyes watered. "She's my sister."

"She's his right hand."

Ariana swiped a tear from her face. "I should've forced her to come with me when I left. I'll never forgive myself for leaving her there."

"Isadora made her choice. This isn't your fault."

"She isn't strong like us, Nathaniel. She isn't ..."

Nathaniel jerked the wheel to the right. The tires protested as he slammed on the brakes.

Reflexively, Ariana braced herself. "What are you doing?"

Nathaniel cut the engine. He unhooked his seatbelt with such force that it smacked against the window. "We have to split up. It's our only chance for survival."

Ariana lowered her head. "I was thinking that too, but I don't know if I can do this without you."

"You can." Nathaniel handed her the keys. "You have to."

"Now? You're leaving me now?"

Without answering, Nathaniel opened the car door and stepped out.

Ariana met him at the hood of the car. "Where will you go?"

"It's better if you don't know. And I shouldn't know where you are either. That way, if they find one of us, we can't give them any information."

"I'm afraid." Ariana shivered and wrapped her arms around herself. "I don't know this world."

"You'll be fine, Ariana. We both will."

***

After they parted ways, Nathaniel went on the run, leaving a trail of bodies in his wake. Restless, he couldn't stay in one place for too long. Nathaniel practically slept with one eye open waiting for Gage to reappear, but it wasn't until years later that he finally did.

Nathaniel was living in the body of Tom Kinsella, mail carrier by day, compulsive gambler by night. The body was adequate, toned from all the walking. He lived alone, which made him a prime target for breaching. And Nathaniel quite enjoyed the gambling, mostly because he was getting pretty good at it.

He had worked all morning and decided to treat himself to a beer at Wally's after work. Locally owned and operated, it was the kind of place where everyone knew everyone, but if they didn't, they left you alone to drink in peace.

The bartender greeted Nathaniel when he walked in. "Hey, Tom. What can I get you?"

"Draft. Thanks." Nathaniel sat on stool at the end of the bar. Moments later, when his beer was served, Nathaniel took a healthy sip and instantly felt relaxed. As he took a second swig, Nathaniel glanced up at the mirror that reflected the entire room just as Gage strolled through the door. The beer caught in Nathaniel's throat and he nearly choked. He forced the liquid down, lowered his eyes, and tried to keep calm.

Gage stood with his hands on his hips surveying the room.

"Can I help you?" the bartender asked Gage.

"No, thanks." Gage shook his head and left.

Only then did Nathaniel exhale. He paid for his beer and slipped out of the bar. He noticed Gage on the sidewalk, looking all around. Stealthily, Nathaniel followed Gage for a few blocks. The streets turned from city to residential. The houses weren't huge, but the neighborhood was nice, well cared for by its residents.

Gage stopped and studied the house in front of him. He walked up to the front window, peered inside, and then quickly backed away. As Gage turned around to face the street, Nathaniel ducked behind a car. Nathaniel watched through the car window as Gage made a phone call. Moments later, a car roared up to the curb. The girl driving was blonde, and even from a distance Nathaniel could see that she was beautiful. He assumed she was one of the other Hunters. Gage got into the car, and he and the girl sped away.

Once the coast was clear, Nathaniel cautiously approached the very house that Gage had just cased. He crept through the yard, praying that there wasn't a mailman-hating dog in his path, crawled up to a window, and slowly slithered up the wall like a vine until he was able to peek inside.

What he saw nearly tipped him over: Ariana.

For several days, Nathaniel monitored Ariana. He had no idea why she was living in her real form. It was reckless and beyond dangerous. Gage had already located her, she just didn't know it. Nathaniel needed to warn her.

The next afternoon, Nathaniel returned to Ariana's house. He stopped short at the sight of a little girl playing in the yard.

"Hi," she said. She appeared to be around ten years old, bright brown eyes, reddish-brown wavy hair, plump cheeks, and a creamy complexion.

"Hello," Nathaniel said. "What's your name?"

"Mercy."

The front door opened. Ariana stepped out onto the porch. She looked different than Nathaniel remembered, softer somehow.

"Who's your friend?" she asked Mercy.

"I don't know." Mercy jogged up the steps and stood next to Ariana. "He didn't tell me his name."

"My apologies," he said to Mercy. "I'm Nathaniel."

Ariana's breath caught.

"Nice to meet you," Mercy said.

"It is a great pleasure to meet you."

"Go inside and wash your hands." Ariana smoothed Mercy's hair, "It's time for lunch."

"Okay. Bye, Nathaniel."

"Good-bye, Mercy."

Ariana closed the door once Mercy was inside the house. She charged up to Nathaniel. "What are you doing here?"

"I could ask you the same thing." Nathaniel couldn't believe it. Ariana had a daughter.

"Do you know the danger you've put us in by coming here?" Ariana's green eyes were frantic.

"Me?"

"Yes, you. You need to get out of here now!"

"Newsflash, Ariana. You've been found. I followed the Hunters here."

Ariana stumbled backward.

"What's going on?" Nathaniel asked, confused. "How are you doing this? You had a child? I didn't even think that was possible."

"I used a human body," Ariana snapped. "Not that it's any of your concern."

"It is my concern. You've led the Hunters right to you. Why didn't you stay in human form?"

Ariana wrung her hands and glanced over her shoulder at the house. "I wanted my daughter to know me. The real me."

"I hope it was worth it."

"It was," Ariana said with conviction.

Nathaniel's heart wrenched for Ariana. He knew what she'd done was risky, but he understood her motives. Ariana wanted a normal life. She wanted a human life. And she had one, even if it was only for a short time.

"Let me help you," Nathaniel offered.

"No one can help me now." Ariana pivoted as if she were going to leave, but then she turned back around and faced Nathaniel. "Promise me something," she said, her eyes pleading. "Promise me you'll stay away from here, from Mercy. She doesn't know about me, and I want to keep it that way."

Before Nathaniel could answer, Ariana went inside. Nathaniel hesitated. He thought about banging down the door and insisting that Ariana let him help her escape. His hand hovered in the air, about to knock, but at the last second he shoved it in his pocket and walked away.

The following day, as Nathaniel watched the news, he cursed himself. Molly Sherman-Clare's, aka Ariana's, face was plastered across the screen. Apparently, she disappeared after dropping her *daughter off at school. The police had located her car, but they hadn't found a body, so she was presumed alive until found otherwise. But Nathaniel knew the truth. Ariana was dead.*

The guilt nearly killed Nathaniel. He may not have brought Gage to Ariana, but he was the one who'd let Gage live all those years ago. If he hadn't, if he'd slit Gage's throat, Ariana would still be alive, and Mercy would still have a mother.

Nathaniel remembered the promise Ariana asked him to make. She wanted him to stay away from Mercy. She wanted him to protect her secret. And he tried, at first. For days, even weeks, he kept his distance. But in the end, he ignored Ariana's last request. At first, it was mostly curiosity. He had to see how Mercy was faring. She was an innocent child who'd lost her mother. He wanted to know that she was okay. But, as the years rolled by, Nathaniel's curiosity transformed into affection for the girl.

So he kept watch over Mercy, all the while looking over his shoulder for Gage. From afar, Nathaniel witnessed Mercy mature from a little girl into a young woman. After her mother's disappearance, it seemed as though a black cloud hovered constantly over Mercy's house, but eventually, the light found its way in. Mercy looked happy again. She appeared to be at peace. It was then that Nathaniel knew he should leave.

But he didn't.

He was drawn to her in a way he couldn't explain. He simply had to be near her. He swore that his need to be around her was driven by his sense of duty. He owed her his life because he couldn't protect her mother from Gage. He knew that someday Gage would come for her, and when he did, Nathaniel vowed he'd be ready.

Chapter Twenty-Four

Mercy

I'm losing my mind. That's the only explanation for what I witnessed tonight. I'm going crazy. Because none of this is possible. My dad can't really be dead. Gage wasn't really kissing Justice.

I can't get out of the police station fast enough. I don't know if I'm supposed to leave, but I don't really care. I have to get out. I need air.

But even in the open air I can't breathe. I don't know how I have any tears left, but more find their way to the surface. Pausing, I lean over, place my hands on my knees, and gulp for air. My chest is tight. My heart is broken. My world is over.

My feet move forward, but I don't know where I'm going. Anywhere but here. I can't be near Gage right now. I don't want to hear his excuses, if he even has any. I don't know why I'm so angry with him. Maybe I blame him for my dad. Or maybe I want to blame him because then I don't have to point the finger at myself. Because that's where it really belongs.

This is my fault.

My dad is dead because of me, because I wasn't willing to do what was necessary. I'm never going to get over this. I'm going to carry this anguish, this guilt, this shame with me forever. It's what I deserve.

Dad. How am I going to live without him? How am I going to come home and see his empty chair? He'll never hug me again, never tell me a funny story, never take me out for pizza because we burned dinner beyond recognition.

I can't walk any farther. I take a moment to look around and see where I am. Somehow, I've wandered to the warehouse. It looks so tall, taller than I remember. Or maybe it's just that I feel so small. Small and weak and helpless.

I trudge through the warehouse until I find the roof access. Once I climb the stairs to the top, I kick open the door and step out onto the graveled roof. I'm still small, but at this elevation, I can at least feel the air hitting my lungs. The rooftop is long and wide, and there's nothing up here, nothing but my thoughts, which are screaming at me. I wish I could block them all out, but they're relentless. I hear my dad calling out to me. I hear the glass shattering, hear the bullets flying. I hear the sickening grunts as the bullets strike him.

Vomit surges to my mouth. I double over and retch until my stomach clenches. The urge to breach lingers beneath my skin, skin I no longer want to wear.

I know I shouldn't. It won't help. In fact, it'll only make matters worse. There's no one here to care for my body. There's no one out there to find me, not with Nathaniel lying in a coma and Gage preoccupied with other things. I am all alone in this, so sadly, breaching would be stupid.

Stepping closer to the ledge and away from the smell of rancid puke, I slide onto my butt and let the brick wall support me. I don't have the energy to pull my knees to my chest and cradle myself, so I just sit there, sprawled, a fatherless bag of bones.

Tears drench my cheeks while snot runs from my nose and over my mouth. Using the bottom of my shirt, I wipe my face, but I'm not sure it's done any good.

The image of Gage lip-locked with Justice flashes through my mind. I have to deal with those feelings sooner or later, so it might as well be now. I know he thinks I feel betrayed by him. And I do. Just not for the reasons he might think. There was a time when I might have thought of Gage in a romantic way, but for some reason, it just never happened. I never felt connected to him the way I do with Nathaniel. Nathaniel and I are linked somehow. He's always in my thoughts, even if only in the back of my mind, and when I thought that we'd, that he and I had ...

"Mercy?"

My head shoots up at the sound of Nathaniel's voice. He's standing a few feet from me, dressed in dark jeans, a dark sweater, his dark eyes full of concern. I want to believe so badly that he's really here with me, but I've been burned before.

"Mercy?" He steps closer, the gravel crunching under his scuffed boots.

I hold up my hand. "Don't."

"What's wrong?"

"Don't come any closer." I pull my knees to my chest and hug them against me.

He stops walking. "Okay. I'll stay here. But will you talk to me?"

I shake my head. "Go away, Nathaniel. Go back to wherever it is you're supposed to be." I want this to end, for the illusion to be shattered.

"Mercy, talk to me."

His voice is so real. Everything about him standing there is so real, and I want to jump up and run to him, nestle myself in his arms, and stay there forever, but I can't.

"You're not here!" I scream. Shutting my eyes tight, I block him out. "You're not here. You're not here. You're not here," I say over and over until I open my eyes and it's true.

Nathaniel is not here. I am on this rooftop alone. Or at least I thought I was.

Gage is walking toward me.

Quickly, I scramble to my feet, wipe my face, then brush my hands on my jeans. "What are you doing here?" I ask coldly.

"I've been looking for you."

Turning my back to him, I say, "Yeah. Well, you found me."

"Mercy, I'm sorry."

"For what?" I sound harsh, even to myself.

"For not telling you about me and Justice. For you walking in and seeing that. It shouldn't have happened that way."

I whip around. "What way should it have happened exactly?

What's the proper way to tell someone you're screwing their evil twin?"

"Don't."

"Don't what? Don't be honest?"

"No. Don't make this about jealousy. Don't make it sound like I cheated on you or something. I didn't."

He's right. We made no promises to each other. We had no relationship between us for him to defy, but I still feel hurt.

"Justice isn't the enemy, Mercy. I tried to tell you that before. She's as much a victim in this as you or I."

"She's …" *Oh, forget it.* I'm too tired to argue with him. "I know."

"What?" A puzzled look flashes on Gage's face.

"You're right. She didn't ask for this anymore than I did. And if she did actually save your life—"

"She did."

"Then I'm grateful." I slide my hands into my back pockets. "You deserve to be happy, and if she makes you happy then I guess I'll have to deal with it."

"You're really okay with this?"

Again, uncomfortable laughter escapes me. "I'm not okay with any of this. I'm so far from okay …" I'm sobbing again.

Gage doesn't hesitate. He rushes toward me and scoops me into his arms.

"My dad …"

Gage holds me up. I will easily fall to the ground without his support, and that's when it hits me. Support. Comfort. Someone to lean on—that's what he's found in Justice, what she's found in him.

I'm angry at how easy it is for them when it isn't easy for me. How did they do it? How did they come together when I am only able to deny my feelings? Because that's what I've been doing this entire time. I've been denying Nathaniel access to my heart because I thought it was the right thing to do. But what if it's not? What if this is the one chance I get at love? Gage went for it. Justice went for it. Why should it be any different for me?

Because it is different for me.

I am not like them. I'm not free to choose. Lucas Church's words echo in my brain. It's not okay to sacrifice the lives of many so the lives of few are spared. I can't let Nathaniel breach in order to be with me. And I can't let my mother do it either. It's not right.

I slither away from Gage's embrace and straighten my posture. "We should go. My mother will be worried about me."

Gage's gaze drop to the ground.

"What? What is it?"

Gage looks over his shoulder and all around, still not wanting to look directly at me.

"Tell me."

"She's gone."

"What do you mean *she's gone?*"

"C'mon. I'll take you home."

I follow Gage to the car. He opens the passenger door for me, and I can climb inside. Gage slips into the driver's seat. He is still a terrible driver, but I can tell he's taking great pains to be extra cautious on this particular trip.

In a few minutes, he stops the car in front of my house. It's still a crime scene. There's yellow protective tape and *Do Not Enter* signs everywhere. I absolutely refuse to acknowledge the bloodstains. I feel Gage's fingers link with mine. He gives my hand a little squeeze before we duck under the police tape to get through the front door.

As soon as I step through the doorway, I know Gage was telling the truth. The furniture, the pictures on the wall, even the pile of dirty clothes I left on the bathroom floor—they're all there. But my mother, she's gone. She packed hastily. Drawers are open; there are hangers on the floor from where clothes were yanked out of the closet. My mother's jewelry case is propped open on the dresser. She left her string of pearls—the ones my father always said would be mine someday. I don't quite know what to make of that gesture.

Circling through the house one more time I let it all sink in before I go back to my room. I find my duffel bag stuffed at the back of my closet. I throw in every pair of jeans I can find, some T-shirts, a couple of hoodies, socks, underwear, and two pairs of Vans. Next I hit the bathroom for toiletries: toothbrush, toothpaste, deodorant, tampons, elastic bands for my hair, and a brush. Screw make-up. If I'm going to face the end, I can do it without mascara running down my face.

When I'm finished, I find Gage waiting for me in the living room. "I'm done."

"Where are you going to go?"

"Lyla's, I guess."

"You can stay with me."

"No," I say quickly. I can't go to their house ever again, not after what happened with Nathaniel, or rather, didn't happen. "But thanks."

"I'll drop you off."

We start for the front door when it opens and Justice walks in.

"What are you doing here?" I ask, forgetting any previous plan I had to be understanding about her new arrangement with Gage. She may have made things right with him, but she and I are nowhere near right.

"Isadora is gone too," she says to Gage.

"You think they're together?" Gage asks Justice.

"They've blown their cover. I don't see why not."

I drop to the nearest chair. "How could she do this?" I ask no one in particular.

"They think you're going to side with Lucas Church," Justice says matter-of-factly. "They couldn't take that chance, so they ran."

"Lucas Church had my father killed," I say, hate seeping through every word. "I will never, ever be on his side."

"Your mother is scared," Justice says, trying to make excuses.

"Don't defend her," I snap. I don't care what her reasons are. She left me, her own daughter, her own flesh and blood.

"There's more," Justice says.

"What is it?" Gage asks.

"Toby is awake."

Toby! How could I have forgotten about Toby?

"We should go," I say to Gage.

"Right," Gage agrees.

"I'll drive," Justice offers.

We exit the house, and as I'm loading my bags into the trunk of the car, I take one last look. This is my home. This is where my handprints are stamped into the concrete in the backyard. Lyla and I washed my dad's car in the driveway for any amount of money he would give us. We sat on the porch and dreamed of our futures together. This place used to be my source of comfort, my sense of familiarity, and it's been transformed into a horrific crime scene smattered with my father's blood. If I never see this house again, it'll be too soon.

Gage's hand is on my shoulder. He and I exchange a look. "I'm ready," I tell him.

Justice drives us to the hospital. The radio buzzes faintly in the background, and I hear the news report about my father.

Mercifully, Gage reaches over and flips it off. I ease into the backseat, lean my head back, and close my eyes. In a few minutes I'm going to talk to Nathaniel. Anticipation makes my stomach flutter. I clench and unclench my hands.

"We're here," Justice says.

I make eye contact with her in the rearview mirror and nod. Climbing out, I try to steady my nerves. I'm jittery and nearly jumping out of my skin, which isn't good because I literally can do that. So I breathe and hold myself steady.

"You should wait here," Gage says to Justice just as we reach the entrance. "We can't risk you and Mercy being seen together."

"Okay," Justice agrees.

We leave her and enter the building.

The elevator ride to the ICU is slow. We stop on nearly every floor to let other passengers on and off. I shift from one foot to the other, making my discomfort known to everyone around me. When the elevator doors finally open to the right floor, I charge out, but I don't know which way to go. Gage puts his hand on the small of my back and ushers me to the left.

"Mercy!" Jay, standing near the nurse's station, sees me and comes running at a full sprint.

We collide into one another, my nose bashing against his shoulder. It is so good to be near Jay, to feel his arms wrapped around me. I want to stay that way for a while, but he lets me go and steps back.

"We heard about your dad," he says solemnly. "I'm so sorry."

I nod as my eyes fill with water and my throat tightens.

"What happened?"

I shake my head, unable to speak. Gage, standing next to me, squeezes my hand.

"Oh my God!" Lyla rushes toward me, a blur of dark hair, blue eyes, and red lips. She grips me so tightly I can barely breathe. "Oh my God," she says again. "I'm so sorry about before. I was such a bitch. We've been so worried about you. I've been calling and calling, and I thought you weren't answering because you were mad at me."

I shake my head again, hiccup into her shoulder, and stop fighting back the tears.

"Come on." Lyla tugs me away from everyone until we're standing in a different part of the hallway. "What happened?"

"It was awful," I say. "They came for me, and he got in the way."

"Who came for you?"

"It doesn't matter."

"I'm so sorry. What can I do? Anything you need and I'm there."

A twinge of guilt pinches my insides when I remember that Nathaniel is lying in Toby's body, that I wasn't able to fix it as Lyla requested. I don't deserve her love and support.

"How's Toby?" I ask.

"He's been in and out most of the day, but the doctors say his condition is stable."

I exhale deeply. "I'm so glad he's okay."

"Me too. I don't know what we would have done if … I'm sorry," she says, resting her hand on my arm. "I'm such an ass."

"We're fine," I say, trying to reassure her.

"How's your mom?" she asks.

I lean against the wall, propping my right foot behind me. "Gone."

"Gone?"

"Yeah. She took off."

Lyla's face crinkles with confusion. "I don't understand."

"I don't want to talk about it right now," I say, and I'm surprised to find it's true. My mother's betrayal can wait.

"Okay. We don't have to."

"What I really want to do is see Toby," I say hesitantly. "If that's okay?"

"Yeah," she says. "Come on."

Lyla leads me back to Jay and Gage, who are standing in uncomfortable silence together.

"I'm going to see Toby," I say to Gage. "Do you want to come with me?"

"Of course," Gage answers.

"I need coffee," Lyla says to Jay.

"And who's surprised by that?" I love Jay for his attempt at humor. "We'll be right back," Jay says to me.

Lyla and Jay take off.

"This way." Gage nods in the direction of room 407.

Chapter Twenty-Five

Gage

Mercy trembles beside me as we pad lightly into Toby's hospital room. His skinny body is lying still beneath several blankets. The machines behind the bed beep the steady rhythm of his heart. So many wires and tubes are stuck to him. The sight of it makes me queasy.

I stand at the foot of the bed while Mercy approaches the top. She looks more uncertain than I've ever seen her. Mixed with the uncertainty is a deep and profound sadness that registers in the hunch of her shoulders and the lilt of her head.

"Nathaniel," she says cautiously.

Toby's eyelids flutter and open. He rolls his head in Mercy's direction and with that one look I am a third wheel.

"Hey." Nathaniel breathes the word as if it takes great effort.

"Are you in pain?" Mercy asks, her voice shaking.

Toby's body shifts slightly and stops suddenly. "Not much," Nathaniel lies. He slowly turns his head so that he's looking at me. "Fill me in."

"We can do that later," Mercy quickly says. "You need to rest."

Though it clearly takes him great effort, Nathaniel looks back and forth between Mercy and me. "That bad, huh?"

Mercy takes a shuddering breath and turns away. I have to get her out of here before she loses it entirely.

"We'll be right back," I say to Nathaniel. Taking Mercy by the shoulders, I then usher her out into the all.

She curls away from me, arms wrapped tightly around her middle. "I can't do this," she says quietly.

"Do what?"

"Any of it." She swipes her cheeks. "I've lost everything, and seeing him in there …"

"Things are bad," I say acknowledging the truth. "But we're not out of this race yet."

"I have nothing left, Gage. My dad is dead. My mom is gone. Lucas Church is hunting us. This isn't just *bad*. This is zombie apocalypse bad, and I'm wearing a shirt that reads *Tasty Brains!*"

I shake my head at her bad joke. "Okay." I clap my hands together suddenly, and Mercy flinches. "Let's be practical about this. One problem at a time. First, we have to get Nathaniel out of Toby's body."

Mercy rolls her eyes at me. "I didn't get the water from the river, Gage. I failed. Remember?"

"True. We were counting on that. But we'll just have to come up with Plan B."

"Oh, okay." Mercy mocks me. "Plan B." She taps her chin with her finger. "Hmm, let's see. Plan B." Mercy shoots her finger into the air. "Got it! You distract everyone while I go in there and kill Toby. Smothering him with a pillow should do it, right? Quick. Easy. Let's go!"

Mercy steps away from me, and I grab her arm. Disgusted, she yanks it back.

"We're not going to kill Toby," I whisper. And then a terrible idea occurs to me. "Oh my God! I'm such an idiot! Why didn't I think of this before?"

"Think of what?"

"Of course! Shit. This has been in front of us the whole time and we just didn't see it."

"See what?"

I'm nearly giddy from my stupid idea.

"Gage!"

"Sorry," I say, returning to the moment. "Do you remember your dream?"

Her face scrunches. "What dream?"

"The one where you told me you could make me a Breacher?"

"Yeah. But Gage, that was just …" Her eyes are as wide as saucers, and her mouth drops open.

I nod along as she registers what I'm suggesting.

"You think it'll work?" she asks.

Mercy is more powerful than any of us; that's what Ariana and Isadora were trying to tell me. It's time to put that theory to the test. "It's worth a try, right?" I'm so excited by this idea, I can hardly contain myself.

"Okay, but Gage, in the dream, I was talking like a crazy person. I mean, it's not like I can just reach in and … Pull. Him. Out."

"But what if you can?"

Mercy paces back and forth, gnawing a hangnail on her thumb while she thinks.

"Look. I don't understand the connection you have with Nathaniel. I don't think any of us can explain it, but we also can't deny that it's there. He was able to find you when no one else could. And he was the one who pulled you from the dead body that one time, right?" Mercy nods. "So how different can this be? You reach in, he finds a way to take hold, and there you have it. It'll be like swiping a tablecloth and leaving all the dishes standing perfectly still."

"Okay, but we still have a couple of problems. One, I can't do anything in my body. We both know I only have those unique powers in my other form. And two, there's no way I'm going to be able to jump on my own, not while I still have binding agent in my system."

"I didn't know you were still taking it."

"It's been a few days, but there's probably still enough to make jumping impossible."

"We need extraction serum."

"There's only one person I know of who has that."

Isadora.

I dip my hand into my pocket and take out my phone.

"Who are you texting?" Mercy asks, but I think she already knows the answer.

"If Isadora has what we need, Justice will be able to find it."

"And you think she's going to help us?"

"I do," I say without hesitation. I believe she will, even if Mercy doesn't.

While we wait, Jay and Lyla return and so does Jay's mom. They check on Toby, and Lyla reports back that his condition has stabilized enough to move him out of the ICU. That's a relief.

After thirty minutes or so my phone buzzes. "She's here," I tell Mercy. "She has what we need."

We say our good-byes to everyone, promising to return soon. I don't know how the real Toby is going to react if this works, but that's not my main concern. Like I told Mercy before, we're going to attack this disaster one step at a time. Right now, we need to get Mercy out of her body so she can rescue Nathaniel.

As soon as we step off the elevator on the main floor, I see Justice.

"Where do you want to do this?" she asks.

"The car, I guess," Mercy answers.

"As soon as you're out," I say to Mercy, "Justice and I will take your body straight to the emergency room."

Mercy nods, hesitation and fear emanating from her. She might be nervous, but I know she's completely capable of doing this.

Justice, as if planning on discretion, parked far from the entrance. There are hardly any cars around, and no witnesses. It's perfect.

Justice sits in the driver's seat while Mercy and I climb into the back. Justice hands me a scary-looking syringe.

"I am so fucking sick of needles," Mercy groans.

"Sorry." Uncapping the syringe, I tap the plunger just slightly and let some of the liquid spill from the tip. "Okay. Ready?"

Mercy nods, stone-faced, as if she's steeling herself for the next part.

"Concentrate on Nathaniel. Throw your energy in his direction, and you should end up near him. If something goes wrong—"

"Gage," Justice interrupts me. "Nothing is going to go wrong. She's got this."

Mercy reaches out with her left hand. Justice takes it. "Thank you," Mercy says.

I don't know what brought on this sisterly show of affection, but it makes my chest swell with hope for both of them.

"Do it," Mercy tells me.

I tip the needle into her arm and hit the plunger, releasing the extraction serum into her veins. Mercy hisses through her teeth. When the liquid is gone, I remove the needle.

"How long should it …" Mercy can't get the whole sentence out before her head falls back against the seat.

Justice shifts and holds Mercy's hand tighter as Mercy cringes and squeezes her eyes shut. She's clearly hurting, but there's nothing I can do to lessen her discomfort. All I can do is hope it'll be over quickly.

Mercy's breathing evens out, slows, and stops.

"Why isn't she breathing?" Justice asks.

"I don't know! Something's wrong."

"Gage, if she dies …"

I know what she's thinking. If Mercy dies, they all die.

"Go! Go! Go!" I yell to Justice. I yank Mercy's legs until they're beneath me. Straddling her, I perform CPR, pumping her chest and blowing breath into her lungs.

The tires squeal as Justice drives the short distance from our parking spot to the ambulance bay. I don't let the car come to a complete stop before I'm throwing open the door and hauling Mercy's body inside. "Help!" I yell into the ER waiting room. "I need help here!"

Chapter Twenty-Six

Mercy

So much pain. I'm on fire and writhing as I peel away from my body. I can feel Justice squeezing my hand until the very end. I push Nathaniel to the forefront of my mind. And then, suddenly, I feel nothing.

I drop, my stomach sliding into my feet, and I think it's never going to end, but then it does. I'm wobbling, and I'm pretty sure I could throw up, but I choke it down and try to steady myself. Holding my hand in front of me, I see that I'm nearly translucent, but I'm still me. I didn't accidentally slip into someone else, thankfully. And I'm in the hospital, which is also very good. Finally, something is going right.

Slipping around unnoticed has its perks. There's no one to stop me and ask me if I belong here, no one to usher me out because I certainly look suspicious.

I luck out that Toby is still in ICU, so I don't have to go traipsing all over the hospital looking for him. My next worry is that Toby's room will be full of people, but mercifully, it's not.

"Nathaniel," I say out loud. "I really hope you can hear me. Because I need you to hear me right now." I push my thoughts into Toby's head.

"I hear you," Nathaniel says. "I can't see you yet, but I hear you, Mercy."

The sound of my name on Nathaniel's lips almost does me in, but I keep going. "I'm here," I say, sliding my hand under his. He curls his fingers around mine and I brighten. "I'm going to try something, okay?"

"Don't kill Toby. I'll be all right."

"I'm not. I mean, I won't. Do you trust me?"

"Of course," Nathaniel says with such conviction that my heart seizes in my chest.

"Do you remember when you pulled me out of that dead girl's body?"

He sighs. "One of my favorite memories."

I laugh lightly. "Really? Why?"

"I have my reasons."

I want to ask him explain, but I don't know how much time we have. "Well, this will be just like that, okay?"

"If you pull this off, you're going to be my favorite person ever," he says sincerely.

"Okay, here goes."

Slowly, I let my hand sink beneath Toby's skin. The urge to breach him entirely is strong, like an undertow. I hold onto the bed rail with my free hand, just in case. Of course I can barely feel it, but it gives me a sliver of comfort.

Warmth spreads beneath my touch, and I worry for the first time that I'm going to pull Toby out of his body instead of Nathaniel.

"Nathaniel, I need you to take my hand," I say, panicking. "Take my hand."

I don't know how much longer I can hold on. My hand is sinking deeper, and I'm being pulled, like a gravitational force, toward Toby's body. "Nathaniel, please," I beg.

Something hits my chest and knocks me back into the wall. I would've fallen over entirely, but there's someone there to steady me. Nathaniel.

It worked. He's standing in front of me. The *real* Nathaniel. Not just some figment of my twisted imagination, not some crazy dream version of Nathaniel—it's really him. In his arms, I fill in completely, no longer a hologram. I'm as real as he is.

A tingling sensation starts in the pit of my stomach, and it quickly runs rampant through my arms and chest and all the way down to my toes. Nathaniel's body is pressed to mine, and the weight of him is intoxicating. My hands are flattened on the wall behind me, and I force myself to keep them there because if I touch him now I don't know if I'll be able to stop.

Nathaniel cups my face. My heart stops beating as his mouth hovers above mine. His chest is heaving as hard as mine.

He exhales sharply, and then he says, "We should go."

I nod slightly, but I don't speak. Words are lost to me. I don't protest when he pulls me from the room. We escape into the elevator without being noticed, which is practically a miracle.

My thoughts momentarily drift to Toby. I know it'll be disorienting when he wakes. The amnesia he'll experience won't be easy, but at least he's alive. He's alive! We actually did it.

I did it.

I saved Nathaniel.

We leave the hospital and hurry down the sidewalk. Nathaniel moves with purpose. He whistles for a taxi and eventually, one stops for us. "Sheraton Grand," Nathaniel tells the driver.

"Nathaniel." I start to say more, but his lips swallow my words.

Nathaniel's mouth is hot and eager, and every second of his tongue against mine is a surge of pleasure straight to my brain.

The kiss doesn't last long, but it's enough. I'm spinning.

The taxi drops us off at the Sheraton Grand, and we hurry inside. Nathaniel's entire body is like an exposed wire, humming with electricity. I don't know what's gotten into him exactly, but I'm not about to ask and ruin it.

"Darling," he says to me. "Would you book us a room?"

"Nathaniel, I don't have money or ..." He smiles wickedly. "Oh. Right."

I inch toward the reservation desk and throw my thoughts to the very pretty girl working the counter. Just for fun, I tell her it's our honeymoon, and graciously, she upgrades us to a suite. We give fake names, of course. She smiles pleasantly when she hands us our room key.

In the elevator, Nathaniel stands in the corner, and I stand opposite. His intense stare is both freaking me out and sending waves of nervous energy through me. "What are we doing here?" I ask.

Gage is probably frantic by now. I was supposed to go straight to him after I released Nathaniel. We should be dealing with the fact that I am not in my body, and that Lucas Church is still very much after us. I haven't told Nathaniel about my dad or my mom taking off. Hell, he doesn't even know that Isadora and my mom are working together. We don't have time for any side trips, and yet, here I am following along after him like a lovesick puppy. Because that's exactly what I am.

The elevator doors part. We head left down the long hall until we come to the suite. He fumbles with the plastic key card, striking out once, twice.

"Here." I cover his hand with mine. "Let me."

The light trips green, and I open the door. It's not even closed before Nathaniel pounces. I'm backed into the door, and he's against me; his hands and lips are everywhere, and I can't breathe. He isn't the only one who's eager. I can't get enough of him.

We stumble away from the door, pausing against each surface until we crash together on the bed. He hovers above me, his right knee between my legs, and I ache for him in a way that I didn't know was possible.

"Mercy." He kisses my throat and then looks directly at me. "I'm sorry it wasn't real the first time."

My breath hitches, and I'm about to speak when he places one finger over my lips.

"Best dream I've ever had," he tells me with such affection that I immediately blush. "And if you let me, I'll make that dream a reality today and every day."

Time slows to a crawl. I swallow hard. "What if we don't have every day? What if we just get today?"

He kisses me slowly, lovingly. Pulling back slightly, he says, "Then today will just have to be the best day of both our lives."

I cup the back of his neck and pull him to me. *Today.* If it's all I get, then I really do want everything. I want to be the me reflected in his eyes. Transferring my weight to my side, I roll on top of him, my knees on either side of his stomach. Nathaniel's dark eyes crinkle at the corner as his mouth turns up in a playful grin.

Today, I think again as I slide my shirt over my head. Nathaniel surprises me by sitting up quickly. He catches me before I fall over backward and plants a kiss between my breasts. I inhale and exhale slowly, arching my back.

"You are killing me," he says hoarsely.

Laughter bubbles to the surface. I hold his face in my hands and kiss him again. I kiss him until my lips are swollen and raw, but I still want more. I pull Nathaniel's shirt off, and his bare skin against mine is even better than it was in the dream because this is real.

There is still hunger between us, but we slow down once Nathaniel rolls me onto my back.

"I can't believe you're actually here with me," I say to him.

"It nearly killed me to be away from you."

"A lot has happened."

A single tear dips out of the corner of my eye. Nathaniel wipes it away with his thumb. "Tell me."

I shake my head. "Later. Right now, all I want is you."

"Then yours I shall be."

***

Nathaniel's skin is sticky against mine. My cheek against his chest, my leg draped over him, Nathaniel strokes my hair, and we breathe together. I don't want this moment to end or to shift from this spot, but there's so much waiting for us *out there*.

He kisses the top of my head. "This won't be our only day, Mercy. I won't let it."

"You heard me?"

"Only because you wanted me to."

I did. Communicating through thought, controlling which ones I want heard, and which ones I don't, is easy with Nathaniel. And it no longer makes me feel violated. Somehow, it makes what I have with him even more intimate.

"Five more minutes," he says.

"Wait," I say, pushing against his chest as a frightening thought pops into my head and disrupts my moment of bliss entirely. "We didn't use anything."

"I used just about everything I have," he says, completely pleased with himself.

My cheeks turn crimson. "No. I mean, what about protection?"

"Neither one of us is human right now. Can't get more secure than that."

"But my mother, she had me." So not sexy to be bringing up my mother, but I can't help myself.

"No, Molly Sherman had you. Human body."

Now I'm even more confused.

"I was confused about that at first too. But your mother explained. She used Molly Sherman-Clare's body to get pregnant, and then she ditched her."

Oh.

The mood slightly killed, I figure there's no reason not to let Nathaniel in on the rest of it. "There's so much I have to tell you."

"Should we get dressed first?"

"Probably."

He hands me my shirt and jeans and all my under things. Even after everything we've done, seeing my bra dangling from Nathaniel's fingertips makes me blush like the virgin I no longer am.

I don't watch him get dressed, and he gives me privacy as well. Once we're put back together, Nathaniel sits in the chair across from the bed and says, "Fill me in."

All the bliss I felt only moments before is gone as I recap everything that's happened. His jaw tightens. His hands clench into fists. Anger radiates from him. But when I tell him about my dad, his anger fades. He swoops off the chair and holds me in his arms. I finish my story by telling him how my mother left me without so much as a good-bye and good luck.

"I will never leave you, Mercy. No matter what happens. No matter how this plays out, it's you and me 'till the very end."

I nod, desperately wanting to believe him. I know that I'm stronger than I give myself credit for, but it's a relief to know I'm not alone.

"Okay," Nathaniel says. "The first thing we have to do is get you back in your body." He reminds me so much of Gage in this moment—so determined, so eager to make a plan and see it through.

We leave the hotel and return to the hospital. We learn that my body is in the ICU, not far from where Toby was. Nathaniel and I have traded places. First he was trapped here, now it's me. I am so sick of this place.

Nathaniel holds my hand tight. I appreciate the assurance in his grip. Being out of my body makes me feel incredibly unstable, but at least with Nathaniel, I feel somewhat secure.

"This way." Nathaniel guides me along the hall.

We enter the room and immediately see an unknown figure. He stands about six feet tall, and he wears a sharp black suit. His hair is light and slicked to the side. I brace myself for the attack.

Nathaniel drops my hand. "Ellis?"

"Nathaniel." They embrace heartily, clapping each other on the back. "It's been too long."

Nathaniel steps back. "I never thought I'd see you again."

"That makes two of us. And yet, here we are."

"It's good to see you." Nathaniel turns to me. "Mercy, this is my best friend, Ellis."

"It's nice to meet you," I say. Is it really? I have no idea. Nathaniel seems completely at ease, but all of my senses are on high alert.

"The pleasure is all mine," Ellis says formally.

"What are you doing here?" Nathaniel asks Ellis.

Ellis's glance lands on me. "I came for Mercy."

Chapter Twenty-Seven

Gage

It's been almost twenty-four hours, and still no sign of Mercy or Nathaniel. Anything could've happened to them by now. Each scenario I imagine is worse than the next. After I check on Mercy's body for the hundredth time, I stalk out to the parking lot to meet Justice, who's waiting for me in the car.

I open the door and flop down into the seat. "She's still out," I say as I pull the door closed.

"And Toby?" Justice asks, her body angled toward me.

"He's awake. Jay says the doctors think he has memory loss."

"That's good."

"Yeah," I say half-heartedly. "I guess."

"He's alive. That's what's important."

Yes. It's amazing that Toby is alive. But I won't feel better until Mercy is back in her body. "What if we didn't get her help in time?"

"We did," Justice says surely.

"She shouldn't have stopped breathing like that."

"We shocked her body with the extraction serum. There's a reason most host bodies die. Mercy may be different, but there's only so much that she can take."

"You're right." I nod. "I know you're right. I'm just worried. Where the hell are they?" My voice is raised, agitated.

"I'm sure they're fine."

"They should've been back by now."

Justice tilts her head to the left. "I'm sure they just wanted some *alone* time."

"For what? We have work to do."

Justice gives me a knowing look. She leans toward me. "I need you to understand what I'm trying to say. They probably needed time *alone*. Together. *Alone*."

"Oh." I sit back against the seat and try to erase the mental picture that popped into my mind. Waving my hands in the air, I say, "Okay, but is this really the best time for," I pause, "*that?*"

Justice exhales slowly. How she can she be so calm? Mercy and Nathaniel are out there, and we need to find them. We need to get Mercy back into her body before something terrible happens. And then we need to put our heads together and figure out how we're going to defeat Lucas Church.

My left leg won't stay steady. I'm practically rattling the entire car. "I can't sit here anymore." I push the door open. "I'm going back inside."

"Okay." Justice exits the car. "Let's go."

My entire body is vibrating with nerves. It probably would've been a better idea to run up the stairs than take the elevator, but it's too late now. Every time the door opens on a floor other than the ICU, I sigh, and Justice flashes me a look.

The elevator dings signaling the floor we need. "Finally," I say charging through the narrow space between the doors, not waiting for them to open fully.

Justice is right on my heels as we enter Mercy's room. I wasn't expecting a crowd, but there they are: Mercy, Nathaniel, and someone else.

"What's going on?" I ask, directing my question to no one in particular.

"We were just figuring that out," Mercy answers.

Mercy and I lock eyes and I relax some. We hug quickly, and I say, "I'm glad you made it."

"And me?" Nathaniel eyes me. "I don't get a proper hello."

"Hello," I say curtly. Looking back at the stranger, I ask again, "So, what's going on exactly?"

"Gage, this is Ellis. You might remember him from …"

"Ellis, right. You're a Guide." Bells and whistles sound in my head like an alarm on full blast. "So that means you're here for …" I can't make myself finish my sentence.

Mercy flashes me a nervous look. "Me," she says. "He came for me."

"She's not dead."

"Not yet," Ellis concedes.

Justice steps between Ellis and Mercy. "She's not going anywhere with you."

I'm surprised that this statement comes from Justice. And I

can tell by her wide eyes and slightly open mouth that Mercy is just as stunned.

"I'm afraid she doesn't have much of a choice," Ellis says. There's no malice to his tone. He speaks matter-of-factly.

"Stop!" Mercy puts her hands up. "I hate it when you all talk about me like I'm not in the room." She throws a look at all of us, which is her way of telling us to shut up and stay that way. "Let's just hear what Ellis has to say first."

Nathaniel grasps Mercy's elbow. "You aren't honestly going to entertain this?"

Ignoring Nathaniel, Mercy says to Ellis, "I'm willing to at least hear what you have to say."

"Thank you," Ellis says genuinely. "I'm afraid the news may be unsettling."

"Just tell me," Mercy insists.

"Lucas Church is threatening to close the bridge forever. He's holding your entire family hostage until you return."

Mercy takes a tiny step back. Nathaniel is immediately there to prop her up. "What do you mean he has my family?" Mercy's voice rattles.

"He's holding your mother and Isadora," Ellis tells her. His mouth twitches, and I know he's about to tell us something terrible. "He has your father as well."

"What?" Nathaniel yells.

We all begin to talk over one another, and the room spins off into chaos.

Mercy charges toward Ellis. Justice is right behind her. Nathaniel steps between Mercy and Ellis, restraining her.

Mercy yells as she struggles to free herself from Nathaniel's grasp, "Why? Why does he have my father?"

"Like I said, Lucas is threatening to close the bridge. Forever. Right now, he's closed it temporarily, and all who have crossed over are hovering."

"My father is in Purgatory?" Mercy's voice breaks. Nathaniel slides his arm around her waist.

"Not yet," Ellis tells her. "Lucas will send your father into the light if you agree to his terms. And then everything will go back to normal. Guides will continue to do their work. The bridge will be repaired."

"And Mercy will be dead," I say.

"I'm afraid," Ellis turns to me, "this is the only way."

"I'll go," Mercy says suddenly.

"NO!" Nathaniel and I bark at the same time.

Mercy slides away from Nathaniel and addresses the room. "This is my father we're talking about. I have to. And if you don't understand why I need to do this then you don't know me as well as you think you do. I won't let him be sentenced to Purgatory. I won't."

Her resolve is unwavering, and my insides contort into knots. I want to stop her. I want to throw myself at her feet and beg her to stay. Screw what Ariana and Isadora think about Mercy being powerful enough to take Lucas Church down. I'm not willing to risk it.

"If I go," Mercy nods in our direction, "what happens to them?"

"We're coming with you," Justice says. "That's what happens to us. If Mercy goes, we all go."

It seems like the best solution. If Mercy is willing to sacrifice herself, then we should be too.

Mercy and Justice exchange a quick look. I can see the bond between them strengthening. It started in the car, when Mercy reached out for Justice's hand, and it's evolving now. The same thing happened between Nathaniel and me. We went from enemies to allies to brothers. I suppose when one is created from the other, a link is inevitable.

"I'm ready," Nathaniel volunteers.

"Me too," I say.

"No," Mercy protests. "This is my fight."

"We're not going to let you face this alone," Nathaniel tells her. "End of story."

Mercy wants to argue, I can tell, but she doesn't.

It's decided.

Everything is happening too fast. I'm not really ready to do this, and I can see that no one else is either, but none of us are going to call the bluff. We're all in.

"Shall we begin?" Ellis asks Mercy.

"Wait!" she cries. "I have to do something first."

"We don't have much time," Ellis cautions.

"I have to say good-bye to Lyla and Jay. Please."

"Let her do it," Nathaniel demands.

"I'll take her," Gage offers. "We'll be right back."

"Be quick," Ellis says.

Mercy nods rapidly. She casts a furtive glance at Nathaniel. Then she makes her way out of the room. I follow.

Once Mercy and I are away from everyone, I say, "Mercy,

have you considered what happens to Nathaniel if he crosses that bridge? His fate is Purgatory."

"I know," Mercy says, sadness drenching her voice.

Dread washes over me. "You can't possibly do what I think you're going to do."

"I love him," Mercy finally admits. "I won't leave him."

"You're going to Purgatory! Are you fucking crazy?" The urge to shake her nearly overtakes me.

"Nathaniel made me a promise. He said we'd stay together 'till the end. I'm willing to keep that promise no matter what it takes."

"No."

"This isn't your decision." She places her hand on my arm. "It's mine."

There are ten thousand arguments circling through my mind. I want to tell her that she's being rash, that she's throwing her life away. But as I look at her resolved face, I know that she won't consider my side. She's made her choice. And I have to live with it.

"Fine," I say. "I won't interfere. But you have to promise me something. If you get the opportunity, you take Lucas Church down. Do you understand what I'm saying to you? Don't hesitate. Just go for the kill."

"Okay." She nods. "Now let's find Lyla and Jay before I lose my nerve."

When we get to Toby's new room, Lyla and Jay aren't there. After a few minutes of searching we find them in a waiting room just down the corridor, curled around each other asleep.

"Shit," Mercy mutters. "Here goes."

I don't know how she's keeping herself together right now.

Something within her has shifted. She isn't hysterically crying, or lamenting her circumstances. She's accepted them, and she's willing to do whatever it takes.

I wait by the entrance while Mercy crosses the room.

"Jay." Mercy shakes his shoulder. "Jay, wake up." Jay rubs his eyes and sits up.

His movements wake Lyla. "What's going on?" she asks.

"Hey," Mercy says.

"Why do you look like that?" Jay asks Mercy.

She's visible, but she's not as whole as she was just moments before.

"Oh my God!" Lyla gasps.

"It's okay," Mercy says reassuringly. "Everything is going to be okay."

"Are you …" Lyla sobs. "Are you dead?"

"Not yet." Mercy tries a smile, but it dies on her lips. "I wanted a chance to say good-bye first."

"No." Jay stands. "This is bullshit. We just got you back."

Mercy tilts her head to the side. "I know. And I'm sorry."

"You can't leave me." Lyla touches Mercy's faded arm and almost immediately pulls her hand away. She takes a step back. Her blue eyes are brimming with tears. "We have prom coming up and summer and our senior year. I'm not doing all that without you!"

"Lyla, I love you," Mercy says. "You are the best friend ever. I will miss you and think of you every day."

Lyla nods and tears splash against her cheeks.

"Jay," Mercy starts. "Thank you."

He sniffs and lowers his head. "For what?"

"For believing me. For keeping my secrets. And for loving Lyla. She's lucky to have you."

"Don't go," Lyla pleads.

"Mercy," I say, stepping forward. Jay and Lyla see me for the first time.

Lyla rushes to me. "Help her! Do something!"

Mercy walks to us. "This is my choice, Lyla. Please don't blame Gage. This isn't his fault." My throat constricts when Mercy touches my arm. "I wish I had more time," she says to Lyla. "But I have to go."

"I'm not ready." Lyla's face is streaked and stained with tears.

"I know. Me either." Mercy forces a smile. "I'm sorry to leave you with this mess. But you'll be okay, Ly." Mercy looks to Jay. "You both will."

I'm sure I'm going to have to peel her away, but Mercy steps back before I have to intervene. "I love you," she says again.

Lyla buries her head in Jay's chest. He rubs her shoulders.

Mercy looks up at me. I wish there was something I could say to her, but words are not what she needs. I slide my hand through hers, and she holds on tight. Together, we walk back to her room.

When Nathaniel sees us, he rushes forward. She lets go of my hand and steps into his arms. She fills instantly, looking completely human again, and I finally get it. Nathaniel is her stability.

Justice slides her arm through mine and leans her head onto my shoulder. These certainly aren't the pairings I imagined, but I'm learning that in the human world things very often don't work out the way they're planned.

Mercy has Nathaniel. I have Justice. Things are as they should be.

"It's time," Ellis says.

Mercy strides toward him, shoulders back, head high. "What do I do?"

"First, you have to reattach yourself to your body. You won't wake up, but you'll take your last breaths, and then I'll do the rest."

Nathaniel helps Mercy climb onto the bed. "See you soon," she says. Lying flat against her body, she disappears inside.

Ellis approaches Mercy's body. His hands hover over her chest as her life extinguishes. I can barely watch. I'm screaming on the inside, wishing for this to stop. I want to go back in time and start over. I want to meet her for the first time again. I want to take her to her birthday party and dance with her all night long. I want to make the last days of her life the best days she's ever had.

Nathaniel grips my shoulder. I cover his hand with mine as we brace ourselves for the next step.

"It's done," Ellis says.

The machine flat lines, and staff comes running. They order us out of the room. Reluctantly, we go. Processing into the hallway, my feet feel like they're moving through sludge.

"Gage?"

I turn and see Justice flicker in and out. "What's happening!" I shout at Ellis. "You're supposed to take us all!"

"You gave us your word!" Nathaniel yells.

"Gage!" Justice cries out again, and then she vanishes.

"What have you done!" I scream.

I lunge for Ellis, but he's gone.

Chapter Twenty-Eight

Mercy

It doesn't hurt. I really thought it would. But death is peaceful. I feel like I've just woken from a Sunday afternoon nap. Sunlight warms my face. I take a second to bask in the sensation.

There's light up ahead, and I am drawn to it instantly. Eagerly, I take a step, and suddenly the light vanishes and the scene pulls into focus. I'm standing on a bridge. At the end, I see Lucas Church and his smug smile waiting for me. He's wearing a deep purple suit with a dark gray shirt, and his tie is the perfect combination of the two colors put together. He looks elegant and proud. I hate him.

Beyond him I see a sight so horrific it stops me cold. My mother, my father, Isadora—they're all encapsulated in an eddy of gray mist that reaches to their hips.

"Mercy. Welcome." Lucas claps his hands together.

Something slams into the back of me, and I fall forward onto my hands and knees. I think at first that I've been hit by an object, but then I see a leg and I realize that I've been hit by someone. Scrambling, I get to my feet. Justice lies on the ground, her body crumpled.

I don't understand.

"Ellis," Lucas directs his comment over my head. "Job well done, my friend."

"You lied to me!" Ellis is furious.

"What have you done?" my mother screams.

Ellis stomps toward Lucas. "I made a bargain with them!"

"It wasn't your place to make promises, Ellis." Lucas smiles like he's winning.

"Nathaniel is my friend!" Ellis roars.

"Then you're in league with the enemy."

Lucas cocks his head sideways. Ellis raises his hands to his throat. He claws at something nonexistent, but he's choking just the same. He drops to one knee and then to the ground as the life is snuffed out of him.

"Stop it!" I yell, but Lucas ignores me.

Ellis dies right in front of me with his eyes wide open. Rage pulses through me. Lucas Church is cruel and unyielding. He must be stopped.

Justice stirs and opens her eyes. "Help me up," she croaks.

I do.

"Where are Gage and Nathaniel?" I ask her.

"Banished." Lucas grins from ear to ear. "Just as they should be."

"Why?" I am ready to hurl myself at Lucas, but Justice catches my arm and holds me still.

"Sweet, Mercy." Lucas clucks his tongue. "I had such high hopes for you." He shakes his head. "But you've forced my hand. You see, there can only be one of us. And I'm not through with my turn yet."

"What are you talking about?"

"You're a Creator!" Isadora yells.

"Hush!" Lucas waves a hand at Isadora, and her mouth clamps shut.

"Is she right? Am I a Creator?"

Lucas shrugs. "The world will never know."

My powers. Saving my mother. My ability to leave a body without harming it. Being able to throw my thoughts and essentially control others. It all makes sense now. No one should have this much power because no one else does, no one but *him*. Of course Lucas wants to destroy me! If he doesn't, I'm likely to destroy him.

My mother, my father, and Isadora fight against their prisons of mist. I have to help them. "Let them go," I order Lucas, anger seething from my lips.

"Of course," Lucas says as if it's the most reasonable suggestion ever.

He waves his hand, and the whirl around Isadora rises and spins at great velocity. My mother screams. Isadora tries to yell, but she can't. The mist pierces her mouth, her eyes, her nose. She's overcome and breaking apart until finally, where once she stood, there is nothing. Isadora is gone. For so long I've wanted her out of my life. But now that she's really gone, I don't feel relieved. I feel rage.

My mother and father struggle, but it's no use. Lucas grins knowingly at me. The grey swirl picks up speed.

"Not my parents! Please!"

He narrows his eyes at me. "You would spare them after all they've done to you?"

"My father has never done anything but love me."

"That's true." Lucas casts a glance at my mother. "But mommy dearest, well, she's not exactly mother of the year is she?" He laughs.

"I forgive her!" As soon as I say the words, I realize that I do. My mother made the wrong choice every step of the way, but if this is it, if this is our end, then I want her to know I love her no matter what. "I forgive her," I say again.

Lucas appears genuinely disappointed.

"You may win this, Lucas," I say, gaining confidence with every word. "But you won't break our bond. Not now. Not ever."

Even in this, the direst of circumstances, I can see my father swell with pride for me.

While Lucas's attention is focused on me, Justice slinks behind him. She's about to make her move when Lucas spins around and grips her throat. He lifts her easily off the ground. She flails against him, but he is too strong.

"Well, what do we have here," Lucas coos.

"Put her down!" I yell.

"You're not telling me you have feelings for *her*?" Lucas casts a disappointed look over his shoulder at me.

"She's my sister," I say. "Whatever she's done wrong, I'm over it."

"How noble of you," Lucas says mockingly. "This whole rib

thing really isn't working out the way I planned." He says to Justice, "You were supposed to destroy her."

"Mercy." Justice wheezes. "I'm sorry." Her face is purple and her eyes are watering profusely. Her arms fall to her side. She's losing the fight.

Lucas delights in torturing Justice. He fixates on her pain like a dog with a treat. As Justice's body stills, it's as if Lucas has forgotten the rest of us entirely.

Gage's voice echoes in my head, *If you get the opportunity, take it.*

Without hesitating, I charge toward Lucas and thrust my hand into his back. My hand slices through his chest. He releases Justice, and she drops to the ground, coughing and sputtering.

My fingers grip what they're looking for: his heart. "This is for my father, you son of a bitch." With all the determination I have, I yank. Lucas turns slowly to face me. His eyes are wide with horror. His still beating heart is in my hand.

Lucas keels over. I back up so he doesn't land on my feet.

"Oh God." I drop the heart. It rolls from the bridge and into the river below.

The gray swirls imprisoning my parents disappear, and they run toward me.

"Mercy!" My father is in front of me. I cling to him like my life depends on it. He smells and feels like I remember. I breathe him in deep.

"Honey," my mother says, trepidation in her voice.

Over my father's shoulder, I see her standing there looking guilty and weak.

"I did this for Dad," I tell her. "Not for you."

"I'm so sorry," she cries.

I sidestep my father so that I can face my mother. "I know. And I do forgive you. I don't agree with your choices. But I forgive you."

"Thank you," she says, not pressing the issue.

"I'm sorry about Isadora," I say honestly. "I know she meant something to you."

My feelings for Isadora are still a bit muddled. Someday, maybe I'll make sense of it all, but not now.

Justice slowly gets to her feet. My feelings for her are unsettling. I was supposed to hate her, but I don't. Her creation might have been sick and twisted, but she came through for me in the end. And that's what counts. She saved my life, and I saved hers. I suppose that really does make us sisters.

None of us seem to know what to do next. We stand there for a few more minutes exchanging glances but not saying a word.

Suddenly, Lucas's body turns to ash, and the ground starts to rumble.

The bridge snaps off at the far end.

"Run!" I yell.

We make it to the other side just in time to see the bridge collapse entirely. Pieces fall and splash, making great waves in the river below. We watch, dismayed as the water rises, swirls, and swallows the bridge. Within seconds the bridge is gone. There's no way back to the other side. For a moment I feel an all consuming panic grip my heart and squeeze it tight, but then I see my mother smiling.

"What is it?" I ask her.

She points to something at my feet. Lucas's pocket watch. I pick it up and roll it back and forth in my hand. It flicks open, and I read the inscription: *To the Creator: The path is yours.* "I don't understand. What does it mean?"

But then I understand. With Lucas Church gone, I am The Creator. Isadora shouted it to me, but in all the chaos, I didn't understand what she meant. Now I do. And I know exactly what needs to be done.

"I have to go back," I say to my mom and dad.

"We know," my dad says lovingly. "This isn't the place for you." He looks around and takes it all in. "Not yet."

"Come with me," I say.

My dad frowns and then smiles weakly. "No." He shakes his head. "I died. I belong here."

"But I can fix it," I say, my voice faltering. "I have the power."

"That's not what your power is for." He grips my shoulders. "I think you know that."

His belief that I will do the right thing is so strong. I don't want to disappoint him. We hold each other until I'm ready to let go.

"You'll be okay," he says, his eyes glassy and wet. "I have faith in you."

I'm crying like the little girl I actually am. "I don't want to live without you."

"You're strong, Mercy," my dad says, his tears pooling and spilling over. "And not just because you have this." He closes his hand over the pocket watch in mine. "You're not my little girl anymore. You're a capable young woman. And I know you can do this. You can do anything."

"But what about you?"

"Someone has to keep an eye on your mother," he says half-heartedly, but he and I know both know he means every word.

"I'm going to miss you," I say. "Every day."

My dad yanks me to him and then my mom joins in the embrace. We hug and we cry and we prepare ourselves for good-bye, or rather, good-bye for now.

When we pull apart, I turn to Justice. "And what about you?"

"I'll do what you think is right," she says.

I know she means it. If I tell her she has to stay, she'll stay. She's willing to do that for me. I can see it in her eyes. But what I feel in her heart is love for Gage. They deserve a chance, and I'm going to give it to them.

"One life," I tell her somewhat sternly. "Only one."

"That's all I'm asking for," she says, a mile-wide grin stretched across her face.

There's Creator business to attend to before we leave: repairing the bridge, making plans to destroy Purgatory and release Isadora and everyone else who was sentenced there, not to mention getting in as many hugs from my parents as I can. By the time everything is settled I'm exhausted and ready to go home.

Justice and I stand at the edge of the new bridge, hands clasped. Turning, I flip the pocket watch in the air. My dad catches it. "You're in charge until I get back," I tell him.

I mouth *I love you* to my parents, and then I face forward, forward into my future, into the light.

Chapter Twenty-Nine

Gage

It isn't supposed to end like this, with Nathaniel and I left behind while Mercy and Justice go off to fight the battle. We should be there with them, not hovering in the hospital, helpless, unsure of what to do. Nathaniel is propped up against the far wall, his head in his hands. All the energy is sapped from my bones, and I can't stand any longer. I slide to the floor. Part of me feels like crying, but I don't think I have the will.

I am completely numb.

Two nurses, one male, one female, pass us. "That was a close one," one says to the other.

"I'm still not used to it," the other one replies. "It's such a rush, saving someone's life like that."

"Pretty amazing, I agree," the first nurse says.

Nathaniel and I lock eyes. He bolts first. It takes me a split second to get up off the floor, but I'm right behind him. We practically crash into each other on our way into Mercy's room.

Her eyes are closed, but there's color in her cheeks. Her chest rises and falls.

She's alive.

Nathaniel sits in the chair next to her bed and takes her hand in his.

Her eyelids slide open revealing her soft brown eyes. I can't breathe, but air is pumping in and out of my lungs anyway.

Mercy looks back and forth between us. "Hey," she says with great effort.

Nathaniel sighs heavily. "I knew you wouldn't leave me."

Mercy smiles weakly. "We won," she says softly. "We did it."

There are roughly six million questions I want to ask her.

"Nathaniel," Mercy says sleepily. "Will you take me to prom?"

I guess Mercy gets to ask the first question.

I realize that I'm intruding on a private moment, and though it pains me to leave her side, I do. Shoving my hands into my pockets, I head back out into the hall.

She did it. She is a complete badass, so much stronger than I ever gave her credit for. It doesn't even bother me that she didn't need my help. And I'm actually happy for her and Nathaniel. They are a good fit, so it's great that things are working out for them. Sure, I wish things had worked out for me as well, but I guess I can't have everything. I have my brother. I have my best friend. That's enough.

"Gage?" Justice walks toward me.

Without hesitation, I hurry to her, hold her face in my hands, and kiss her. I don't care if we're in public, or that I'm making a complete spectacle of myself. I keep on kissing her until we both desperately need air.

She grins. "I guess you're happy to see me."

"You could say that." I can't stop touching her. And if she lets me, I'm never going to stop.

"I love you," she says.

I'm surprised to hear her express such affection, and I'm even more surprised that I want to say it back. "I love you too."

"Mercy awake yet?" she asks.

"Yeah."

"Good. I'm ready to go home."

"And where is that exactly?"

Justice laughs. "I have a lot to tell you." She tugs my hand. "Come on."

"We can't leave," I tell her. "Mercy—"

"Is just fine."

"But—"

Justice leans up and kisses me. "Stop worrying," she tells me once our lips part. "We're free."

Worrying is kind of what I do, and I'm not sure I'm going to be able to stop anytime soon. I need to know what happened. I need to know that Mercy is safe, that we're all safe. I'm about to pepper Justice with questions, but as soon as we step outside, I realize that fresh air, and her by my side, is all that I need in that moment. The questions can wait.

"Are you hungry?" she asks me.

"I guess."

"I'm starving." She flattens her hand against her stomach. It growls.

"All right then."

We walk a few blocks and talk about nothing important. Justice comments on everything we see, things I've never noticed before. She's fascinated by architecture, graffiti, life in general. At first I think she's kind of nuts, but her enthusiasm is endearing. She's new to this world, practically an infant. Come to think of it, I'm relatively new to this world as well, and I'm seeing it through new eyes, her eyes, and it's amazing.

We decide on a Japanese restaurant because she wants to try sushi for the first time. Justice devours everything we order, which is about half the menu. The raw fish doesn't sit quite as well with me, but I like some of the rolls. I might even like it enough to eat it again.

Despite the fun we're having, I can't keep the questions at bay. "Are you going to tell me what happened?"

"I guess I've stalled long enough, huh?" She takes a swig of tea. "It's all still kind of hard to process, you know?"

"I can only imagine."

"Basically, in a nutshell, Mercy is the new Creator."

"I'm sorry," I say, not quite comprehending. "How is Mercy the new Creator?"

"Well, apparently, only one can exist at a time. Obviously, Lucas Church knew this. So he tried to kill her. And he failed. Big time."

"Is Lucas …"

"Dead? Oh yeah. Mercy ripped his heart right out of his chest. Super gross, by the way."

It is gross, and yet I feel oddly proud. "What else?"

"Well, things didn't end quite so great for Isadora."

"Meaning?"

"Lucas sent her to Purgatory. But Mercy's trying to figure a way to destroy Purgatory once and for all."

"Can she really do that?"

Justice shrugs. "No idea. She's got her mom and dad looking into it."

"Her mom and dad?"

"Right. So they decided to stay behind and make sure everything runs smoothly. Well, mostly her dad is in charge. She gave him the pocket watch to hold while she lives her one life here."

"The pocket watch?"

"It was Lucas's. Now it's Mercy's. It's like a source of power, you know, holding time in your hand and all."

I shake my head trying to unscramble all of my thoughts.

"You should've seen her rebuild the bridge. That was freaking awesome!"

"I guess that means the bridge was destroyed?" I ask, trying to keep up.

"Oh yeah. Crumpled like a piece of paper, but then Mercy went all Creator and ..." She pauses. "It's hard to describe. You had to be there."

"Sounds like it."

Mercy is the new Creator. The bridge is restored. Mercy's parents are technically dead. This is a lot of information to get in a few minutes.

"How is she?" I ask, trusting that Justice knows I'm asking out of concern, not because I'm still holding onto my feelings for Mercy.

"She's been through a lot," Justice says. "We all have. But she's going to be fine. She has Nathaniel." She lets the implication hang in the air.

"And I have you," I tell her, hoping to quell her doubts about us.

Justice brightens. "And all is right with the world."

"Is it really over?"

"The hell with Lucas Church? Yes. Our lives? Just beginning. According to my dear, sweet sister, we get one lifetime. So I say let's make the best of it." Justice leans in closer. "And I know exactly how to do that."

"Okay." I laugh. Justice's enthusiasm is infectious, and I can feel myself getting swept up into it. "What do you want to do?"

"See the world! Doesn't that sound amazing? I want to see it all, Gage." She grins and takes my hand. "And you're coming with me."

"I am?"

"You'd rather go to high school?" Justice makes a face like a two-year-old child being force-fed lima beans. "Mercy is crazy for going back, but she has this whole prom dream. And I get that. But the rest? No thank you. Homework is so not for me."

She makes an excellent point.

My head is swimming. We've been fighting and running for so long I can hardly believe it's over. Do I really get to live? To travel the world with Justice by my side?

"So, you in?" she asks, chipper and eager as ever.

"Yeah," I say. A genuine smile parts my lips as I realize that the future is finally wide open. "I'm all in."

Epilogue

Mercy

I'm standing in the cramped bathroom at Lyla's house—my house now too—checking my reflection in the mirror. My hair is swept up in a sophisticated knot. My face is painted with rouge, eyeliner, mascara, four shades of eye shadow, and lipstick. I'm not sure I like it.

"We got another postcard from Justice and Gage." Lyla enters the tiny space, waving the card in the air like a fan.

I lean over the bathroom sink and dab my cheeks with tissue, hoping to peel off at least one layer. "Where are they now?"

"The Great Wall of China." Lyla shows me the card, and reads, "Miss you. Love you. Wish you were here. J & G." Lyla rolls her eyes. "I can't believe she sends postcards. It's so 1953."

"I think it's sweet," I say.

"Whatever." Lyla sets the postcard on the counter. "Okay."

She taps me on the shoulder. "Let me look at you."

I turn and wait for my inspection. Lyla and I dress shopped for weeks, but in the end, I chose the black dress I've had hanging in my closet all this time. I always said I was saving it for a special occasion, and I can't think of an occasion more special than this.

Prom. I actually made it to prom.

It wasn't an easy adjustment coming back to this life. I miss my mom and dad. I barely made it through my dad's funeral, but Lyla, Jay, and Nathaniel were there to hold me up when I needed it. And they were there again when my house sold. It killed me to let it go, but I didn't really have any other options. I may be The Creator, but I have to keep those powers in check if I want to make my life in this world work. A typical teenage girl wouldn't be able to afford a mortgage, so I sold the house and moved in with Lyla and her sister Kate, and Kate became my legal guardian. She's still in the dark about me, and I intend to keep it that way. It's nice to have at least one person in my life treat me like I'm normal.

Nathaniel, of course, wanted me to live with him, and someday I will, but not yet. I don't want to rush ahead in this one life I get with him. Sometimes, when Lyla is driving me nuts, or she wants to be with Jay, I stay over at his house. But I try to keep those occasions few and far between.

Lyla tucks a few stray hairs back into my up do. She takes the can of hair spray from the counter and coats my head.

"Okay. Okay," I say, waving the fumes away. "That's good enough. How's my makeup," I ask her.

"Perfect. I did it."

I check my reflection one more time. "It's not too much? I feel like it's too much."

"Mercy, you look beautiful. Nathaniel is going to drop dead when he sees you."

I can't help the sour face I make.

"Poor choice of words," she says. "Sorry."

The doorbell rings.

"The guys are here!" Kate yells from down the hall.

"We're coming!" Lyla calls. She primps for a few more seconds. "Okay, let's go!" She's practically squealing as she ushers me out of the bathroom.

Nathaniel and Jay are waiting in the living room. Jay looks great. He cleans up good. Of course, he's still Jay, so he's wearing beat-up Chuck Taylors with his tuxedo, but on him, it works. I never did tell him about Nathaniel being inside Toby's body, and every time I see him I feel slightly guilty because of it. Sometimes I have the urge to confess, but I know it'll only cause him pain while I soothe my own guilt, and that's not what I want to do. I never want to cause Jay or Lyla harm ever again.

I bite my lip when I see Nathaniel, mostly because I'm thinking ten thousand different dirty thoughts, like how skipping the prom and going back to his house instead is starting to sound like a really good idea. I push my thoughts to Nathaniel and raise an eyebrow, inviting him to agree with me, but he shakes his head.

Fine. Prom first.

Kate snaps picture after picture, and we all groan but secretly love every minute of it. I wish my mom and dad were here to see this, but someday, I'll tell them all about it when we're together again.

After the pictures, we climb into the limousine and head off to dinner. Nathaniel chose the restaurant, which means it's incredibly fancy and overpriced, but the food is delicious. Now that he's told me about his other lives, I make him cook for me all the time. And when he's not in the mood to eat at home, it's up to him to pick the restaurant. I never thought I could love food this much, but with Nathaniel, it's easy.

For kicks, I order a bottle of champagne. Nathaniel shoots me a chastising look, and I shrug my shoulders. Yes, it's technically wrong to abuse my Creator powers, but it's *prom*. I'm allowed to have a little fun.

Dinner eventually ends. The limo drops us off in front of Memorial Auditorium. Prom is even better than I imagined. The room is dimly lit and decorated with silver and navy balloons. There's a huge disco ball hanging from the ceiling, and who knew, but Nathaniel can actually dance. I look like a dork. But I so don't care. I am having the best night of my life.

A slow song comes on, and Nathaniel takes my hands and wraps them around his neck. He holds my waist and nuzzles my neck. Being with Nathaniel is better than I expected. Every day he frustrates me and annoys me and brings me more joy than I ever thought possible.

Looking up at him, I say, "Tell me honestly, do you miss it?"

"What?"

"Breaching? I mean, I never even asked you if you wanted to give it up."

"Do we have to talk about this now?" Nathaniel spins me around.

"No. I'm sorry. Forget it."

He puffs out a short breath. "I never wanted to lie forever, Mercy. You know that."

"I do, but I should've asked you first if you were ready to give it all up and be human."

Nathaniel abruptly stops dancing. "You should have. I mean, you took away my ability to kill innocent people," he says sarcastically. "You made me into the man I've always wanted to be. Shame on you."

I pull him to me, forcing him to sway to the music. "I can't help wondering why didn't Lucas Church do it? Why didn't he just grant you one life and then let it end?"

"That's simple." Nathaniel pulls me in close. "He wanted me to suffer. He wanted all of us to suffer for betraying him."

"He should've just let you cross the bridge."

"But then I wouldn't have you." He kisses the tip of my nose.

We dance some more, my head resting on his shoulder.

"I think you should ask me now," Nathaniel says. "You know, since you technically never did."

"Ask you what?"

"Ask me to spend the rest of my last life with you."

I know he's teasing me. But I indulge him anyway. "Nathaniel Black," I say officially, "will you spend your last life with me?"

"Nothing would make me happier."

I kiss him and, above us, the disco ball spins.

The End.

ACKNOWLEDGEMENTS

To everyone at Month9Books, especially Georgia McBride, thank you for turning my dreams into reality. I love being part of the #Month9Squad. Thank you to the editors, cover designers, and publicity coordinators—you are all awesome!

Thank you, family, for being the greatest support system ever. I could not do this without you. Thank you for embracing my weird, and for loving me even when I ignore you. Sorry about that, by the way. Husband, you are my person. And girls, Mommy loves you. Make good choices.

Jill, thank you for laughing with me as I explained that I needed to "go into the map." I'm so grateful that you get me. Thanks for being you.

Jennifer, you are my rock. Thank you for reading drafts and giving me much needed critiques. I am so blessed to call you friend.

Lastly, thank you readers! Without you, there is no purpose to what I do. Happy reading!

CAROLINE T. PATTI

Caroline T. Patti is the author of *Into the Dark* as well as the
Nettie series. She is a mother, a procrastinator, and an avid Green
Bay Packer Fan. She most likely regrets eating that box of candy,
but she did it anyway. Caroline lives in Northern California with
her husband, her two daughters, and her Yorkie, Captain Jack
Sparrow. You can visit her at carolinetpatti.com.

Stuck in her best friend's body, only one can survive.

INTO THE DARK

CAROLINE T. PATTI

OTHER MONTH9BOOKS TITLES YOU MIGHT LIKE

SERPENTINE
EMERGE

Find more books like this at Month9Books.com

Connect with Month9Books online:
Facebook: www.Facebook.com/Month9Books
Twitter: https://twitter.com/Month9Books
You Tube: www.youtube.com/user/Month9Books
Tumblr: http://month9books.tumblr.com/

SERPENTINE

A JUNIOR LIBRARY GUILD SELECTION

CINDY PON

MER CHRONICLES
BOOK 1
She will risk everything to stop him from falling in love with the wrong girl.
Emerge
TOBIE EASTON
"The most fun I've had reading in a long time!" —Wendy Higgins,
New York Times bestselling author of the *Sweet Evil* series